Hoodwinl

A Racing Thr

By

Charlie De Luca

Per ardua ad astra

To JB,TB,HB,MCH,MEH and LC with love

Hoodwink

Verb

Past tense: **hoodwinked**; past participle; **hoodwinked**

Deceive or trick

"staff were **hoodwinked into** thinking the cucumber was a sawn off shotgun."

More books by Charlie De Luca;

Rank Outsiders

The Gift Horse

Twelve in the Sixth

Making Allowances

See www.charliedeluca.co.uk for more details.

PROLOGUE

The blue skies and the heat haze over the rolling Yorkshire Wolds at the shared gallops in Walton, suggested the current scorching weather would continue for a few weeks to come. Two men stood watching a busy scene unfold. One was small, hints of an ex-jockey perhaps, the other taller and both were dressed in cotton trousers and short sleeved polo shirts. Ahead of them were three paths. To the right racehorses arrived at the gallops having walked and trotted from their yards in neat strings, all identifiable by the matching shirts and caps of their stables. Directly in front of them a polyplastic gallop rose and turned out of sight, and to the left was the all-weather gallop which ran uphill in front of a copse of trees. In between the tracks was a grassy hill with a small set of starting stalls at the bottom and further up the hill, several flights of hurdles and a few bigger chase fences. There was all the equipment needed for the twenty or so racehorse trainers who shared the gallops, to train both flat and national hunt horses.

It was a charming, bucolic scene; strings of jostling and jogging horses, circled in front of the gallops waiting for a signal to begin their work. There was the odd snort, the jangle of bits and from behind the main road, the hum of traffic as Walton, the small market town, woke up. Sinews strained; most animals were alert, poised for action. Even when suddenly released, they moved quickly and elegantly as the riders let their charges onto one of the gallops and urged them into fluid strides, fast yet attuned to their riders' wishes. Most horses were varying shades of dark brown, or bay, with the odd chestnut, grey and black animal thrown into the mix. The brightly coloured caps the riders wore, added to the earthy mix of the greens, blue skies and browns of the natural colour palette in front of them. Most of the horses galloped on the flat but there were a few working over by the hurdles. It was officially the flat season and these horses were noticeable by their small stature compared to the rangier hurdlers. Although the National Hunt season did not officially start until October, there were some jump meetings over the summer and about ten horses were cantering in circles before they tackled the fences.

The bulk of the animals were currently in training on the flat. Every so often the two men barked out instructions to the riders. One of the men was taller, more confident, clearly in charge of proceedings, whilst the smaller man listened intently to his companion.

'Let's try Rocky in George's hood, see if that will stop the bugger bolting. George is alright if he's following and I reckon he won't get past Rocky.'

The shorter man called to one of the riders, who dismounted from one of the large bay horses and removed the black hood, which held the blinkers in place. The blinkers allowed the horse to see in front, but its peripheral vision was limited, thus reducing distractions, which could sometimes hinder a horse's performance. Horses are pack animals and rely on their peripheral vision to see possible predators and outrun them. The blinkers cancelled out this line of vision and helped the horse concentrate on his own race. The shorter man placed the hood on another bay horse. The two horses were virtually identical. After fiddling about with the velcro and webbing straps that kept the hood in place, the rider was legged back on his mount. The two horses peeled off from the group and trotted off.

'Right off you go…' shouted the taller man. 'Straight up onto the top field.'

Both men watched intently as the two bay horses set off up the incline at a half gallop. The leading bay had a shorter, choppier stride whilst the second horse, Rocky, lolloped along, moving more easily but pulling hard. Halfway up the incline his rider moved to the left and at some secret signal the horse began to speed past the leader showing impressive acceleration. The horse continued to pull away easily, but it was clear that his rider was in control.

The older man turned to his companion. 'Well, will you look at that! He hasn't bolted and is going much better.' The smaller of the two whistled appreciatively, his eyes still trained on the two horses, as the gap between them widened. 'I reckon the hood might just work on the course too.' There was an air of suppressed excitement between the pair.

His companion grinned. Like the weather, he felt his mood brightening. Horses were sometimes like that, you just had to find the key to unlocking their potential and the blinkers seemed to have done the trick with Rocky. Instead of spooking and bolting he had maintained his speed and listened to his rider's aids. If it worked on the racecourse then the sky was the limit. They were really going to go places with that horse now, he was sure of it.

Chapter 1

'So, how's it going in the world of jockey coaching? Have you met anyone nice?' Finn's sister, Jenny, sat forward in her chair. Her tone was casual, but her eyes were like lasers. Of course, she meant had he met anyone female.

Drew, her husband, gave Finn a sympathetic look that spoke volumes.

'Well, the jockeys, the trainers, of course. I have met some great people, all in all.'

Jenny sipped her red wine and widened her eyes. 'Good.' Her eyes took in his smart appearance and came at it from another angle. 'So, you look well. Haircut suits you and your clothes too...'

Drew snorted and raised his eyes heavenward. 'I think what Jenny's trying to say is what's her name?'

Jenny flushed and elbowed her husband. 'I did wonder if you had met someone. You and Harriet seem close and you're always together.' She turned to her husband. 'Anyway, he is my brother and I'm allowed to be interested and ask awkward questions about his love life, you know. Big sister's prerogative and all that.'

'Yeah, but that's just it. You're not asking, I just did because you were so bloody gormless...' Drew was a thickset Yorkshire man, whose large hands were strong and capable. He had a no-nonsense attitude and a heart of gold. He had worked as a chef but then taken everyone by surprise by going one step further and opening Avocado, an organic fast food venture. He had started by going to events with a trailer, but business was so good he hoped to open a restaurant in the near future. Drew had big plans of Michelin stars and exotic menus. Jenny worked as a teacher, so at least one of them had a reliable source of income. Finn hoped it would work out. He loved his sister and liked Drew enormously.

Finn grinned as he listened to the bickering. He had been considering toying with Jenny, but then she would only invite him to another one of her dinner parties. One where there was always a spare female looking awkward and then hopeful as soon as Finn appeared, and they saw that he was more than presentable.

'Anyway, we are having another dinner party. Just a small supper and we'd love you to come.'

'God, another bloody dinner party,' exclaimed Drew. 'In case you hadn't noticed I'm a bloody chef and the last thing I want is to cook at home, too.'

Actually, Drew loved cooking at home, Finn thought wryly. He loved experimenting and trying his new dishes out on his friends. If the reactions were positive, he'd try them out on his stand, so it really was a win win situation.

Jenny looked suddenly crestfallen. 'Do you really hate them? I can cook if you want...'

Finn came to a decision. He wasn't going to say anything but how could he not? At least it might stop a full-blown row between the pair.

'Actually, I have met someone. Her name is Kimberley, she's an actress, and I met her at the races.'

Jenny nudged Drew; her face transformed into a wide smile.

'That's fantastic, Finn, it really is.'

Drew took a swig of beer. 'Great, Finn. Bloody marvellous, actually. I thought after what happened with Livvy, that you'd never go out with anyone again and Jenny would never stop worrying about you.'

Jenny clapped her hands in delight and then proceeded to pump her brother for information about how they had met, would Kimberley have been in anything she might have watched, and how long they had known each other.

'Christ, Jen. Just give the man a break, 'exclaimed Drew. 'There he is just popping round to give you Lola's birthday present and you grill the poor guy…'

Jenny looked chastened but only a little.

At the mention of the reason for his visit, Finn produced an expertly wrapped gold parcel tied with a huge gold and cream spotted bow and handed it over to his sister. Finn had waited until after nine on a Thursday night when his six and four-year-old nieces would be safely tucked up in bed, before coming around with his gift for his younger niece's birthday.

Jenny put the parcel to her ear and shook it gently. 'It's beautifully wrapped. What is it?'

'It's a Frozen castle complete with play characters.'

It had been expensive, but he could picture Lola squealing with delight as soon as she opened it. Both of his nieces adored Disney films, especially Frozen. Even he had sort of enjoyed it when they insisted on him watching with them, over and over again. They never seemed to tire of it and now there was even a new Frozen 2 film that they would no doubt want him to watch.

Jenny hugged him as he left.

'Thanks, Lola will love it. You do rather spoil them. I think you'd make an excellent father.'

Finn laughed. 'Steady on, there. I have only just met Kim. It's far too early to be thinking about all that.'

Jenny grinned. 'Hmm. We'll see. And I'm serious about that supper invitation. You and Kim must come around very soon. How is Harriet anyway?'

'She's fine, just finishing up at Uni, but still just a friend.'

Jenny gave him a sceptical look.

Drew was not able to respond as his phone rang and he was suddenly talking in an animated fashion. He disappeared into the hallway.

Finn looked inquiringly at his sister.

'Oh, he's always on the phone these days, talking to suppliers, making deals and so on.' She rolled her eyes heavenward and for the first time Finn noticed the strain on her face. 'If you're self-employed, you're always at work.'

'Is everything OK?'

A shadow passed over his sister's face momentarily and then she smiled.

'Fine.' She replied. 'I mean it, we'd love to meet Kimberley.'

'I don't doubt it. But don't be too hard on Drew. It is going to be hard setting up a new business, it's just the way it is. It will be worth it in the long run, though.'

Jenny nodded, a little uncertainly.

'Of course. Anyway, we'll fix up a time for you and Kim to come around.'

Finn nodded.

He knew that Kim would be examined and fussed over, and that all information would be fed back to his mother who would issue her own invitation, not to be outdone. He only hoped that Kim wouldn't object to such scrutiny and decided that she would stand up to it very well.

Chapter 2

DI Gabriel Taverner was glad he hadn't grabbed a quick breakfast en route to the crime scene. Even after all his experience, you never knew when nausea would creep up on you in this job. At least he would be with DS Wildblood who, he knew, was a sensitive soul underneath her practical, sensible exterior and would struggle far more than he would. He had been in North Yorkshire for about six months now and had moved from the Met in London. At first, he had found it hard to adjust, but now he loved the rural landscape, and had warmed to his Yorkshire colleagues with their friendly but no-nonsense attitude. He had made the move for family reasons which hadn't quite worked out as he hoped, so far. But that was old history and he didn't want to think about it today. He had a job to do. Taverner ran his hands through his dark, wavy hair, took several deep breaths and approached the layby, passing a young uniformed officer who was clearly preserving the area. SOCO were already there, wearing white coveralls and working quickly and efficiently. Taverner nodded at an officer he recognised vaguely, flashed his badge and took in the scene.

He'd seen some sights, but this one was one of the worst. The victim, a man, probably in his thirties lay on his back, a large gunshot wound between the eyes and a look of surprise on what was left of his face, in a layby outside the small market town of Walton. The wound was large, so large that it had to be from a shotgun at close range. The brain had spilled out at the back of the head, so it looked like the man was lying on a bed of liver, brain and hair. The features were all but obliterated. He caught the metallic whiff of blood and gristle and turned away to avoid gagging. It was such a contrast to the idyllic scenery. Even at eight in the morning, the sun was streaming through the trees, the heatwave was, according to the weather forecast he'd heard on the radio, set to last at least until the weekend. Taverner scanned the scenery, taking in the rolling hills and the calm, verdant panorama. Over the hill was the quiet stone village of Langford where he rented a cottage. A rural idyll is how the estate agent had described the area. Walton was billed as the 'food capital of the North', but the town was also famous for racehorses and Taverner knew that many trainers, about twenty or so, were based in and around the small market town. He'd already spotted the shared gallops and heard the steady clip clopping of hooves in the early morning as strings of thoroughbreds made their way to them. It was a typical Yorkshire market town and the last place where one would expect to find a murder victim.

'Christ, what a mess,' said Anna Wildblood, his DS, coming to stand alongside him. 'A shotgun wound, by the look of it. Poor sod.'

'Yes, I'd say so. Any ID?'

Anna consulted her pad. 'Yep, James Clary, that's his van.' She nodded at the small Ford with the legend 'Clary's Farm Foods' on it, next to graphics of fruit and vegetables. 'His wallet containing his driving license was found in the van, so it looks like it's him alright.'

DI Taverner nodded at her, taking in her wan complexion, tousled hair and puffy eyes. Christ what was it this time? He knew life was hard at home with her toddler twins, but her husband and her mother-in-law were on hand to pick the boys up. He sighed and swallowed down his questions. He could find out more when they'd sorted out the poor dead man.

'Who found him?'

'Old bloke walking his dog.'

DS Wildblood nodded over to where an elderly man sat with a small terrier on his lap in the front seat of a panda car. A uniformed officer was crouched at his feet by the open door, dispensing tea and sympathy, no doubt. A dog walker, of course. It was always a bloody dog walker. Taverner wondered why the stable staff hadn't found the body first, but then saw that the entrance for the horses was some three hundred feet further up the road, so they wouldn't have necessarily seen or heard anything depending on the time of death.

He studied the landscape. There were several tracks, all on an incline, and some steeplechase fences to the left. The whole place looked well maintained and professional.

'These are the local shared gallops, I take it?'

DS Wildblood nodded. 'Yes, perhaps our victim liked a bet on the old geegees?'

Taverner nodded, various lines of inquiry forming in his mind.

A scrunch of wheels heralded the arrival of the pathologist, Dr Tony Ives. The tall, patrician looking man put on a white, disposable forensic suit and strode over towards the body nodding briefly at Taverner and Wildblood. A jocular Scot, he was a skilled professional and something of an amateur detective too.

Bending over the body, he muttered his observations into a dictaphone. The DI watched the scene and shook his head. This was his second murder since taking on his job as DI in the North Yorkshire force, and he was determined to carry out a thorough investigation. He'd done well on the last case and wanted to do the same with this one. His team had been a little suspicious of him initially and thought he was a 'southern softie' who had left the Met under a cloud. His degree and interest in criminal psychology, had set him apart from his peers, until they discovered his love of football and northern roots, which had helped break down the barriers. His team were competent and seemed to respect him now. DCI Sykes would be the Senior Investigating Officer, someone he had a more fractious relationship with, but even so, the pair had worked together successfully, and he hoped that his progressive policing might yet impress his superior officer.

Taverner felt his phone vibrate and took the call.

'Yep, right will do,' he replied and then added, almost as an afterthought, 'Sir.'

'Trouble?' asked Anna.

'DCI Sykes's in court today so it'll just be you and me. We need to completely seal the site, organise a finger-tip search and arrange door to door inquiries. So, Anna, what was Clary doing here in this remote layby, do you reckon?'

Anna shrugged. 'There's no café around, his van looks OK, so no breakdown. Perhaps he was meeting someone, having a pee or watching the horses?'

'Maybe. No sign of a phone though, so until we find it, we're a bit stuck. We'll need a roadblock and Traffic will need to put in a diversion whilst we remove the body. Then can you direct Haworth to find out all he can about Clary's Farm Foods, what deliveries were done yesterday, find out what's in the van, all that kind of stuff? And get Ballantyne onto speaking to the locals, not that there's many around here, but someone may have heard a shot, maybe even one of the work riders, depending on the time. I'll get onto ballistics, plan the incident room and then you and I will see the family.'

By now more police vehicles had arrived and the scene was a hive of activity. Taverner knew he had to assume control, coordinate the teams smoothly and make it look as if he knew exactly what he was doing. He did in theory but doing it in practice was different especially since the attack. He had lost confidence since then. He winced and rubbed his thigh. His old injury always seemed to flare up when he was under stress, almost like a fault line. How was it that a wound could heal so beautifully from the outside and yet still ache and burn so much inside? He forced himself to walk without a limp, heel toe, heel toe, as the physiotherapist had instructed. The muscle eased a little and he breathed a sigh of relief.

Taverner approached the pathologist.

'First thoughts?'

The doctor continued talking into his dictaphone then eyed the DI as if he resented the interruption.

'Cause of death, obvious. Time of death, can't rightly say until I've done tests, but I'd probably between two and five this morning, but I presume the shot was heard, so you can get a better estimate, no doubt.' Ives narrowed his eyes and pursed his lips and Taverner sensed further revelations.

'I'd say our man had been in a recent fight. He has bruises and cuts which could predate his death, not sure by how long. I'll know more after the PM tomorrow. It's a shotgun injury so there's huge trauma and less evidence for you lot. It wouldn't have been possible for the victim to inflict a wound like that on himself, of course, so we can rule out suicide. The cartridges are standard enough. Half the farmers round here will have a shotgun, of course, so that's not going to help.' Ives sounded almost pleased at this impediment to their inquiries. He nodded at the gallops. 'Where are you going to start? I wonder if he worked in the racing yards, or maybe he was a racing enthusiast? Probably, it happened before the horses arrived.'

'Perhaps. We'd better get on. I'll see you tomorrow.' Taverner nodded and then strode over to the police van. He didn't want to encourage speculation at this stage and needed to set the wheels of the complex investigation in motion, so couldn't afford time to gossip. A man was sitting in the van with the door open, a small Border terrier at his feet. He had a full head of grey hair and Taverner had the impression of a bulky figure dressed in jeans and a polo shirt.

'So, you found the body, Sir? Which makes you an important witness...'

Taverner smiled as the man sat up straight, enjoying the drama.

'Aye, I was just walking our Jinx. Marie's been took bad, says this heat is making her hip play up something shocking, it ached all night, poor lass so I says, 'I'll walk Jinx, you try and get some rest love,' so I did...'

Taverner nodded as if interested in Marie's hip. 'So, what time did you and Jinx leave the house?'

'It'd be around seven, just listened to the first news bulletin 'ont radio...'

'And home is where?'

The man turned and gestured behind him. 'Bungalow up yonder. 'Almarie'.'

'And you came upon the body and phoned us on your mobile.'

The old man's face split into a grin. 'Aye, me daughter bought me the smartphone for me birthday. Can't get me head round all the new-fangled things it does, don't want to neither but I can phone folk.'

'And did you hear anything unusual last night or this morning, anything remarkable?'

'Aye, I was up with our Marie and I heard a gunshot, thought it was old Maurice out after rabbits again. Just before five, I reckon it was. Heard the church bells just afterwards, loud they are, when the windows are open.'

'Thank you, Sir, that's all for now. We may need to ask further questions, so we'll be in touch.'

'Aye, but aren't you going to ask me about Jimmy? He delivers all that organic what have you, the wife gets her veg boxes off him an' all. He was married to me niece, lives over the hill, she does. Course Jimmy divorced Caroline, got a fancy woman from down south in tow now...'

Taverner took down the details of the niece who he figured would still be classified as Clary's next of kin. He felt a stirring of interest. 'In that case we'll definitely be coming to talk to you and Marie again. Thank you very much, Sir.'

So, it seemed the victim had a complex personal life. Great, thought Taverner. In his experience, love or money was behind most murders, so a jealous husband or thwarted lover was as good a place as any to start.

After a busy morning and a Tesco chicken salad sandwich, Taverner was driven into Walton to visit James Clary's next of kin, Caroline. DS Wildblood pulled up outside a small detached house on a new estate on the outskirts of the town. There was a small hatchback on the neat driveway.

'Looks like someone's at home. Right, you know the drill, Anna.'

The two detectives rang the doorbell and waited. Taverner noticed the hanging baskets were in full bloom, someone was obviously nursing them through the drought. There were also flower borders

14

edging the drive and a pink child's scooter with streamers flowing from the handles, thrown on the grass. Taverner mentally rehearsed his speech, thinking that this part of the job never got any easier.

The door was opened by a pretty woman, dressed in a T shirt and leggings. Her mid brown hair was twisted up into a ponytail and she looked, thought Taverner, wholesome and healthy.

'Hi, can I help you?'

They flashed their warrant cards. 'Mrs Caroline Clary? North Yorkshire police, can we come in?'

Taverner noticed the homely atmosphere of the place, as he followed the woman. She turned to look at them, having gently shut the door through which the sound of a child's cartoon programme could be heard. She had already guessed that something serious had happened.

'You might like to sit down, or I could call someone?'

'It's just me and my daughter, look out wi' it, summat's wrong isn't it?'

Taverner took a deep breath. 'I'm afraid we have some bad news. The body of a man we strongly believe to be your husband, James Clary, has been found this morning. I'm very sorry.'

The woman sighed and perched on one of the stools placed around the breakfast bar in the homely kitchen.

'You know we're separated, right? It's still a shock, he's Amy's father, you know. I always thought we might get back together, thought he'd see sense about that Perdita. He was around here the other day. God, what do I say to Amy?'

'Are you sure there isn't anyone we can call?' DS Wildblood was already filling the kettle and as Taverner had expected, flicked into practical mode. Patient and kind, she seemed to gain Caroline's trust quickly. Phone calls were made, Caroline's mother was called and was due to arrive shortly.

Caroline looked up; her eyes clouded with tears. 'What happened?'

'We are viewing his death as suspicious. Is there anyone you might think of who would wish to harm your husband, Mrs Clary?'

Caroline sipped her tea and seemed to be struggling to hold the cup and control her trembling hands. 'No, no, he's popular is Jimmy, well liked, no enemies at all…'

'And where were you last night Mrs Clary, sorry I have to ask, it's just routine of course.'

'Here with Amy, all night…'

'Can anyone confirm this?'

Caroline shook her head. 'I'm a single parent, so there's only me and Amy.'

'Does Jimmy have any other relatives in the area?'

'His brother, Gavin, works at Hunt's place as a conditional jockey.'

'Right, we'll need to see him too.' Taverner thought it might be better for Gavin to identify the body, rather than impose the task on the ex-wife, or maybe they would use DNA. He thought back to the man's obliterated features and shuddered.

A woman arrived, obviously Caroline's mother and after a short time Taverner and Wildblood left.

'Any thoughts?' asked Taverner as the DS drove back to their base in York.

Anna shrugged. 'Don't think his wife's involved. She seems genuine enough, upset and shocked. If they split up a while ago then why wait 'til now and you know the stats on females who kill. I suppose the Family Liaison Officer will find out what's what. Reckon we need to talk to his brother and colleagues.'

'Yes, we'll set up the incident room and get cracking. Ballantyne and Haworth should have some information by now too.'

As she pulled into the car park of their headquarters, Anna cleared her throat.

'Look sir, did you remember about me leaving early today? I know it's bad timing, but it's been arranged for a while. We have to take one of the twins to the hospital...'

Taverner remembered the twins from a brief glimpse a few weeks ago, robust and lively boys dressed in dungarees with rosy cheeks. How could one of them be ill? He nodded.

'Of course. Nothing serious I hope?'

Anna gave a huge, heartfelt sigh and Taverner was struck anew by how exhausted she looked; the skin around her eyes looked bruised and paper thin. 'Jasper has had breathing problems, maybe asthma, we don't know yet. I've been up with him these last few nights and barely had a wink o' sleep...'

Taverner was left to wonder how on earth Anna coped with all these worries, not to mention the lack of rest. He just prayed that Jasper would recover, and his DS would return to maximum efficiency very soon. At her best Anna was a consummate professional, efficient, dogged, with excellent people skills. He knew without a doubt that he was going to need all the help he could get if they were going to get a result and find out who had murdered James Clary and why.

Chapter 3

Harriet Lucas arrived at The Singing Kettle Café in Walton and made her way to the kitchen past a few early breakfasters, carrying several bags.

'Hi Hattie, we've got part of the kitchen sectioned off for you and we've reserved tables over there by the alcove. Eight people, wasn't it?'

Dottie Mitchell was the owner and manager of the shop and had been keen to get involved with Hattie's scheme of holding a cooking demonstration for local jockeys. A shrewd and hardworking businesswoman, Hattie thought she might just be trying to build up her clientele. But beggars can't be choosers she told herself, as two other cafés in the town had turned down her proposal.

Hattie nodded and took a deep breath. This morning was important. As she was about to qualify as a dietician, Hattie was trying to find a job and was busying herself trying to make her CV look better. A few months ago, she had become involved in solving a racing fraud with her friend, jockey coach, Finn McCarthy. Now with Finn's help she had set up this demonstration of healthy, low calorie cooking for several of the conditional jockeys Finn mentored, which was to be followed by eating the meal in the café. There would be Finn, herself and five conditionals based at local racehorse yards in and around Walton. Conditionals were those training to be National Hunt jockeys, as opposed to apprentice jockeys who were training to ride over the flat.

As she and Finn had discovered, healthy eating, surely a no brainer for aspiring jockeys, was not always a young person's first thought when trying to maintain their riding weight. Even though National Hunt jockeys can ride at higher weights than their counterparts on the flat, it can still be hard. Too many resorted to saunas and illegal methods such as diuretics, amphetamines and worse to keep the pounds off, despite the plethora of sound advice from the horse racing authorities. She was fascinated with jockeys' diets and wanted to help them make better choices, so as a part of her undergraduate degree she was undertaking a project on healthy eating with local jockeys. She knew that poor diets caused low bone density and a range of other health problems as jockeys aged. She wanted the project to go well and realised it was making her tense. She took a deep breath and entered the warm fug of the café's kitchen where resident cook, Betty, was busy frying eggs, her burly arms wielding a spatula with skill.

'Morning, Hattie. Listen, I'm not sure your veg box has arrived, haven't seen Jimmy here or his mate. You might need to give them a ring, love.'

Hattie sighed. God, that was all she needed. She'd gone to the trouble of ordering local, organic produce from Walton and needed the vegetables for her low calorie chicken stir fry meal. Damn, she'd better ring Clary's and see what was happening. It was 11.30 am already and the jockeys were due to arrive at midday after their morning duties. She grabbed her phone and rang Clary's Farm Foods.

The phone rang but no one answered, and it clicked onto the answerphone. Hattie left a quick message and resolved to give them ten minutes before dashing down to Tesco's.

'Here love, have a coffee. Probably, they're just running late.' Betty inclined her head over to where a jug of coffee was simmering on the hob. Hattie poured herself a cup and took a mouthful. Then her phone rang, and she answered expecting it to be the company phoning back. It was Finn.

'Hi Hattie, listen we'll be about ten minutes late. There's a police roadblock on the Langford road, must have been an accident. We're going around the back way.'

Hattie relayed the news to the cook.

'Well, finish that and then nip down t'shop. If Clary shows up, reckon we could use his veg here, so don't fret lass.'

Hattie nodded and drained her cup.

By 12.45 the party were all tucking into the low calorie meal, albeit not made from organic produce. All the jockeys had helped, many just by stirring the vegetables and chicken in the wok, but the mood was buoyant. She'd showed them how to make a low calorie sauce which they had helped her with. Hattie was pleased to see two of the jockeys she knew well, Sam Foster and Connor Moore. Sam looked well and appeared happy, which was good news after the difficult time he'd had at his old racing yard.

'So, everything OK at your new place, Sam?'

'Yep, my new guvnor Robert Johnson's decent. We've got some good horses and I'm really looking forward to next season.'

'Great, I'm so pleased. And you, Connor?'

'I'm at McMahon's now. Yeah, it's grand. Me shoulder's healed now so I'm ready to take you on Foster, so I am,' he replied in his thick Irish brogue.

Everyone laughed. The jump racing season had not started officially, although a few courses ran meetings throughout the year. The season proper started in October. All the conditional jockeys were sponsored by a trainer and rode for their bosses' yards and needed to rack up seventy-five winners before they could take out a professional licence. It was a competitive business and Finn had explained that only 20% of the hopefuls made it.

'So, guys do you reckon you could knock up this stir fry yourself?'

Several of the young men nodded.

'It's easy peasy and actually very tasty,' commented Finn encouragingly.

'I think cooking proper meals is really gonna help, you know,' said Sam thoughtfully. 'We should take it in turns and cook for each other, it'd be cheaper too, wouldn't it?'

Hattie smiled. She guessed that Sam was trying to help her out here. He really was a nice young man.

'Don't forget I've got a few recipes for each of you here. There's lots of healthy but quick stuff.'

It was, Hattie realised, all going well. So far, so good. She had several more ideas and recipes to suggest and was also planning to loan out some recipe books. She had asked the jockeys to try her low calorie meals for a month and keep a log of their weight to see whether or not they were able to dispense

18

with other practices that might be harmful to their health, such as making themselves sick, known as flipping, saunas and running with heavy clothing on in order to lose fluid. These weight loss methods caused dehydration and loss of minerals which could be very harmful. She was passionate about jockeys being taught different methods of maintaining their weight so that they could improve their health and functioning. When they left racing, they didn't want to be left with a whole host of health problems. Eventually, she also hoped to write her own cookbook, getting each of the conditionals to contribute a favourite meal.

Finn and the jockeys had headed off and Hattie was just washing up when an ashen faced woman popped her head round the door. It was Daisy, her best friend.

'God, Hattie! You'll never guess who the police have found stone dead!'

'No, who?' Hattie had no idea, but she knew from just one look that her friend was deeply shaken. She strode over to her side and touched her arm.

'It's Jimmy Clary, you know Gavin's brother.'

'How did he die, a car accident or something?' Finn had said something about a diversion, hadn't he? That's what the police did when there was a car crash. Daisy sighed and sank down in a spare seat.

'No, that's just it, he was murdered. Shot in the head, by all accounts.'

By then Betty had come into the room, probably alerted by the loudness and urgency in Daisy's voice.

'Not Jimmy, I only saw him the other day! Who the hell would want to murder him?'

Daisy let out a sort of strangled sob.

'I don't know, but the thing is Neil had fallen out with him. They had a big row last week, in the pub of all places, so everyone saw!'

'But surely you can't think Neil would do such a thing?'

Daisy gave a long, sorrowful sigh. 'No, of course not. Poor Jimmy.'

'Did you know him well?'

'No, not really.' She bit her lip. 'It's just with Guy Montague moving his horses to the yard and him sponsoring Neil, we could really do without any bad publicity and the police are bound to come around asking questions, aren't they, when they find out about the argument?'

Hattie tried to be reassuring. 'I'm sure everything will be fine, you're worrying unnecessarily.'

Daisy nodded but it was clear she wasn't convinced, and neither was Hattie. At least Clary's death explained what had happened to her organic vegetable box. It was only later that Hattie realised that amid all the drama, she had completely forgotten to ask what the row with Jimmy had been about.

Chapter 4

Finn McCarthy drove to Robert Johnson's yard to visit his young conditional, Sam Foster. He worked as a coach to support conditional jockeys who were training and needed the support of a seasoned professional, like Finn, to keep an eye on them. Sam had had a bad experience at his first yard with trainer, Henry Teasdale, and he had found himself in the midst of a race fixing scandal where he was expected to play a leading role by pulling horses. Sam felt under enormous pressure, had defied his instructions and been beaten up as a punishment; then he had run away to avoid further harm. Finn and his friend Hattie had joined forces to try to find him when they realised what was happening. Sam was a talented rider and Finn had managed to find him another guvnor, Robert Johnson, in Walton and he was on his way to see how he was settling in.

It was a bright June morning, the sun was flickering through the trees as Finn drove through the North Yorkshire countryside. He had been in his job for about eight months now. He thoroughly enjoyed it. It had been hard giving up the thrill of race riding, but it also had its compensations; like being able to eat, being injury free and he loved passing on his knowledge and skills to the next generation. It was the next best thing to race riding. Conditional jockeys relied on their trainers to pay their expenses, offer rides and treat them decently and most trainers did, but there were always exceptions to the rule, and this left young lads and lasses highly vulnerable, as in Sam's situation. He had hand-picked Robert Johnson as Sam's guvnor and really hoped that the lad had settled down. Johnson had a good reputation and seemed a decent enough chap, so he shouldn't go looking for trouble when there wasn't any. His first three months into the job had been very testing as they tried to find Sam and unravel why he had gone missing, only to find that he had to run away to avoid being implicated in a race fixing scandal. But everything was going to be a breeze from now on, because lightning would never strike twice in the same place, would it?

He pulled into the gravelled yard just as the string were making their way back from the gallops. Although the National Hunt season started in October, Johnson had a few flat horses and there was plenty for the conditionals to do in terms of schooling and no trainer wanted their hurdlers to get fat over the summer break, so they needed some exercise. Finn looked out for Sam amongst the lads who were riding into the yard. Most of the horses were calmer after their exercise but some were still jogging and jangling their bits in their mouths. Finn spotted Sam aboard a large bay horse and raised his hand in welcome. The string made their way to the yard where a stone house was positioned behind the L shaped stable block.

Sam untacked his mount and Finn made his way over to him whilst Sam ran a brush over the gelding.

'So, how's it going?'

Sam grinned. His smile said it all. 'Great. The guvnor is really sound, I get on well with the staff and the horses, so it's all good. Can't wait for the season to start properly.'

'Any rides coming up?'

'Might be going at Bangor next week but it depends on the ground.' Sam frowned. 'This is Rocky.' He nodded at the horse he was grooming. 'He's a flat horse but needs a strong rider, so I've taken him on. He can bolt, you see.'

Walton was famous for its communal gallops, which all the twenty or so trainers used. Finn wondered what had caused the horse to spook.

'What was it a flock of birds or something?'

Sam shook his head. 'No, he just gets scared around other horses. He's bolted pretty much every day until he was ridden in a hood. He's been much better since, even won. We took it off Saint George, the horse over there, because we didn't have a spare until the tack order came through. Old Georgie is nervous and one paced, whereas Rocky has been brill since we tried him in the hood. Suppose it helps him concentrate. He didn't even spook at the police sirens, you know. Place was crawling with coppers after that murder.'

Finn gasped. The charming country town of Walton was the most unlikely murder scene he could imagine. It was incredible.

'Murder? Who was killed?'

News travelled fast in a small town and Sam was well informed.

'It was the delivery chap, Jimmy. He was found in the layby near the gallops. He was shot in the head by all accounts.' Sam narrowed his eyes. 'His brother is Gavin Clary, you probably know him, actually.'

Finn certainly did. He was one of his latest conditionals, not that he had met him yet. Gavin was at Vince Hunt's yard. Finn's brain was whirring with possibilities. A cold-blooded murder in Walton, his conditional's brother! He remembered the roadblock earlier. So that's what that was about. He resolved to visit Hunt's place to see how Gavin was coping. The lad would need a lot of support. The location of Jimmy's van was not lost on Finn either. Sam said he was often parked in the layby, which could be because he enjoyed watching the horses work, but maybe there was more to it. Still, the police would no doubt be investigating everything, so he'd leave it to them. He stayed for a while to talk to Sam and his guvnor. Finn was delighted when Robert spoke highly of the lad. As he left, his thoughts turned to the shocking murder and he texted Hattie, who he was due to meet next week, saying he was in the area and perhaps she wanted to bring their meeting forward. The reply came back almost immediately. He grinned at her typically enthusiastic response.

Great. Look forward to it. Tomorrow Blacksmith's, 8?

Chapter 5

Gabriel Taverner stood and waited for the team to settle, feeling like he imagined a new teacher would when faced with a noisy class.

'Right, listen everyone. DCI Sykes has been seconded to a disciplinary hearing in Northallerton for the next few days, so I'll be keeping things going here for the time being.'

He glanced around the team. There were several new faces, DCs seconded in to help with the investigation, intermingled with the usual members of the team. Ballantyne, the gloomy Scot, blew out his ruddy cheeks and shrugged. Haworth, the joker, chewed gum and looked relaxed. Anna Wildblood smiled encouragingly, and Patel nodded from behind his computer screen. DC Natalie Cullen, a bobbed haired, keen young officer, sat with her pen poised. The incident room had been hastily assembled. There were several computer monitors dumped in one corner that had yet to be claimed. Gabriel noticed that the more established members of the team had positioned themselves towards the front of the room, nearest to the DCI's room and his own small office.

Anna had pinned a photo of James Clary in the middle of the links board. Gabriel pointed to it, took a deep breath and began.

'James, 'Jimmy' Clary was shot yesterday. Probably between 2am and 5am yesterday, but we can narrow that down to 5am as shots were heard then. I'll know more after the PM this morning. Right, what do we know about Clary? Any info from the door to door inquiries, Ballantyne?'

The Scottish detective consulted his notebook.

'His current partner, Perdita Brittain, was too upset to speak.' He made a gesture with his hands indicating a large belly. 'She's about six months pregnant, I'd say, didn't want to push her with the bairn nearly due...'

'Very wise. Try again today, take Anna, she might respond better to a woman.'

Christ was that sexist? Gabriel hoped not. He scanned the team, no one seemed about to complain.

'Any other people work at Clary's?'

'Jimmy owns the business and employs three staff. Ms Brittain went into hysterics, though, and sent everyone home...'

Gabriel surveyed the DC. He was an old-fashioned copper, a man's man with a dour manner. Still, he had a good reputation, albeit in this provincial force, so it was all relative. He probably wouldn't cope in the Met but then who would? Not even Gabriel himself, as it had turned out.

'Mmm. OK, go again today. Get a list of employees if they're still closed and get round and interview them all. I want to see the books, decide if the business was doing well or not. Right Haworth, got any more on Clary?'

Haworth stood up and grinned. A joker, he kept the team's spirits up, but beneath his jocular exterior, he was actually pretty shrewd.

'Yep, he's got previous, charged with Actual Bodily Harm four years ago, Aggravated Burglary and Possession of an Offensive weapon. For the last three years he's been clean. Oh, and he used to work in one of t'racing yards around the time of the offences before setting up Clary's Farm Foods. Intel suggests he's something of a wheeler dealer, and does not play it absolutely straight, shall we say.'

Taverner absorbed these facts.

'Good work. Right, so I want to know who he pissed off, who his potential enemies were. Find out who had a motive, who stands to gain from Clary's death. I want to know about his family, his friends, his interests. I want to know how his ex and his new partner got on, I want to know his shoe size, his favourite film, song, his finances, everything you can rake up about him, because it just might be relevant. He is separated from his wife and is in a relationship with Brittain. And I want his phone, keep looking, because you and I know it could hold the key, right?'

Gabriel glanced at the photo of Clary. The victim looked inoffensive, handsome even, smiling uncertainly into the camera. His looks were certainly deceptive given his history and charge sheet.

'Theories anyone?'

Anna put her hand up. 'It could be something to do with racing? He was found in a layby just near the entrance.'

'Possibly. I did check and from where he was parked, he wouldn't have been able to see the horses given the hedge. Nothing in fact, but he could have been in the habit of parking up and walking onto the gallops. If that was the case, then someone must have seen him. Check out if the yards are aware of spotters in the area. Any other theories?'

Ballantyne smiled. 'I heard that this food festival thing in town's big business, maybe Clary was treading on someone's toes, a competitor maybe?'

'Yeah, my veg is better than yours. More organic, better looking,' quipped Haworth with heavy sarcasm. The team tittered and Gabriel let them run on for a few minutes with jokes about suggestive looking carrots. Dear God.

Suddenly Gabriel had heard enough. 'Any news from ballistics?'

Patel coughed. 'Not yet. A shotgun was used and won't yield much in the way of evidence except DNA, of course. There were a couple of cartridges left at the scene too, so there might be some prints on them. They also found some tyre tracks in the layby which they need to follow up on.'

'Good. Right get to your jobs. We'll meet again at 8am, Thursday. I've got a PM to go to.'

He strode off wondering how that had gone. He'd had an uneasy start when he first arrived in North Yorkshire and was well aware that his new colleagues were suspicious of his previous role in the Met and his degree. Yet he had won them over and the team had done well to work together and find the killer of a young student some months earlier. He had expected life to be quieter in this rural idyll and hadn't thought he'd have to investigate another murder so quickly after the last one. Still, with DCI Sykes away, it did give him an opportunity. He ran through a delicious fantasy of the DCI being delayed for several more days and returning to find that the team had already got their man, with watertight evidence which would stand up to the closest scrutiny. But investigations took on a life of their own, as he very well knew, and took all sorts of unexpected turns. He just had to keep an open mind and follow the evidence.

Standing watching the PM, Taverner ardently wished he'd brought someone else from the team along. One of the young DCs perhaps, not Wildblood who he knew hated post-mortems even more than he did; in fact, they had even bonded over the fact. Jesus, with his mouth running with saliva and his legs as weak as plasticine, he forced himself to focus on the pathologist, Ives' back, averting his eyes from the view of the body. He was already breathing through his mouth and trying hard to block out the horrible squelching noises as Ives removed some internal organs. The doctor recorded his findings as he went about his business. Taverner caught the odd comment.

'Hmm, he's got a hernia there, he's broken several bones in the past. Last meal a curry I'd say, heavy smoker too. Healing bruising to his jaw and chest...'

How much longer, thought Taverner, before he could in all decency claim he had things to do and slip away? His brain processed what Ives had just said.

'So, he'd been beaten up earlier? How long before he died?'

Ives pursed his lips. 'Maybe forty-eight hours or so. Looks like he was in a scrap and he hit back judging from the scrapes on his knuckles.'

Taverner pondered on this. So, the other party would no doubt be nursing bruising too. It certainly gave them a motive of sorts. They needed to find out who he had been arguing with and why.

'Inspector?' An insistent voice called him to attention. 'I think our man may have been a drug addict in the past. Maybe clean now as these marks are all healed. The toxicology results will tell us, but this scarring suggests regular injections. Look, here and here…'

Taverner felt himself sway and staggered to correct himself.

'That's all for now. I'll send you my report. The cause of death is obvious, of course.' Ives studied the entry wound, then glanced at Taverner. 'Pretty standard shotgun wound, massive trauma, death would have been instantaneous. You look like you need some air, Inspector…'

Taverner nodded as he tried to focus on Ives's words. He scuttled out into the daylight and gulped in the cool air until he was sure he was going to be OK. It was always the same when he was confronted by corpses. At times like this he wondered if he was really in the right job, he was a sensitive man, had empathy in spades which made him good with people and an excellent listener. It was amazing how much you could pick up by just listening. But being sensitive was also a curse. Briefly he wondered whether his skills were inherited, what *she* was like and then brushed aside his thoughts. He needed to focus on the investigation. Clary had been involved in a fight a few hours before he died, and hadn't Ives said that he was also a drug user? He sighed. That one fact blew the whole investigation wide open to a whole load of other potential suspects. Jimmy could have drug debts or been dealing, annoyed other local gangs; there were endless possibilities. He found himself revising his initial theory that Clary's death was to do with racing. There were now several theories running through his head. They needed to get down to work in earnest.

Chapter 6

Hattie was keen to meet Finn and made her way to The Blacksmith's Arms with a spring in her step. Her red hair glimmered in the sunlight and her movements were fluid and athletic. She was wearing a flowery dress and a denim jacket, with flat brown sandals on her feet, and her mood was upbeat. Finn was waiting with a drink for her, a racing paper by his side. His face split into a broad grin.

'How are you, Hattie? How's the dissertation going?'

To be honest Hattie was a bit fed up studying and living hand to mouth. She was desperate for a proper job, with a proper wage. It would be bliss, to be able to splurge on clothes and luxuries once in a while.

'Oh, so so. I'm still waiting for a job at the PJA to come up. I'm really hoping that my research on jockeys' diets will swing it.'

The Professional Jockeys' Association employed dieticians and Hattie would really like to work for their organisation.

Finn nodded, opened the paper and peered at an article.

'It's a shame you don't know this guy, Jake someone or other. I've never heard of him, but he's a chef making a name for himself with his new clean diet. He advocates less dairy, organic fruit and vegetables and very healthy snacks. Reckons he can help people lose pounds by this clean eating.'

Harriet looked over at the article. There were so many new diets out there which were fads and not nutritionally sound that she was immediately sceptical. Then she saw the photo of a healthy looking man with wavy dark hair, worn to his collar, slight stubble and blue sparkling eyes and did a double take. She certainly approved of this particular chef. He also looked vaguely familiar then she realised why.

'Hey, that's Jake Delamare. He was a finalist in 'Cooking up a Storm', the professional chefs' show. Everyone thought he would win. He was great and cooked some amazing meals. He goes out with that model, Tatiana Black.'

Finn looked baffled. 'Well, he reckons he can help athletes with their diets. Something about protein balls.' He frowned. 'Protein balls, called Life balls.'

'Perhaps, he can help jockeys too?'

Hattie laughed at Finn's expression, accompanied as it was by a look which indicated that he had never heard anything so stupid in his life. She scanned the article.

'Blimey, he's going to be at York races at the weekend to give a cooking demonstration. Hey, we should go.' She scanned the article and began to read aloud.

Sadly, Tatiana and Jake have parted due to pressure of work. Jake said: 'She's a great girl and of course we are still good mates, but we just couldn't make it work with our busy schedules.'

Hattie shrugged, knowing that Jake was unlikely to remain single for long, he was just so good looking, with his blue black curls and ice blue eyes. He looked more rock God than food guru, with a dash of continental playboy thrown in there for good measure. An image of Tatiana came into her mind, of high cheekbones, almond eyes and legs up to her ears. They certainly had made a handsome couple, but she suspected that Tatiana was probably heavy going and certainly not into eating, judging by the size of her. Imagine going out with a chef who cooked up delicious meals and never being able to eat? That was a problem she would never have. She drifted off drooling over Jake Delamare and suddenly focused when she tuned into what Finn was saying.

'I'm going to the York meeting with Kim, might catch you there.'

Harriet felt momentarily deflated. She was used to meeting up with Finn, usually at the races, after she had completed her work for the Racing to School charity. Not that she had worked for them recently, with exams and a dissertation deadline looming. She worked part time for the organisation, which aimed to introduce school children to racing and help them educationally. So, she had met up with Finn frequently after her work had finished. Finn was often there supporting the conditional jockeys he mentored. She and Finn enjoyed each other's company, so much so, it was easy to forget that he was actually in a proper relationship. It made Hattie feel that she should be moving on with her life too. Not with Finn; not that she thought about him in that way, at all, but it was nice to have a stimulating companion, all the same. She plastered a smile on her face; she was happy for Finn, she really was. They chatted on about this and that, racing and life in Walton. Then she remembered the news she had heard recently.

'So, did you hear about the guy who was shot in the layby? Jimmy Clary?'

'Turns out he's the brother of one of my new conditionals, Gavin Clary,' replied Finn, his face serious.

'Oh yes. Gavin is at Vince's, isn't he? Daisy told me they needed more staff after Guy Montague moved his horses there.'

'Guy Montague, from Montague's stud?'

'Yep. He's even sponsoring Neil's show jumpers, so they are thrilled.' Guy's family were fabulously wealthy. He was Lord Montague's youngest son but also managed the family's equine assets. Montague loved racing but had rarely been seen lately as he was very elderly and in poor health. His eldest son, Tarquin, was going to inherit, but was rumoured to be more interested in saving the planet than anything else. Guy seemed much more suitable. He was already very rich and had a computer software company, Smart Thinking, which had made him a fortune when it had been floated on the stock market. Some people have all the luck, thought Hattie. Sadly, not Jimmy Clary, though.

'Who do you think shot Clary? I heard it was murder.'

Finn frowned. 'I don't know. I really need to go and see Gavin and make sure he's OK.' He caught Harriet's expression. 'I don't know what the gossip is. The police will be investigating, no doubt.' He noticed Hattie's hopeful expression. 'Don't even think about it. It's definitely not one for us.'

'No, you're probably right.' Harriet couldn't help but feel deflated. After the pair had foiled the race fixing scam a few months ago, she had wondered if they might be called upon to repeat their feat. She had to admit she had never felt so alive. 'The police will be all over it.' Harriet had a great respect for the law, especially since her father was an inspector, now retired, and her brother, Will, worked in the force.

'Has Will said anything?'

'Not really. He's tight lipped, has to be, I suppose.' She told him about the conversation with Daisy and the concerns she had about Neil because of his argument with Clary. 'But Daisy is worried as they really need to clear Neil's name otherwise Montague might renege on his promises.'

'What did Clary and Neil fall out about?'

Hattie shrugged. 'I'm not sure.' She hadn't really asked, but she needed to find out in case she could help her friend.

Finn looked serious. 'I'll let you know if Gavin says anything. No doubt the police will talk to him anyway.'

'Yeah. I'm just worried about Daisy. Still, the police will sort it out, of course.' Hattie felt they should talk about something more uplifting, like relationships. Not that she had a lot to say; her love life certainly needed revitalising, CPR was definitely needed on that front, but she was curious about Finn's. 'So how is Kimberley these days? Things going alright?'

Hattie wasn't sure about Finn's new girlfriend. She been surprised when he'd first introduced her. But it wasn't as if she liked Finn herself, they were never going to get together, so why not? But she took an interest in him, like you would your brother's romances. It was just that Kimberley with her perfect hair and makeup didn't seem to suit Finn, with his love of horse racing and down to earth lifestyle. But who was she to question his taste in women? Not given to introspection, Hattie did not stop to think why the presence of Kimberley Western had had such an impact on her.

'Fine. It's early days, of course,' replied Finn with a shy smile before adroitly changing the subject. 'So, I hope that they catch whoever did it. It's a bit of a shock to hear about such a crime in sleepy old Walton.' Finn frowned. 'I'll pass on anything I find out. I'll see you at York. Listen, you just take care, Hattie.'

Hattie frowned, puzzled.

'You know, with a murderer on the loose.'

'Oh yes, of course.'

Far from feeling scared though, Harriet felt increasingly frustrated. She had to admit that she had expected that she and Finn might be able to work together, albeit behind the scenes, to make some inquiries in a small way, but annoyingly Finn had pre-empted her and dismissed the idea. She also wanted to help her friend Daisy. Besides she was curious and still shocked. A murder in Walton? It was unthinkable.

At home, where she still lived with her parents, Hattie let herself in. Her mother, Philippa, was tidying up the kitchen.

'Nice evening?'

'Yep.' Hattie made her way over to the cupboard suddenly overwhelmed by hunger.

'Guess who's been round? Honor!'

'Is she OK?' Hattie could not help feeling guilty. The racing fraud she and Finn had uncovered had had ripple effects locally for lots of people, including Honor. But the less said about that, the better. Hattie still felt weird about it. She had always liked and respected Honor and hoped she was alright.

'She's fine. Surprisingly upbeat actually. She's bought and taken over a beauty salon in Walton. You know the one, Secrets. She used to be a beautician, after all. Anyway, you and I have free vouchers for a day's pampering on Friday. So, what do you say?'

Honor clearly was upbeat and was feeling generous.

'Cool.'

An image of the super fit Jake Delamare flashed into her head, all tousled dark mane with his toned body and pouting lips. It wouldn't hurt to look her best if she was going to see Jake's cooking demonstration at York. Maybe he had a vacancy for an assistant? Now that would look fabulous on her CV, wouldn't it? Not to mention the thrill of being in close proximity to such a God. Her spirits lifted like a helium filled balloon. Maybe he could provide the emergency care her flagging love life desperately needed?

Chapter 7

York was a classy, flat racecourse located on the outskirts of the city. Home of the famous four day Ebor Festival, it was the third largest racecourse in England and boasted impressive races with prize money only topped by Ascot. It was a cooler June day, compared to recent temperatures, but the sun was flickering from behind the clouds, promising to shine later. Finn was a regular at York, it was his hometown after all, and he thoroughly enjoyed racing. Finn had been a successful National Hunt jockey and adored the thrills and spills of riding over fences, nothing could compete with that. Flat racing didn't quite cut it as far as he was concerned, the races were over in a flash, the favourites more often than not won, but he had to concede it was probably more glamorous than National Hunt racing. For a start, the fixtures were held in the spring and summer, so that allowed for race goers to be more adventurous in terms of their clothing, rather than dressing for warmth, which was often the case in National Hunt racing. Certainly, Kimberley looked stunning in a dusky pink shift dress and matching jacket, the outfit topped off by a small, cream fascinator. He strode up to greet her, planting a kiss on her lips.

'You look amazing, as ever,' he added. She did too. Not only was she stylish, she had dark tumbling curls, dark eyes and the creamiest skin Finn had ever seen in his life.

Kimberley smiled. 'You don't look so bad yourself. Now let's get a drink before the first race and check out the runners.' She tapped the racecard she was clutching. 'I want to know about everything and I'm hoping you can give me all the inside info.'

'I'm not an expert on flat racing, you know that,' Finn protested.

'But you know about racehorses and you're sure to know loads more about flat racing than I do,' Kimberley added. 'I am keen to learn everything!'

Finn had met Kimberley a few weeks ago at York. She had been with some owners he used to ride for, they'd been introduced and had got on amazingly well, so much so, that Finn had left with her phone number. They had been on four dates since and things were progressing nicely.

Finn ordered wine and picked up a menu from the bar.

'So, how's work?'

Kimberley pulled a face. 'Oh, you know, a bit dull but I did have an audition this week, though. I had to lie to the office manager about having 'flu to get there, but never mind.'

Kimberley was currently temping as an administrative assistant for a firm of solicitors but had studied drama at university and was desperate to break into acting. She described herself as 'resting' but as far as Finn was aware, she'd had very few acting roles since she had finished her training, apart from a few positions as extras in a couple of soaps and some advertising roles. Still, with her good looks and ability, he thought it was only a matter of time before she triumphed. Finn was a straight down the line sort of guy though, and he didn't hold with lying to bosses. Still, probably everyone pulled a sickie now and again, except for him. Maybe he just had too high standards, he decided, so he thought he'd keep his opinions to himself.

'It's a nursing role in one of the medical dramas, Emergency 999,' Kim told him as she crossed her fingers. 'It went very well, so I'm hoping for great things.' She frowned at the menu in the bar. 'My agent, Damien, says, I need to lose some more weight though, so I'll just have a salad, I think, no carbs…'

Finn frowned. Kimberley had an excellent figure.

'Really? Your agent is a fool. But I might be able to help you there, though. You remember my friend, Harriet? She's a dietician and she's going to be here today. I said we'd meet up. I could always ask her to recommend a diet for you, if you like…'

A look of annoyance flashed across Kimberley's face then she smiled. 'OK, you're so sweet. I can't wait to see her again.'

Finn was pleased that the two women had appeared to get on well. He would have hated it if they hadn't. For some reason he couldn't quite fathom, he didn't want to alienate Harriet. She had become a good friend, especially after everything they had been through together in their last investigation.

'What salad do you want?'

'Smoked salmon,' Kimberley replied smoothly. 'Thanks, Finn.'

The racecourse was filling up and Finn had seen a few familiar faces. He saw another at the bar, a bookie friend he hadn't seen for years. Melvin Vine was a thickset man, dressed in a suit with a grey wool overcoat and trilby. He was probably in his sixties but looked hardly any different from when Finn had last seen him, which had to be at least two years ago. He graduated from a small pitch locally, to a chain of betting shops.

'Now then Finn, me old mate. How's things going? I heard you work for the BHA now, coaching the young 'uns.'

It was no surprise to Finn that Melvin knew about his new role. Melvin had the memory of an elephant and made it his business to find things out about people. It was this curiosity and shrewd instincts that had led to him becoming such a successful businessman, he supposed.

'It's going well, I'm enjoying it actually, more than I thought I would. How are you doing, do you have any tips for me?'

Melvin sighed and lowered his voice. 'It's more what you could do for me as a matter of fact. I'm looking into summat, see. There are some jokers about, trying to outmanoeuvre us so I'm keeping me ear to the ground, that's all.'

'Oh, anything I can help you with?' Finn was well aware that there were often attempts to get one over on the bookies, but he also knew that whoever tried it would need to be exceptionally smart to succeed. Sometimes, bookies did try and deal with such matters themselves and he had known Melvin, and his associates refuse to take bets from anyone being caught out trying to swindle them.

Melvin smiled enigmatically. 'Just look out for someone putting money on the pitches and making a show of it, will you and let me know if you recognise 'em.' He produced a business card together with a wad of notes and looked over to where Kimberley was waiting.

'Now, let me buy you a drink and one for the lady.' He handed the business card over to Finn. 'Anything to eat?'

'A salmon salad as well.' Finn patted his pockets in search of his wallet.

Melvin waved his hand at him. 'Nah, this is on me, Finn. Now don't forget, not a word to anyone, but if you do find anything out then give me a ring. It's hush hush and very important.'

Finn was intrigued. 'Course, I'll let you know. How long has this been going on?'

'A few months, too bloody long. A different person every time but the same MO. You can't miss it.' Melvin looked mournful. 'I'll get these sent over to you.'

Finn stared at his friend. Melvin had by imperceptible nods and winks managed to order the drinks and food, despite being way down the queue for the bar. He was a man who conducted every aspect of his life by making contacts and using inside information. For someone who was so well connected, the betting coup should be easy to resolve and yet Melvin was clearly rattled. It occurred to Finn that he hadn't found out what the modus operandi actually was, just that different people were involved every time. Damn. But when he looked round, Melvin had long gone. There was nothing for it. He resolved to stand near the bookies' pitches and see for himself.

Harriet and Kimberley greeted each other politely enough. In contrast to Kimberley, Hattie was dressed in layers; a green asymmetrical top and long skirt with a multi coloured necklace, topped off with a green matching headscarf tied in her auburn curls. She looked stylish and as if she hadn't tried too much, which he suspected was the case. He also noticed that her skin glowed and she exuded health and vitality. His friend was not as groomed as Kimberley, but she had, he acknowledged, a real natural beauty and her own unique style. Black, wedge heeled boots, finished off the outfit.

'Now, did you find anything more out about the shooting?'

'Not much more, except for the fact that although likeable, Jimmy probably had lots of people wanting to harm him. There are unconfirmed rumours of drug use, so if he was a small-time dealer then it could have been gang related,' explained Hattie.

'Hmm, interesting. He sounds like he might have had lots of enemies,' added Finn. He felt strangely disappointed. He had been convinced that the murder was something to do with betting, due to the location of the body, but the drugs information widened the whole case. Drugs gangs had their own way of dealing with issues, and meted out their own punishments, he knew. He was suddenly aware of Kimberley clutching his arm, her eyes wide with curiosity.

'Shooting, drugs, what on earth is going on, Finn?'

He felt Hattie's eyes boring into him too. Why hadn't he talked to Kimberley about the murder before? Probably, because it wasn't exactly a topic for a date, was it?

'Oh, it's nothing. Just someone was killed in Walton where we do most of our work. I just wondered if Hattie had heard anything about it, that's all.'

'Oh, the layby shooting.' Kimberley immediately lost interest. 'I heard about it on the news. Bet it was a drug debt or jealous husband or something. Now let's see the horses in the next race.'

They followed Harriet striding ahead in her sturdy boots whilst Kimberley took much smaller steps in her stiletto heels. Finn patiently waited for her to catch them up. The race was underway by the time Harriet caught up with them and Finn had a winner whilst Kimberley's horse was fourth. Finn had arranged it so that they had stood close to the bookies' pitches and he had scanned the scene constantly and not seen anything remotely unusual. He glanced around him, but there was no sign of Melvin. What was it he had said? *You can't miss it.* Well, so far, he certainly had. It just seemed like another race day with the usual set of punters, besuited young men studying form, groups of seasoned race goers and herds of shrieking women, picking horses simply because of their names. Then, it was time for the second race.

Hattie pointed out some Walton flat trainers who had runners which were in the parade ring. She chose Haberdasher, a nice looking but undersized chestnut trained by Robert Johnson whilst Finn went for the grey, Byzantine, trained by Hattie's friend's father, Vince Hunt. He always had a few flat horses but had decided to take in more recently. He had also landed a rich, new owner, Guy Montague, who after the death of his old trainer, had moved four hurdlers and five flat horses to Vince's.

'Which one do you like?' Finn asked Kimberley. She pouted and cast her eye over the horses. 'Well, they're all lovely. Hmm.' She turned to her race card and puzzled over the row of numbers underneath each horse's name.

'This row is the form from previous races. Byzantine is likely to be the favourite, followed by Haberdasher and Shabby Chic.' Finn pointed at the racecard.

Kimberley looked at each horse as it passed them.

'What do I look out for?'

'Well, I always like a busy walker and a horse that looks well in itself, you know, shiny coat, maybe a bit on its toes even.'

They made their way through the thronging crowd towards the bookies' pitches when suddenly with about twenty minutes towards the off, he saw Melvin at the corner of the stand, his eyes trained on someone. He turned to see who it was and saw a flamboyant man with collar length curls, deliberately studying the odds. He was wearing a long fawn coloured coat with a fur collar, cream trousers, checked cream and black waistcoat over a cream shirt and a red bow tie. He strode about before approaching Melvin's pitch and pulled out some cash. He placed it in a copy of The Racing Post, a sizeable amount by the look of it, and mumbled something to the bookie. Finn had advanced towards him and overheard that he had backed the lot to win on number 7 in the last race. Finn checked his racecard. It was the third favourite, Florette. The odds on this horse was 7-1 so he made a mental note to see what would happen next. It seemed a strange thing to back a horse in the last race just as the second was about to start, but the man had made such a show of it, there were already other punters circling Number 7 in the sixth race, nudging and nodding at the man, as though he knew something they didn't. A series of whispers began to circulate. He heard an older woman suddenly remark to her friends that she had had a tip about Florette, whilst her friends then flicked through their racecards to find the horse. The whispers about Florette were circulating faster than influenza, which Finn guessed was exactly what was intended. He made a mental note to check to see if the odds changed by the time the last race came and was willing to bet that they would have shortened considerably. Everyone put their bets on for the second race, Finn went for Byzantine, Harriet, Shabby Chic and Kimberley, Absolute Beginners, as a fine drizzle began to fall. Kimberley huddled up to Finn, looking miserable.

'Why don't me and Kimberley get a drink in and we can watch the race from the bar?' suggested Hattie. Kimberley gave her a grateful look.

Finn handed Harriet a twenty pound note. 'I'll meet you in a minute. Can you get me a white wine and whatever you want? I just need to talk to a friend.'

When he looked round, Melvin had vanished. The tall, long haired man was just about to disappear too, presumably to the bar. On impulse he took a surreptitious photo of the man with his smart phone, just capturing his profile as he left. In the warmth of the owners' and trainers' bar Harriet and Kimberley were chatting about Kimberley's audition.

'I'll keep my fingers crossed for you,' Harriet added kindly. 'Hey, did you hear that Kimberley has the same agent as none other than Jake Delamare!' Finn couldn't help noticing the dreamy expression that drifted over her face. 'I'm hoping to get him to do a talk for the jockeys on healthy, clean eating.'

Kimberley smiled. 'I don't actually know him, it's just that Damien was going on and on about him. He poached him from another agent after they had a row or something. He's his biggest client by far.'

'He's tipped as the next big thing on healthy eating and dieting. His Life protein balls are absolutely delicious. They are supposed to contain all the nutrients you need in one day and are packed full of energy.'

Finn rolled his eyes. The damned things were being advertised everywhere and as for the title! God, how pretentious could you get!

'Well, I'm sure they are good for you but £3.50 per ball, it's a bloody rip off!'

Hattie regarded him steadily. 'But they are packed full of goodness and will keep you going all day, so really it's very good value when you think what you'd spend on lunch. Mind you, I'd like to read the science behind it all. If he's right, then I think the jockeys could use them to help them maintain energy for riding. In theory, they could still lose weight.'

'Hmm. You'd lose weight alright, because they are so bloody tiny!'

'Oh, I'll definitely try them then,' added Kimberley.

Finn looked appalled.

'Anyway, the race is about to start!'

They trained their eyes on the horses urging them on. It was a close run six furlong race, but Byzantine beat Shabby Chic by a short head. Kimberley's horse, Absolute Beginners, came in last.

'Damn. Still I'm pleased for Vince.' Harriet was gallant in defeat. 'Anyway, the winner gets another round in, don't you agree, Kim?'

'Absolutely.'

Finn returned and made his way to the bar. He looked out for Melvin but there was no sign of him. He was beginning to wonder what all the fuss was about anyway. So what if someone backed a horse early on in a loud, obvious way, surely that couldn't distort the odds enough to make a difference, could it? Melvin did not reappear, so he forgot about the man in the coat with the fur collar and decided to enjoy the rest of his day.

Within the hour, the rain suddenly dried and the sun shone. Hattie waited by the winner's enclosure for a brief glimpse of Jake Delamare, whose cookery demonstration was due to start any minute. She was near to the front, having hung about between the fifth and sixth race whilst Finn and Kimberley went to look at the horses. She thought they would like some time on their own. Finn showed little interest in seeing Jake and had suggested that he and Kimberley go for a drink with some friends.

Suddenly, there he was, flanked by Tim Ryedale, the race day presenter. In the flesh Jake looked even more impressive, thought Hattie. He was tall, well over six feet, with a lean, toned body. Dressed in trademark tight black jeans and a white shirt, with his lightly tanned face and tousled, collar length black hair, he exuded energy and vitality and made Tim look like a hospital patient. True, Tim was a rotund man in his mid forties with a drinker's nose and high colour but despite this, Hattie felt a quiet thrill wave through her and was pleased she'd spent yesterday at the beauty salon. The eyebrow design, whatever that was exactly, facial and hot oil hair treatment had all worked to make her look as if she also belonged to the Jake Delamare exclusive, clean eating brigade.

'So, ladies and gentlemen, allow me to introduce Jake Delamare.' There was a riotous round of applause from the quickly assembled crowd, nearly all of whom were female. They all had their eyes trained on their hero.

'Now Jake, you have been busy, fresh from off your success on 'Cooking up a Storm', we hear you are spreading the clean healthy eating regime, in particular the Life balls…' Tim held up a small purple pack, about the size of a book of postage stamps which bulged in the middle.

Jake leaned forward to reach the microphone. 'Well Tim, the Life balls are small protein snacks which contain a unique blend of, obviously protein, vitamins and minerals.' He had a good voice, clear, slightly husky and deep, like an actor.

Tim waved the pack around waggishly. 'Yes, but what makes this special, Jake?'

Jake gave a self-deprecating laugh. 'Well Tim, they make great snacks. Eaten over a period of time, they help the body by stopping it craving sugary, fatty and unhealthy food. A diet of my special Life balls for just a fortnight, at breakfast, lunch and a small dinner will make you lose weight rapidly, without effort or cravings…'

'So, jockeys could use them?'

'Absolutely. I'm thinking of trialling some new super protein balls with athletes and jockeys are athletes, right? I just need a few volunteers, of course.'

'Oh, I'm sure that won't be a problem, Jake,' brayed Tim. 'I mean what these people do to keep down their weight with saunas, running, starving and what have you, I'm sure they would be more than willing to give these a try…'

Hattie felt the first stirrings of disquiet. Were these being marketed as slimming aids? Surely, they needed to be tested and how could two balls be enough for anyone to survive on? What about fibre, fruit and vegetables?

'Obviously the main aim is not for slimming, it's to supplement a healthy diet primarily…' added Jake, as though reading her thoughts.

'You look good on them, that's for sure.' Tim guffawed into the microphone. 'I might try a few myself, Jake…' He patted his tweed encased paunch. 'Anyway, what are you going to do for us today?'

A table with an array of ingredients had been brought into the arena and placed next to the two men.

Jake tossed his dark locks. Hattie saw that his shirt was unbuttoned to reveal a muscular chest. His bright blue eyes surveyed the crowd and there was a pause before he began. He's playing the fans beautifully decided Hattie, but she didn't mind. Anyone as easy on the eye as Jake deserved their full attention.

'Today I'm going to show everyone how to make one of the simplest protein balls. Obviously, the Life balls have a complex set of ingredients, a few secret ones, actually.' The crowd murmured, thrilled somehow with this information. 'But the peanut ones I'm going to show you today, still pack a nutritional punch and you can use them to snack on instead of chocolate, crisps and all the bad foods which I urge you to avoid.'

A female voice behind Hattie quipped, 'I'd even give up chocolate for him…'

The woman next to Hattie was leaning heavily over towards her and elbowed her sharply in the waist. Suddenly, Hattie wasn't sure until later how it happened, she found herself yelping. She looked up at the same moment as Jake was scanning the crowd and his eyes caught hers. His sympathetic glance and conspiratorial smile seemed to imply that he'd seen the elbow barge.

'I need a volunteer. Now let me see.' There was a pause and several women involuntarily put up their hands like they were back in school.

Jake gave a slow, lazy smile and his eyes locked onto Hattie's.

'The woman with the beautiful auburn hair, would you perhaps consider helping me out?'

With a nod Hattie found herself pushed forwards and walking up towards Jake.

'Well done, darling,' he whispered. 'All you need to do is fashion the dough into balls, it's just like plasticine, alright?' Jake winked at her. 'By the way, what's your name?'

Hattie told him. She was close enough to his tanned face to see his thick dark lashes that framed his blue eyes and she breathed in his spicy cologne.

'I think we need to make it snappy chaps,' warned Tim, 'just a few more minutes.'

This reminder seemed to galvanise Jake who, with sudden professionalism, began tossing ingredients into a large bowl in the centre of the table, all the time keeping up a commentary.

'So, use organic, ethically sourced ingredients, of course. Add peanut butter, choose an unsalted variety with no added sugar, toss in chopped apricots, desiccated coconut, cinnamon, chopped dates, vanilla essence and blend it.' At this point Jake rolled up his sleeves to reveal toned forearms and there was a faint gasp as he plunged his hands into the mixture and began kneading. 'I find it easier to do it by hand. Obviously, I washed my hands thoroughly before I came out,' Jake explained.

A thin woman dressed in black who Hattie hadn't spotted before, carried a bowl of water over towards her and she was urged to wash hers.

'Now my able assistant, Hattie will roll the mixture into balls, about the size of a walnut. Now you can roll them in chopped nuts, coconut whatever you like and then put them in an airtight container in the fridge. They'll keep for two to three days and I think you'll all find them a great, healthy and delicious snack. They'll definitely enhance your life, my Life balls.' He gave a little laugh.

'We've put the ingredients on our website, I believe,' added Tim,

Hattie rolled the mixture, which was like cookie dough and obediently, dipped them into a small bowl containing coconut flakes, making about ten balls in total.

As she finished off, she was aware of Jake watching her closely. Realising this was a great opportunity, she said, 'I'd love to know more about how these things work. I'm just about to finish studying as a dietician and I'm doing a dissertation on jockeys' diets. I know a lot of them, so I might be able to get you some volunteers.'

Jake studied her thoughtfully as though coming to a decision. Damn, thought Hattie, flushing as she realised how pushy she sounded. She was aware that she was holding her breath. He probably had all sorts of weirdos throwing themselves at him and was likely to be very adept at dealing with unwanted attention. Then he smiled and it was like the sun coming out, as her embarrassment melted away.

'Hey, Hattie, that's amazing. This could be the start of a beautiful friendship. I'll get my people to speak to you and see if we can hook up. But I have to dash, I have another engagement.' He nodded at his assistant.

The thin woman appeared with a clipboard and asked for Hattie's email address. She also passed over a paper bag with some of the protein balls inside.

Tim was winding up the demonstration. 'I'd like to thank Jake here, I'm sure you'd all like to give him a proper Yorkshire round of applause.'

Amid the clapping and even whoops, Jake took Hattie by the hand and lifting their arms, pushed her into giving a slightly awkward bow in front of the audience.

As he left, he kissed her on both cheeks.

37

'You've been amazing, Hattie. I'll be in touch.' His slight stubble brushed her skin and then in a whirl he was gone, and Tim was ushering her out of the enclosure where she was greeted by Kimberley and Finn. Kimberley stared at her with new respect.

'Hattie, you lucky thing. He actually kissed you…'

Finn rolled his eyes and looked disapproving.

'I told him about my course. He's going to get in touch.' She was babbling incoherently now. 'I said I could get him some jockey volunteers.' She noticed Finn frowning. 'Once I've established that the Life balls are the real deal, of course.'

'I could ask Drew, my brother-in-law who is a chef, to have a look at them, he could probably recreate them and help analyse the contents. I'll get him to give you a ring,' suggested Finn.

Kimberley ignored him. 'Wow Hattie, this deserves a drink, don't you think Finn?'

Finn shrugged and managed a smile, but Hattie was too excited to spot his thoughtful, even troubled expression. As he queued for the bar, he looked around for Melvin, but he had not reappeared. He looked at the large TV monitor, which was installed in the bar, as he waited in line. It was coming up to the last race and the commentator went through the lineup of horses. He couldn't help noticing that Florette's odds had reduced to 2-1, so she was the red hot favourite. Was that significant and had the man's actions caused this? He wasn't sure but he filed the information away in his brain, momentarily distracted by a poster of Jake Delamare smiling his devastating smile from the noticeboard behind the bar. He shuddered. There was just something about him that made his skin crawl.

Chapter 8

DI Taverner and DS Wildblood were on their way to interview show jumper, Neil Horton. They were at the early stages of their investigation but from what several people had reported, Neil and the dead man had an argument that resulted in blows being traded in the Blacksmith's Arms, of all places, in full view of several other punters. This was a couple of days before Clary was murdered. It was rumoured that Neil was warning James off from conducting a relationship with his groom, Kerry, and the general opinion was that Neil was a good bloke who wouldn't hurt a fly but did object to James messing his trusty staff member about. DS Wildblood was far from impressed at the information they were beginning to uncover about Jimmy; he liked the ladies and was a ne'er do well, by all accounts. She was also irritated that his mobile phone still had not turned up which meant that they would have to rely on the network records, which would take longer.

'Honestly the more I hear about this victim, the more I can see why he was murdered. He's a proper Lothario.' She scowled. 'There's an ex-wife, a pregnant girlfriend and now another bloody woman that he's been coming on to. Then there's drugs, possibly dealing and God knows what else. We'll have a suspect list as long as your bloody arm!'

Gabriel shook his head. 'I know, but we mustn't speak ill of the dead. He was murdered and no one deserves to meet such a gruesome end in my book.'

His tone was light, but the rebuke was still there. Anna hung her head.

'I know sir, I'm sorry. I'm just tired, that's all, what wi' the twins and that...'

'How are they?' Gabriel had experienced parenting by proxy from close friends who had kids. He liked them in small doses but looking after them full time would no doubt drive him to drink.

DS Wildblood grinned. 'They are absolutely fine, in good health now. It wasn't asthma just the usual viruses. It's just knackering, double trouble, that's all.'

Gabriel was glad that the twins were at least healthy, but he did appreciate it must be very tough on Wildblood, as well as working in a demanding job. Just as well she had a mother-in-law and supportive husband to help out. He swung the car into the neat stable yard.

'Right, here we are. We had better make a start. Do you want to lead, and I'll chip in?'

Anna grinned as he knew she would. It was a master stroke. Anna relished a challenge and her sheer professionalism would overcome any errors due to tiredness. He absolutely knew that now he had her full attention.

'I'm quite looking forward to seeing some horses,' Gabriel added. 'Horton keeps his at Vince Hunt's place.'

Anna gave him a strange look. 'Really? Nah, I don't get why anyone likes them, 'specially racehorses. My father was a gambler and we were often left with no money for the week because he spent it on a sure thing at York. It's a mug's game, if yer ask me.'

'But he must have had some winners, surely?'

Anna shrugged. 'Maybe he did but he seemed to lose far more than he won, and then took it out on all of us.'

'Still, they are beautiful creatures and you don't have to bet on them.' For some reason Gabriel felt drawn to horses, he always had been.

Anna shook her head in firm disagreement. Clearly, her father's exploits had had a profound effect on her.

'So, did you or did you not say to James Clary that 'he'd better watch himself or else', after you had kicked him and bloodied his nose?'

Neil, apparently a show jumper, in his late 20's, attractive in a blond floppy haired sort of way, looked deeply uncomfortable.

'Well, yes, I did. But he just stood there sneering whilst I was talking to him about staying out of Kerry's way, cocky as you like. He's got a wife, a pregnant girlfriend and now he's hanging around my groom.' He flushed and realised what he'd said. 'I mean he *was* hanging round her…'

'And what time did the argument take place?' asked DS Wildblood.

'Around nine. We were in the pub when Clary comes up, cocky as anything, buying Kerry a drink, touching her bum. God, he made my blood boil!'

'And what precisely is your relationship with Kerry Mullen, Mr Horton, for you to become so angry?' Gabriel asked softly.

Horton licked his lips. 'She is an excellent groom, one of the best, a great girl all round…' Gabriel cocked an eyebrow and Neil grasped his meaning. 'No, nothing like that. There is nothing romantic going on between me and Kerry, far from it. I'm engaged to Vince Hunt's daughter, Daisy. I rent some stables from Vince for my show jumpers and keep a few of my youngsters there too. Daisy and I have been together for years.'

'So, you're dependent on Mr Hunt, I take it, and wouldn't want to upset him or his daughter?'

Neil nodded. 'That's true enough. But look, I particularly didn't want Kerry being upset by a loser like Clary. I'm competing abroad this year, if I can get the sponsors, and I have a good chance of making it big on the circuit with my youngster, Special Agent, so I'm going to need a good groom. She's an emotional girl and I don't think she'd even contemplate coming abroad with a twit like Clary playing her off against the other women in his harem.' Neil had seemed to recover his sang froid. 'I told him to leave her alone, and he goaded me with his annoying remarks about being able to have her any time he liked. It was disrespectful. I kicked him, he kicked me back and made some crude remark or other, so I punched his nose, he hit back so I punched him again. I certainly didn't kill him. Believe me, he wouldn't be worth the bother.'

Anna scowled as she peered at her notebook. 'So, did you also say, 'I'll fucking kill you, you twat."

Neil flushed and shrugged. 'I may have done, but it was just a figure of speech, that's all. I certainly didn't do anything, if that's what you're implying.' He paled when he realised that this was exactly what the two officers were thinking.

'Where did you go after you'd hit him?' persisted Anna.

'I went for a walk round to calm down and then went back to the yard and spent the evening with my girlfriend, Daisy.'

Anna pursed her lips. 'Who was in the pub at the time who would have witnessed the incident?'

Neil went through a list of names, mainly stable staff apparently, plus the landlord and a few regulars. Gabriel noted that Neil's girlfriend, Daisy, was not amongst them and wondered what she had been told about the argument.

Anna frowned. 'Hmm, and what time do you get up in the morning, Mr Horton?'

'At 4.30am precisely. The horses need skipping out and grooming. Then they need exercising. I usually have a break at about eleven and then start schooling.'

'And you never left the premises on Thursday morning?'

Neil shook his head. 'No, and what's more everyone saw me. Daisy was around all morning, so you can ask her, and Vince and the other stable staff too. They'll tell you.'

Anna nodded. 'Perhaps, you can tell us their names and we will do.'

Anna made a list of employees.

'Can I ask if you ever saw Jimmy up on the gallops or hanging around the yards?' Taverner wanted to rule out the possibility that Jimmy was spying on the horses at work, given where his body was found.

Neil shrugged. 'No one has ever mentioned anything, not Vince not anyone, so I don't think so.'

Taverner studied Horton's hands. His right hand had the bloom of faint bruising across his knuckles, suggesting he had used some real force to hit Clary, but had he murdered him? He wasn't sure.

'I think that's all for now, Mr Horton,' added Gabriel. He pondered on the best place to see the witnesses and decided that he would rather the staff members were interviewed away from the yard, so they were free to say what they wanted without being under the watchful gaze of their employers. They were far more likely to get the truth out of them. He decided to change the subject.

'It's a fascinating place you have here…' Gabriel scanned the well-kept, neatly brushed yard. Several horses had their heads over the door, looking about them. In another corner there were some horses out at grass, and there was an arena beyond, with a course of brightly coloured show jumps arranged in a figure of eight. They were absolutely huge, maybe five feet high, thought Gabriel, impressed. In another corner there were two small horse lorries and a much larger, newer one with *Neil Horton- Show Jumper* written into the fancy green and gold coach paint. The whole setup looked professional, organised and successful. Still, it was possible that given the number of staff the yard employed, all engaged in different tasks, Neil could easily have slipped out to the gallops unseen and reappeared without anyone noticing, especially very early on.

'Would you like a guided tour?'

Neil had visibly relaxed when he thought he was off the hook, for now at least, and he could afford to be generous.

Gabriel glanced at his watch. 'Well, just a very quick one and then we'd better get back to work.' He looked at Anna. 'We'll send some officers out to speak to the witnesses at their home addresses, so as not to bother them now, if you could give me a list.'

He did not need to look at his colleague to know that she was scowling.

Chapter 9

Hattie had placed the protein balls in the fridge. She'd given half of them to Kimberley who had been thrilled and keen to try them, so she could lose weight for future acting roles. She found herself replaying the scene where she had met Jake back in her head, like a video clip, over and over again. She had been staring at him in awe from outside the arena and when he was looking for a volunteer, his eyes lingered over her, she had felt goosebumps, when he had asked her to take part in his cooking demonstration. When she had blurted out about her degree and how she could get him some volunteers from the conditionals she knew, she really thought she had blown it and pushed him too hard, but had been amazed when he had actually agreed to contact her! She luxuriated in thinking about Jake; she remembered every detail of her encounter with him. The memories were like an exquisite piece of jewellery that she pulled out from time to time to relish and admire.

Her parents were out at a dinner party and Hattie flopped on the sofa with exhaustion. A day at the races was so tiring, probably the mixture of loads to see, lots of walking and fresh air, she mused. She made a cup of tea and flicked through the TV channels. There was nothing on but game shows which bored her silly. With a sigh she picked up a copy of 'Alive' magazine left by Nuala, Will's wife. Flicking through, her eye was caught by none other than Jake Delamare, photographed at a party with Tatiana before the split. God, you idiot, she chided herself. She needed to get a reality check. She'd really been taken in by the guy and yet here he was in a national magazine. He was clearly a bit of a poseur. She had to admit that his ex-girlfriend looked amazingly glamorous. As if he'd contact her! He probably said that sort of thing to everyone. Her initial enthusiasm began to dim, and she started to think more rationally, at least for now.

And what about these Life balls? Was it any more than a gimmick? There was a brief profile about Jake. He was twenty-nine and was born into a money, there was even a photo of him in front of a large country house. Clearly Jake was privileged, probably from some sort of landed gentry type family. No wonder he'd sounded so posh. He'd shone at his private school and went on to study at LSE. Then, after dabbling at work in the city, where he was something in banking, he'd seen the light about his unhealthy lifestyle and become a real advocate of healthy eating and retrained as a chef. Now he was on a mission to improve the health of the nation with his Life balls. Hmm. What exactly was in the things? She had been taught to be critical of fad diets and miracle ingredients in her training. What was it that Finn had said about his brother-in-law? Drew might shed some light on the ingredients. She sent him a quick text suggesting they meet up, then reached for her laptop and was just settling down to research them, when the phone rang.

It was Daisy. 'Hell, Hats, we've had the bloody police here today!' There was a stifled sob. Her friend was clearly holding back tears.

'Well, they will have to ask questions, won't they? If, as you say, Neil argued with Jimmy Clary they would have to check out the story. Surely it's just routine?' Hattie knew from her father that detectives took statements, checked them and looked for inconsistencies. Over the course of a murder investigation many, many people would be questioned.

'That's just it. The inspector, someone called Taverner seemed OK with Neil's explanation. I wasn't there on the evening of their argument as I was teaching. Neil told me about it, but the thing is, he missed out the most important bit. It wasn't just a row, they actually traded blows and got into a fight.'

'Oh…' Hattie could see how this might look bad. 'But if the police were OK with it…'

Daisy sounded despairing. 'They might have been, but I'm not. The fight was over the bloody groom, Kerry. I mean, what engaged man gets into a fight over another woman? And now we've had an almighty row and he's only buggered off…' Daisy's voice broke and she began to sob.

'Look,' said Hattie, 'do you want me to come over?' Her reverie about Jake and the research into the Life balls, would just have to wait.

Chapter 10

Gabriel Taverner was struggling to hold his tongue. His superior, DCI Sykes had scheduled this brief Sunday morning meeting and together they were going through the evidence. Sykes, Taverner suspected, had a very simplistic, crude approach to policing.

'So, arrest this ruddy show jumper,' he paused, 'what's his name, Horton. He'd fallen out with the victim, got into a fight and threatened him before Clary wound up dead. He has motive and opportunity. So, job done.'

Taverner sighed. 'Yes sir, but he has an alibi for Thursday morning. All the staff at the yard and his girlfriend agree that he was there all morning and Ballantyne and Haworth interviewed them at home, so there was no likelihood of them being overheard. We've got no reports of him leaving until the afternoon and some of the staff were there from before 5 in the morning.'

The DCI gave a snort and his jowly face wobbled as he made his point, as if to a slow child. 'But he is the future son-in-law of their boss, so they probably would say that, and we all know that wives and girlfriends are not reliable as witnesses. Anyway, Horton probably didn't do it but ordered someone else to do his dirty work. Come on Taverner, from where I'm standing it looks like an open and shut case. Arrest Horton and see what you can get him to tell you. Go through his phone records, put the frighteners on him and talk to the girlfriend at the same time. I don't know how you used to do things in the Met,' he added, 'but here you'll find things are pretty straightforward. Best not to complicate matters, that's what I always say.'

Taverner opened his mouth to protest but closed it again. OK, he wasn't certain that Horton their man, but he supposed it was worth probing further. He had wanted to pursue more leads before narrowing his search down. But he couldn't see what Horton's motive would be. Being protective of his groom was surely not a sufficient reason to murder someone? Unless there was something else going on, of course. If he was having an affair with the groom, then maybe. Perhaps, they just needed to conduct more searches of Horton's phone records?

'Right Sir, I will.'

DCI Sykes nodded and handed him the file. 'Anyway, how are things here? How's your father?'

Taverner's father had had a heart attack a few weeks ago, so he'd had a few days off. It had also made him re-evaluate his plans to meet his birth mother, who came from York originally. He felt it would be a huge betrayal after everything his adopted father had done for him, so he had put his plans on hold. His adoptive mother had died a few years ago, and he felt terrible guilt at even contemplating meeting his birth family. Yet the curiosity nibbled away at him, never quite going away.

He nodded. 'A lot better. He's out of hospital and is pretty much fully recovered.'

'Good, glad to hear it.' Sykes looked ill at ease. 'And are you still going to meet her, you know, your mother?'

45

Taverner shrugged. 'Maybe, when things are a bit calmer.'

Sykes nodded gravely. 'Hmm. Blood is thicker than water, though, isn't it?'

'Yes, sir, I suppose so.'

The older man eased himself up out of the office chair. 'Right, I'm off to play golf. Do you play Taverner?'

The DI shook his head.

'No? Perhaps you should try it? I'll be off. Let me know how it all goes. I'm going to be tied up for at least another week, I'd say, with this damned inquiry. Keep me informed then. Good luck, Taverner.'

'Thanks Sir.' Taverner pondered over Sykes's words. God, that was all he needed, Sykes dishing out advice. It was hard to know which version of Sykes he preferred; the authoritarian boss, or the understanding, nice guy. Still, he was right in a way. He had neatly shelved his plans to meet his birth mother when his adopted father became ill, but the plan still loomed large in his mind as unfinished business. He had a murder to investigate and that took precedence now, but he did need to make arrangements for when things were quieter. He glanced at the links board and went back to his desk, brooding over the case. He'd told the rest of the team to rest today but he needed to press on, so he decided that he should stay put and work on a few things.

Several hours later, Gabriel was still trying to piece together the last known movements of Jimmy Clary and going through the statements collected by the team. They knew from Perdita Brittain, that Jimmy worked as usual until around 2pm on the day before he'd been shot. He'd been in the pub until about 10 pm where he'd been all over Kerry like a rash. Perdita Brittain said he'd returned home, was in bed by 11pm and up before 4.30 am. Was he lured to the layby on some pretext or other? Perhaps, he was in the habit of watching the racehorses working on the gallops, but then again, he wouldn't have been able to see much from the layby. Everyone said that Jimmy was a wheeler dealer and liked to live close to the edge. Gabriel fervently wished he had Jimmy's phone. Patel had found the number from his friends, but the mobile was dead when they'd tried it. Patel had also found that it was crucially a pay as you go type, virtually impossible to trace, of course. Gabriel made a list of leads to follow and prepared for the briefing tomorrow. He wanted Wildblood to talk to the groom, Kerry Mullen. Ballantyne was too blunt, he had not seemed to get a great deal out of Jimmy's girlfriend, too upset, he'd said. Wildblood was good at the empathy, sisterhood stuff which might work well with Perdita and Kerry. He also felt sure that the brother, Gavin Clary, might know something. He should go and talk to him too. By then Patel and Cullen should have unearthed details of Jimmy's private finances. They already knew that Clary's Farm Foods was not a great success, probably running at a loss. Then there might be more information about the tyre tracks and a report from ballistics too, and they still had yet to find the murder weapon. Then, after pursuing these leads, he might feel inclined to bring Horton in for questioning. Gabriel flicked through his notes and jotted down the name of the pub where Kerry and Jimmy had met the day before his death. The Blacksmith's Arms in Walton. He decided to call in for a pint on his way home.

The Blacksmith's Arms was a cosy type of place, all beams and horse brasses, with what Taverner took to be blacksmithing type utensils hung up around the walls, interspersed with photos of horses. It was one of the smaller pubs, there was also the larger Yew Tree and The Coach and Horses on the other side of the town. The Blacksmith's Arms was positioned in the west and he assumed serviced the yards in the area. Taverner decided to order some food and sat quietly for a bit, taking in the atmosphere. Over a pint of bitter, washing down steak and ale pie with chips, he surveyed his fellow customers. There were family parties eating Sunday lunch in one area and over in another, what looked like regulars, some of whom he thought were horsy types. For one thing they all tended to be either pretty short of stature or very skinny, often both. He also noted the type of clothes they wore, jodhpurs, stretch jeans and chunky boots. And there was a blonde haired girl he thought he recognised from Hunt's yard. The place was busy, there was a pleasant atmosphere and Taverner flicked through a newspaper as he ate, happy that no-one seemed to have noticed him. Or so he thought. The crowd began to thin, and he was just considering ordering a coffee when the middle-aged man from behind the bar wandered over.

'Now then, I wonder if you'd like to order a dessert? Or coffee maybe?' The man looked him up and down and said in a low voice. 'I reckon you're either from the police or a journalist, here about Jimmy's murder, I'm guessing...'

Taverner felt his cheeks reddening. God, how stupid to imagine he'd been undetected in a quiet place like this. He gave a shrug and grinned. 'Rumbled... the former actually. Listen, I'd like a coffee and maybe a quiet word if that's OK?'

The barman jerked his head towards the end of the bar where there was an empty stool. 'I'll put your coffee there and then we can talk. I'm Henry Wilson, by the way.'

Taverner shook his outstretched hand. 'DI Taverner. So, I understand Jimmy was a regular?'

'Yep, he dropped in a few nights each week, I'd say.'

'And he was here last Wednesday?'

'Yep, he was.'

Taverner remembered the camera he'd spotted in the car park. 'But you've got CCTV? OK if I send one of my men round tomorrow?'

The nod was imperceptible. It was as if, thought Taverner, the landlord wanted to be helpful, but also wanted no trouble, like most people trying to run a business, he supposed.

'Anything else you can tell me, Mr Wilson?'

'Huh, he was OK Jimmy, a bit complex, didn't really know him well, but he was pleasant enough.'

Taverner did know. Everyone said the same thing, except for Horton.

'Bit of a ladies' man, I gather... Did you see the argument that happened between him and Neil Horton?' Taverner threw this in tentatively, wondering if Wilson would have an opinion.

'Yep. Couldn't miss it. There were fists flying, a couple of tables knocked over. Told the pair of them to get a grip.' Wilson scratched his head. 'I gave a statement to one of your officers…'

Taverner nodded. He had read it minutely.

'Do you know what happened to Clary's phone? In the statement you said it flew out of Jimmy's hand?'

'Yes, that's right.'

'Where were they standing?'

Wilson pointed to an area near the bar.

'Where did the phone go? Did Clary pick it up?'

'Maybe, I'm not sure.'

'Was Clary an argumentative type then? Was he into fighting?'

'Not generally. He was a lovable rogue mainly, more of a charmer than a fighter. You wouldn't want him hanging round your daughter, put it that way.' Wilson gave him a man to man stare.

'What about Neil Horton?'

'He seemed very het up about his groom, maybe a bit too much. Listen, I reckon if you're struggling with this case you could do worse than contact Finn McCarthy. He's an ex jockey, coaches the conditionals now. He's often in Walton. He helped sort out that bad do about a few months back. You know the betting thing…'

Taverner nodded, taking this in. Wilson wandered off to pull pints and he was left deep in thought, sipping his coffee. He looked at the area near the bar where the argument occurred and made a mental note to ask one of his officers to search the area, as it was too busy to conduct a search now. He was torn between annoyance at the assumption that he didn't quite know what he was doing and a sort of grudging intrigue. He'd remember the name Finn McCarthy in case he needed it and resolved to find out exactly what had happened in Walton a few months ago and how McCarthy had been involved. He threw down enough coins for the coffee and left. Time to try and relax because tomorrow was going to be manic and he needed to make progress with the case before Sykes got back. He knew that the DCI was ferocious once riled, and he wanted to keep on the right side of him. Wilson had hinted that maybe Horton was overly protective of his groom, so it would do no harm to bring him in for more questioning and it would help him score some points with the boss. After all, his job, was about the only thing in his life right now, and he just had to make the move north work and pick up the shattered pieces of his life somehow. When his father became ill, he had shut away all the questions he had about his identity, but he knew that they would seep out eventually. He was acutely aware that now was not the time for such soul searching, so he had to keep working. After all, he had a murderer to catch.

Chapter 11

Finn had been allocated Gavin Clary who was a conditional at Vince Hunt's yard. He was clearly aware that his brother had been murdered, so he rang Vince to see if the lad was up for a visit. Apart from anything else, Finn's role was partly pastoral and if Gavin needed time out to help his family and grieve, then this could be arranged, and he could help support him. It could prove very tricky having Neil around, especially since the police viewed him as the chief suspect.

'Well, you can visit for me, Finn. The lad is down, but more than that, it's as if he feels responsible. I'm a bit out of my depth, actually. I suggested he have a few weeks off, but he said that would make matters worse. More time to think, he said. So, I'll tell him you'll meet him at 10, shall I?'

Finn agreed and wondered about Gavin's presentation. Probably, he was just grieving and daren't take leave because he was worried about his position at the yard. He had previously worked as a stable lad and had only just been given a conditional licence. The National Hunt season didn't start properly until October, so he could afford to have the time off. Vince had both Flat and National Hunt horses, so would be concentrating on the former at the moment. Finn could reassure him on that score and suggest that he took compassionate leave. Maybe he knew why his brother had been murdered and if that was the case, then he would advise him to contact the police. Even though he and Hattie had helped solve a betting scam that involved many locals, a murder was something else. He did feel curious about the motive behind Jimmy Clary's death, but then from what he heard he had a lot of enemies, including several women that he was having simultaneous relationships with, so any one of them could have turned nasty. Then, there were the rumours of dodgy business interests too. Besides a murder was definitely one for the police.

He arrived at the yard to find that the horses had been exercised and there was a handful of lads mucking out and sweeping up. He found Vince running his hands up and down the legs of a large, chestnut horse.

'Ah, Finn. I'll introduce you to Gavin then call into the house if you would and have a coffee with us. I want to speak to you about something.'

Vince led him to a tack room which smelt of neatsfoot oil, leather and the distinctive smell of horses. He disappeared and came back with a pale, slim youth with dark curls and thickly lashed blue eyes. He had a haunted expression.

'Now, this is Gavin Clary, your coach, Finn McCarthy. I'll leave you to have a chat, shall I?' Vince, Finn guessed, felt awkward about discussing a complex emotion like grief with the lad, and Finn wasn't too sure how to go about it either.

Finn extended his hand and Gavin shook it with surprising firmness.

'I heard about your brother. It must be a real shock. I'm so sorry.'

Gavin nodded, his expression grim.

'So, I just wondered what your plans are? Do you need to have some time off, maybe visit your family? There will be a funeral at some point…' Finn presumed the police would not release the body until they had finished conducting tests for the post-mortem, so it may take a while. Gavin gulped, a wave of emotion washing over him.

Finn touched the lad's arm. 'Look, don't worry about your job at a time like this. I can square it with Vince and besides the National Hunt season hasn't started properly yet, so it won't do any harm to go off for a bit. I imagine your family would like to see you.' He knew how close Irish families were. And it must be very awkward having Neil around.

Gavin swallowed hard, biting back tears.

'It's like if I just keep working, keep going, you know, it's as though it never happened. I keep on expecting him to walk into the room, I just can't take it in.'

Finn let the paroxysm of emotion die down and just listened. It was easy to jump in with platitudes but he realised that listening and saying nothing was far more difficult, but hopefully more helpful.

Gavin looked up; his face contorted with misery. 'He was me big brother and I loved him, looked up to him, you know? I hear what they're all saying about him, he liked the ladies, the horses and that, but he was me brother, I just can't believe it. Today is his birthday, he'd be thirty-five.'

He sat down, his head in his hands. Finn looked at him helplessly. It seemed all the more poignant that today would have been Clary's birthday.

'So, do you know why anyone would want to harm your brother?'

Gavin looked up. For a second a strange expression flitted over his face, as if he knew exactly what had happened, then it was gone.

'No, of course not. And I'm not worried about Neil, by the way. The police are way off beam. He wouldn't harm a fly, anyway.' He rubbed his eyes. 'I'll carry on working a wee while and when the funeral is arranged, I'll go back to Ireland for a couple of weeks. In the meantime, I'll go to Church and pray for me brother's immortal soul.'

Finn nodded. He realised that having a strong religion would probably be a huge comfort at a time like this. He wished sometimes that he had the firm convictions that went hand in hand with religion. He fished into his pocket for his business card.

'OK. If you need me, here's my number. I can put you in touch with specialist services, if you want, or if you maybe need to chat, then just ring me. I know counsellors, doctors, just let me know. I wouldn't want you to struggle. I'll catch up with you in a couple of weeks. I'm sure the police will be in touch. Take care.'

Gavin managed a smile and put the card into his trouser pocket.

Finn walked up the farmhouse with a feeling of disquiet. He had a horrible suspicion that Gavin knew far more than he was letting on and what was more, he seemed certain that Neil was not involved.

How did he know? Still, it was a murder investigation and he felt sure that the police would work tirelessly to bring the murderer to justice, so he would let them get on with it.

In the Hunt household, Finn realised that Jimmy's death had implications for the whole family. Vince showed him into the kitchen where he was greeted by Rose Hunt, Vince's wife, Daisy, Hattie's friend, her younger sister, Alice and Neil, Daisy's fiancé.

'How was Gavin?' asked Vince.

'As well as can be expected, I suppose. He doesn't want any time off just yet but may do later on after the funeral.'

Rose handed him a mug of coffee and produced a coffee and walnut cake. Finn took a small slice. He saw that Daisy looked far from her usual ebullient self and Neil was ashen. Finn wondered what the family wanted.

Vince cleared his throat. 'Well, Finn. We want to talk to you about Jimmy Clary, not just because of Gavin although, of course, we are worried about him and it is awkward with the police questioning Neil.'

Daisy rolled her eyes at her father. 'It's just that the police think Neil is a suspect because he had some argument with Jimmy the night before he died in full view of the whole pub…'

Finn looked inquiringly at Neil. 'I just wanted to stop him making a fool of my groom, Kerry. He was all over her and I know for a fact he has, had, at least two other women on the go. Now they think I murdered him because I punched him.'

'Right.' Finn had heard the gist of the story from Hattie and could see that this would be awkward for Neil, not to mention for Daisy. It seemed an extreme reaction to hit Jimmy over his attentions towards a member of staff. He imagined that Neil had had a lot of explaining to do and not just to the police.

'Anyway, they think Neil is chief suspect number one and even though he has an alibi for the morning that Jimmy was murdered, they still seem to think that he could have slipped out or hired someone to shoot him,' Vince added.

Finn shook his head. It sounded ridiculous unless, of course, there was something they weren't telling him, which he suspected was highly likely.

'Well, I'm sure the police will eliminate Neil from their inquiries, and everything will be fine.'

Vince shook his head. 'But that's just it. I'm not sure they'll try that hard. It's easy to pin the blame on Neil and it means the police won't have to look any further. It will be a simple prosecution. That's why we want you to do the job.'

Finn nearly spat out his coffee. 'What job?'

Daisy looked at him steadily. 'We want to pay you to find out who murdered Jimmy Clary and therefore exonerate Neil. Should be straightforward for a man of your skills. You could ask Harriet to help you. After all, you did a pretty good job with the missing jockey and all that stuff with Dr Pinkerton.'

Finn opened his mouth to speak but Vince interrupted him.

'We know all about miscarriages of justice and dodgy police evidence, so we really need someone to act quickly. You have the right skills but you're not local, so you would be perfect!'

Finn looked at the sea of faces, with their serious expressions and wondered what on earth to say.

'Well, you see the thing is, dealing with race fixing is one thing, but a murder is quite another. Besides, the police are involved, and the ball is in their court. They are the proper authority to investigate, so I'm afraid I can't help you.'

Vince sighed, his eyes intent. 'Sleep on it, see how you feel tomorrow. You and Harriet were amazing in that other case. We'd just feel so much happier if you were involved and we'd pay you the going rate, of course.'

Daisy took Neil's hand and squeezed it, then gazed at Finn imploringly.

'Please, Finn. You are our last hope.'

Five pairs of eyes bored into him, but he had to stick to his guns.

'I'm sorry. I was directed by the British Horseracing Authority to investigate the last case because there was clear evidence that conditionals were being adversely affected. From what I understand, there is no suggestion that Clary's murder had anything to do with racing, therefore I have no authority to act.'

Vince sighed. 'But if there was evidence to suggest otherwise then you'd consider it?'

Finn shrugged. 'If the racing authorities wanted me to, then, maybe...'

The family looked devastated. Finn was firm, however. That would be the end of that, he decided, as he left. Jimmy's death was unlikely to be anything to do with racing, and the police would find their killer. How wrong he was.

As he was driving home to York his phone rang. He used the hands-free kit expecting it to be Kimberley or Hattie. It was his boss, Tony Murphy.

'Now then, Finn. I've heard a whisper that there's been a murder in Walton. Do you know anything about it?'

'Yes. It was a chap called James Clary who runs an organic vegetable business.'

'Yes, yes, but wasn't he found by the gallops in Walton? And isn't he the brother of one of your conditionals?'

It seemed that Tony was remarkably well informed, which made Finn decidedly wary.

'Yes, that's right. Gavin Clary.'

'How's the lad doing?'

'I've just been to see him actually. He's upset, holding it together, just. He'll probably take some leave as soon as the body is released for the funeral. I'm just trying to support him and negotiate with his guvnor, that's all.'

'Hmm.'

Finn could hear the mental cogs working.

'Well, the thing is Finn, the bosses have asked that you make some inquiries on behalf of the BHA. I can't say too much but RaceStraight have had a few hints about something amiss, and if there is the slightest suggestion that Clary's murder was anything to do with racing then we want to know about it. You are well placed to make inquiries with you covering the area.'

'But surely it's a matter for the Integrity Unit?'

The BHA policed racing very thoroughly and had a specialist team, the Integrity Unit, who dispatched staff to various areas, sometimes taking on different undercover roles in stables, in order to investigate anything that threatened the reputation of racing.

'No, no, it would take too much time to establish undercover staff and you're already well known in the area, so you're ideal. All I'm asking is that you keep your ear to the ground, do some low key investigations, don't get in the way of the police and report back anything that relates to racing. You can still carry on as a jockey coach, in fact, it is essential that you do. Don't worry, we have cleared it all with the local DCI. You did such a splendid job last time.'

Finn was beginning to wish he hadn't done quite so well. He also wondered what 'low key' investigations were exactly.

'Look, do you know something for definite about the murder?'

'No, just the usual whispers and rumours, nothing concrete. But we have to keep abreast of everything so that we can deal with the fall out. It could be a PR disaster.'

'And what do I get out of it?'

'Of course, you'll be paid handsomely, and you'll be defending our way of life.'

Finn sighed. Tony certainly knew which buttons to press. Both men were staunch defenders of the reputation of racing and were acutely aware that bad press could be very damaging. It could also be risky for him personally, given the fact that someone had been murdered. He was clearly dealing with a highly dangerous criminal.

'Well, I insist that given the obvious dangers, I am provided with a gun.'

Tony paused as he considered this. After a while he came to a decision.

'Fine. I'll get one of the Integrity Unit staff to issue you with one. Do you know how to use one?'

'Well, I haven't used one in a long time, but I used to shoot.'

'Fine, I'll sort someone out to give you some training, no problem.'

Despite his misgivings, Finn found himself agreeing to taking on the role.

He could sense approval ebbing over the radio waves. 'Excellent, Finn. I knew you wouldn't let us down. I'll be in touch about the weapon training, and in the meantime keep your wits about you. And it goes without saying that this is strictly confidential.'

'Of course. Can I ask Harriet to help?'

'The girl who helped you before, in the Pinkerton case? Well, I'll leave that to your own judgement, in fact from what I hear she could prove useful, as long as she's sworn to secrecy too, of course.'

Finn promised him she would be. He could think of no-one he'd rather work with. He signed off, wondering exactly what he was getting himself into. He almost rang Vince Hunt to tell him the good news before he realised that that was exactly the wrong thing to do. It was essential that they carried on as normal and maintained their cover. All he had to do now was tell Hattie.

Chapter 12

It had been an odd forty-eight hours reflected Hattie, as she put the kettle on and made tea for Daisy and her parents in the kitchen at home. She'd spent most of Saturday evening consoling her friend after the row with her fiancé, Neil. When she'd found out Neil had been in a fight with Jimmy Clary about Kerry, his groom, Daisy had called him, 'a two-timing little shit' and other worse things. The fact that there was no evidence that Neil was in some sort of relationship with Kerry, had not deterred her friend. But when, on Monday evening, Neil was taken to York police station for questioning, Daisy's views had undergone a complete transformation.

'So, why would they take him to the police station, Bob? I mean it's obvious he hasn't done anything. Poor Neil, can I get a message to him? Supposing he thinks I've abandoned him over this stupid row over Kerry and takes his own life in the cell?'

Daisy was now cradling her tea and gazing at Hattie's father as if he was the oracle. Tears threatened and her bottom lip trembled. In her holey navy jodhpurs and baggy jumper, Daisy smelled faintly of horses and looked dreadful. Her dark hair was scraped back into a small ponytail and her pale face, eyes devoid of makeup, had violet smudges underneath. She looked close to breaking point.

Bob Lucas gave a sigh. 'Look Daisy, as far as I can make out, he's not even been arrested. Clearly the police will see him as a person of interest and want to talk to him more, if as you say, he saw the victim a couple of days before and argued with him.'

'But supposing Neil gets blamed for it, they set him up, plant a gun on him or something?'

Bob's eyes widened and Hattie could see him suppressing a smile.

'I'm sure he's got nothing to fear in that way. My advice is to go and get some rest and then you'll be fresh and ready to help Neil when he leaves the station.'

Hattie's mother, Philippa, was busy chopping onions at the battered pine table. She looked up and took in Daisy's demeanor.

'But before that you must have something to eat. When was your last meal, Daisy? Several days ago, I shouldn't wonder…'

Hattie went to the fridge and found the bag of Life protein balls.

'Mum's right you know, everything's better if you eat properly. Have one of these while I help Mum cook, it'll keep you going.'

As she knew it would, the Life balls distracted Daisy for the time being. Her friend ate three in quick succession.

'These are alright, where'd you get them?'

Hattie explained.

'Oh Christ. What a rotten mate I am! Something really cool happens to you like meeting Jake Delamare from 'Cooking up a Storm' and before you can tell me all about it, I dump all my crap on you...' Daisy's eyes filled with tears.

Philippa stopped mid stir. 'Damn, Hattie, I forgot to tell you. You had a message from someone called Tracey. She's something to do with that Jake Delamare. I've written down the number. Something about popping in to see him at The Marsden Hotel for a meeting....'

Hattie felt her cheeks flush. 'When was this? I haven't missed it, have I?'

Philippa found a post-it note, where she'd written the details in her italic handwriting. She passed it over and went back to stirring.

Hattie scanned the note.

'Wednesday. 10am meeting at Marsden'.

'What's this love?' Bob asked.

Hattie suppressed a grin and tried to play it down.

'It's only a meeting with Jake Delamare. When we met at York, I asked if he could tell me more about the protein balls. I was thinking we could try some with jockeys, you know how they struggle with their weight, do some research really. You know I'm doing my dissertation on jockeys' diets? He said we'd have a chat about it.'

'Get you!' shrieked Daisy. 'You do know who he is? Alice is crazy about him. He was great on 'Cooking up a Storm', he even dated Natalia Black, didn't he? His food is to die for and so healthy and nutritious. Those Life balls were absolutely delicious.' Hattie couldn't help but notice that the protein snacks were suddenly far tastier when Daisy realised who had invented them.

'Hmm,' Bob seemed unimpressed.

 Philippa was checking to see if the pasta was cooked. 'Might be something to put on your CV, darling.'

Over spaghetti bolognaise and a nice Valpolicella, Daisy seemed to revive and chattered in a disjointed way.

'Oh Philippa, this is delicious, totally to die for. Didn't know I was so hungry. You'll have to tell me all about Jake, he's so cool.' She shoved more into her mouth and then said, through half a mouthful. 'You know s'pose I should be pleased, 'cos Neil really landed one on Jimmy, knocked his phone out of his hand and everything.' Hattie frowned, not following. 'I mean, at least Neil can handle himself.'

Her father glanced at Hattie, they had often talked about the importance of phones in police investigations these days and she could guess what he might be thinking.

'Did the phone break or anything?' Hattie asked casually. 'And did Jimmy have it when he left?'

'Neil said Jimmy was too scared to look for it, so he just vamoosed. It's probably still there in the pub under a table or something. It wasn't expensive. It was only one of those little ones, like you give to kids.'

Hattie's ears pricked up and she made a mental note to search the pub, though surely the police had done that already? She supposed it depended if Neil had told them about knocking the phone out of Jimmy's hands. Mostly, she guessed they would have concentrated on investigating his home and business. Interesting. But then her mind went back to her meeting on Wednesday. What should she wear? What on earth should she say? She was both delighted and terrified at the prospect.

Dragging her mind back to the present, she realised it would really help if she could locate Jimmy's phone and she now knew just where to look. OK, so they weren't investigating his death, but it would do no harm to help the police along with their inquiries, would it? She sent Finn a message.

'Meet you at the Blacksmith's sometime this week? Think I know where Jimmy's phone is. H'

Chapter 13

Taverner called the team together on Tuesday at 5pm to review the case. The team were chatting and the mood, as far as he could tell, still seemed quite buoyant. He tried to look upbeat, although his thigh was playing up and he'd had to wander down to The Langford Arms near home last night, to buy several whiskies to anaesthetise the dull ache.

'Right, we brought Horton in for questioning yesterday but we haven't got enough to charge him. But he remains a person of interest in the ongoing investigation. We still need more to link him to the crime, so we mustn't leave any stone unturned. We need to go through Neil Horton's phone records and do an ANPR number plate check. If he was in a relationship with Kerry, they would meet well away from Walton, and he's bound to have contacted her on his phone, so that is something to look out for. Anything else?'

Ballantyne put up his hand. 'We've been through the CCTV from The Blacksmith's Arms. It confirms that Clary was there with Kerry. Eyewitnesses said that they looked pretty cosy.'

'OK. Anna how did you get on with the women in Clary's life?'

Anna sprung to her feet and flicked through her notebook. Taverner was pleased to note that she looked better rested and seemed her efficient self once more. 'Well, the FLO hasn't got anything significant to tell us about the ex-wife Caroline. Perdita Brittain is more interesting. She claims to rubbish the rumours that Jimmy was playing around with Kerry, but she is pregnant with Clary's child, so that might have tipped her over the edge. She's also got previous.' There was a pause while she found the right place in her notebook and a hum of expectation came from the group.

'She was done for a variety of Public Order offences dating from the last three years. Protests about housing developments, fracking, climate change and so on. During this time, she was dating that eco warrior, I think some of you may know him as 'Wolf', as he likes to call himself.'

Haworth stopped chewing his crisps and let out a guffaw. 'Sure, I know him. I've arrested him a few times. He is aka Tarquin Montague, eldest son of Lord Montague. Anyway, Tarquin's supposedly still in love with Perdita. She reported him for stalking a few months ago and uniform went to warn him off.'

Haworth pulled up a photo of a grubby looking guy with red dreadlocks and very pale skin. They all craned their necks to get a better look. It was hard to imagine anyone who looked less like the son of a Lord than this man, who upon his father's death, would inherit the title and entire estate. Taverner listened carefully.

'Hmm, it might be worth us asking him a few questions. Print off the photo and put it on the board, will you? Find out where this Wolf character was last Thursday. You get onto it, Haworth, since you know a bit about him. And by the way, did you find Clary's phone in the pub?'

Haworth shook his head. 'No, I haven't managed to get there yet, but I'll make it a priority.'

'OK. Make sure you do. What did the groom have to say for herself?'

Anna opened her mouth to speak and Taverner nodded for her to continue.

'Kerry Mullen, the groom was upset. She just kept sobbing. Says she and Jimmy were just talking, that was all, and Neil got the wrong end of the stick. Reckons Perdita is jealous of her too. Thinks Perdita is a stuck-up cow. She's from a top brass family too, her father's a Colonel. Christ, I wouldn't like to see these three together in a room, would you?'

'A right cat fight, I reckon,' added Ballantyne.

Haworth gave a snort. 'He put it about a bit didn't he, our Jimmy. Wonder what his secret was, didn't look much…'

'Probably made them laugh and listened to them,' said Anna, 'bet he cooked too, you should try it, your wife might thank me.'

There were several jeers at this. Haworth was known to be something of an old fashioned guy, who regarded cooking as beneath him. Ballantyne tossed a screwed up ball of paper over at him, by way of agreement. They knew each other well and it was a way for staff to let off steam, away from the pressures of investigating some terrible stuff. Taverner let the banter run for a while, then got them back on track.

'OK Patel, Cullen, where are we on ballistics and tyre tracks?'

The young bespectacled man was a genius with technology and gadgets, and he was ably assisted by Natalie Cullen, the young DC who had recently joined the team. Patel peeped around from his computer screen.

'Well, we know that the wound was caused by a shotgun, so there will be little evidence to help us identify the gun. There are loads of licensed gun owners in the area, they're mainly used for sport, hunting and so on. So, lots of people locally could own one and it would be easy enough to modify.'

'Can you go through the list of gun owners and ask if anyone has had a gun stolen recently?' asked Taverner with a sigh.

Patel nodded. 'I'm on it, boss.'

'And the tyre tracks?'

Haworth cleared his throat. 'Thought to belong to a four by four. There's a couple of possible tyre brands but they're fairly common with half the locals driving them, it might not tell us much, but there is some distinctive wear, so that might help.'

'OK, let's see what Patel comes up with and what the door to door inquiries throw up. Someone, somewhere, must have seen something. I suppose the lads from the yard wouldn't have been there at that time, but it's worth going through their statements again. Cullen, you can help Patel out and talk to the locals about guns. Say we're doing spot checks and I want to be sure all the guns are accounted for. Do we have an address for this Wolf character?'

Anna read it out. 'I phoned the family today. He wasn't there, at a demonstration apparently and expected back tomorrow.'

'Right, you and Ballantyne go and visit him tomorrow, just to introduce yourselves. Haworth can take the statement later, two visits from us should put the wind up him. In the meantime, stick to the jobs I've given you and we'll reconvene same time tomorrow.' Taverner glanced round the team. 'I'm confident we **will** get this killer, by painstaking work and effort. We all need to pull together and pretty fast. I have faith in each and every one of you. Now scram.'

Taverner wished he'd still got the bottle of Macallans in his desk drawer, but that was at the Met, here he was trying to stay healthy and so far, his bottom drawer had stayed resolutely free of whisky. Taverner read through his notes, did a bit of filing, started a mind map about Wolf but kept being interrupted by Sandra, the office cleaner. When she wasn't hoovering, she was singing loudly. There was, he decided, only so many versions of 'Show me the way to Amarillo' a person could stand with or without the accompaniment of her hoover.

Taverner drove back home, squashed into the red Fiat 500. It hadn't been his choice of car; it had been Georgia's, his ex's. He had acquired it after popping down to London to pick up some belongings from the flat. The train was late, then cancelled due to a signaling issue, so he'd come back in it. He'd return it one day soon but wasn't sure it would be missed. He guessed the Hedge Fund manager, Jeremy, she was now seeing could easily buy her a new car, something more fancy which was what she'd wanted all along apparently. After some initial ribbing, he decided to commute to and from work in it, as the fuel economy was much better than his Mercedes.

His cottage was quiet, rather chilly and didn't feel like home. Taverner made himself a ham sandwich and flicked through the TV channels. TV detectives on most sides. How come they got the drama so wrong, made it all look exciting and quick? They had taken the boring bits out, that was how.

By 9.30pm he was down at The Langford Arms near to his cottage. It was a stone building with a flagged floor and wooden beams. It hadn't been changed or modernised much over time. The walls were decorated with old pictures of horses. An old bloke sat in the corner, he wore a blue beret and stared silently into his pint.

He ordered a whisky and the old man sidled up.

'Ah, you're living in old Matheson's place. Are you here for work of pleasure?'

Taverner grinned. 'Just work.' He really didn't want to talk about the job as he might attract the wrong attention or put people on their guard. He struggled for some conversational gambits and studied the paintings on the walls.

'It's a lovely place. Racing seems to be a massive thing hereabouts. I suppose some of yards have had some really good horses?'

'Oh yes. Henderson, behind yon hedge here, is a right good trainer. He has had lots of Group One winners and a couple of Cheltenham Gold Cup ones too. There's loads of good trainers here, lad.' The blue eyes studied him.

'Well, I hope you get some tips, I expect you do, drinking in here.'

The grey head nodded. 'Aye, we do. A couple of the lads will let summat slip every now and again and there's always some chaps spying on the gallops, trying to get information.'

It occurred to Taverner that maybe that was what Clary had been trying to do, but then he couldn't have seen much from the layby. Perhaps he had intended on walking higher up to get a better vantage point, or maybe he was on the phone or about to take a leak? Despite Clary's disreputable past, he shouldn't ignore this as a line of inquiry.

The old man extended his gnarled old hand. 'Reg Taylor. I reckon you've come in here to find out about Jimmy Clary, have you?'

Taverner was about to protest, as he realised that the anonymity he craved was about to go up in smoke again.

Reg tapped his nose. 'Word gets about in a small place like this, see?'

Taverner nodded, cursing these small towns where everyone knew everyone else. In London, no one knew anyone, not even their neighbours.

He shook Reg's hand. 'Taverner. So, is there anything I need to know about Jimmy Clary that might explain why he was murdered?'

Reg nodded and bent his head towards him, nodding at the glass.

'Ah, he's an interesting character, rather was.'

'Do you think his death was related to racing?'

Reg shook his head. 'No, he had other fish to fry, I reckon.'

Taverner got to his feet and picked up the pint glasses. It was going to be a long evening.

Chapter 14

Finn met Hattie at Hunt's place at around noon. They chose the time when the lads would have finished for the morning. It was handy because Hattie still rode Daisy's ex-show jumper, Kasper, and she took him into the arena. Finn decided to put Harriet through her paces and after warming up, had her jumping three fences on the bounce, coming at them from different directions and speeds.

'It will really help your horse with his balance and confidence,' he'd added.

Hattie started off quite poorly but managed to improve after several attempts. She needed to become fitter, though, Finn noticed, as she and her horse were breathing very heavily.

'Right, I think that's enough for today. Let's cool him down and then we can get going. Where do you think Clary's phone is?' he hissed.

'The lounge at The Blacksmith's Arms, apparently. Let's have lunch there.'

'Great.'

'So, did Vince speak to you and are you helping Neil?'

Finn shook his head. 'Not exactly, but I'll explain later.'

Hattie frowned but didn't press him further.

When they made their way back to the stables, Vince was showing round a well dressed, dark haired man with a florid complexion. His suit was made from tweed and looked expensive, probably straight from Saville Row, his accent cut glass and his whole demeanour screamed landed gentry.

'So, I'm confident that your horses will settle and with our excellent facilities such as the swimming pool and solarium, then we should look forward to a great season.'

'Splendid. I presume I can pop in and check on their progress?'

'Course. Anytime you want, just give me a call.'

Vince noticed Finn. 'Can I introduce the conditional jockey coach, Finn McCarthy. He coaches several of the jockeys in the area. Finn, Guy Montague and this is Hattie Lucas, a family friend, who rides Kasper, my daughter's old horse, from time to time.'

Guy shook Finn's hand. 'Finn McCarthy.' He looked slightly awed. 'I'm delighted to meet you. My father won a lot of money backing you.' He shook Harriet's hand. 'Lovely to meet you too, Harriet.' His eyes slid back to Finn. 'Who do you coach here?'

'Gavin Clary and Connor Moore.'

'Fantastic. I am a great supporter of young jockeys, and of course their weight allowances can come in very handy too. I hope they'll be able to ride some of my horses, guided by you, naturally. My father and I followed your career with interest. It's great to meet you in person.'

'And you too.'

Vince and Montague drifted off. Harriet glanced behind her, noticing the man's brand new Land Rover parked in the yard.

'Hey, he's a bit posh. No wonder Vince wants us to exonerate Neil. He obviously don't want anything to jeopardise having him as an owner. He looks like he has some serious cash.'

Finn nodded. 'Hmm. Well, the family are loaded. The estate is huge. I remember his father, Lord Montague. He had a good eye for a horse, so let's hope his son has his skill. He runs Montague Stud but also has a fortune from his software company 'Think Smart.''

'So, he's a good businessman, too, by the sound of it.'

'Yep. His older brother Tarquin is the complete opposite, he's one of those eco warriors or something. He is set to inherit when his father dies but a lot of people feel Guy might have been a better bet. There was some scandal about the family a couple of years ago, but I forget what exactly. Last time I saw him he looked like an extra in Brave Heart, all red curls and bulging biceps. He's definitely passionate about conservation and the environment. I think he's been inside a few times because of demos and animal rights stuff.' Finn glanced at his watch. 'OK. We had better get on and find that phone.'

It was later than he thought, and he wanted to stop Harriet being distracted by gossip about the Montagues. He wasn't particularly impressed by people with money, especially if it was inherited. It was what was in people's hearts that mattered, and money had very little bearing on that in his experience.

The Blacksmith's Arms was fairly quiet mid-week, so they settled down in one corner, sipping wine, in Hattie's case and Coke in Finn's, waiting for their food to be cooked. There was an older man, behind the bar and a young fresh-faced barmaid who eyed Finn appreciatively.

'So, you're not going to take Vince's job?'

'Not exactly.' Finn leant forward and lowered his voice. 'You see the thing is my boss Tony rang me and the BHA want me to investigate Clary's murder as I'm already working here.'

Harriet's eyes lit up. 'I knew it!'

'But the thing is we can't tell anyone, not even Daisy.'

'No, no, I can see that. Hey, did you say we?'

Finn nodded. 'Yes, I cleared it with Tony, but it's going to be dangerous and if I think it's too dangerous for you to be involved then you must stay at home. No ifs or buts. Right?'

Harriet nodded. 'Of course. So, does the BHA think that Clary's death is linked to racing?'

'I don't think there's anything concrete, just some rumours and information from punters and RaceStraight. From what I understand, Clary could have had a lot of enemies anyway from different of walks of life, so we probably won't have to do much anyway. And of course, we have to keep out of the police's way.'

'Hmm.' Harriet's eyes raked around the bar. 'So, what about Clary's phone?'

Finn cast his eyes around the room. It was a typical country pub with a large inglenook fireplace, horse brasses and rural water colours adorning the stone walls. There were French doors, which led to an aromatic beer garden with hanging baskets, frothing with vibrant pink and purple fuchsias.

'Where did Neil sit, do you think?'

Hattie thought for a bit. 'Not sure. Now imagine you're Jimmy and you walk in and see Kerry. It depends where she was sitting, I suppose. 'Harriet frowned in concentration as she re-enacted the scene in her imagination.

Finn shook his head. Sometimes Hattie was too dramatic for her own good. He could do without a theatrical reconstruction of the whole thing. He stood up and wandered about, bending to shine his phone light under a sideboard and then under various tables, systematically as he approached the bar. He kept a surreptitious eye on the staff and made to tie his laces when bar staff appeared. He went to investigate various paintings, mainly of horses and scenes of Walton at the turn of the century and used this as an excuse to explore and have a good look around. As he approached the bar, he dropped a pound coin on the floor and moved to investigate the underside of a bookcase at one side as he went to pick it up. It was then that he spotted two silver objects glistening from the torchlight.

'Bingo.'

He quickly fished out some freezer bags and used them like gloves. After some manoeuvring with a laminated menu, when the barman's attention was elsewhere, he held the silver phone gingerly and replaced the battery and back, which had come off when the phone hit the floor. He put it in a bag and placed it on the table.

Harriet was amazed and smiled at his use of the freezer bags.

'Great. I can't believe you found it so quickly and that you came prepared.'

'Well, it was easy to find. I suppose we should give this to that Inspector?' he added. 'Taverner, wasn't it?'

Hattie nodded. 'The battery will be dead after all this time I should think anyway. I'll pop it into the station when I'm next passing through.'

Still wearing the bag, Finn's fingers hovered over the silver button at the side. He pressed it and the screen leapt into life in a blur of noise and colour.

Finn and Hattie stared at each other, accomplices in what was about to happen.

'I suppose it won't hurt to have a quick look. I'm wearing these', Finn added. He scrolled through the phone, both heads together, eyes trained at the screen.

'What do you suppose his passcode was?' He scowled at the phone as he realised they had reached a brick wall.

Harriet frowned as she considered what it might be.

'What was Clary's date of birth? I use that for mine.'

'God knows.' Finn thought for a bit and tried to put himself in Jimmy's shoes. He had no idea what Jimmy's date of birth was. What else would someone like Jimmy use? Then it came to him. Of course! What was it that Gavin had said when he visited him? It had been Jimmy's birthday, he remembered.

'What was the date last Tuesday?'

Harriet frowned. 'Hmm, June 10th, why?'

He keyed in 1006. The phone sprang into life as Hattie looked on in surprise.

Finn scrolled quickly through some of the contacts and messages. There was one that stood out. In fact, there were loads of messages between Jimmy and another person. He showed the screen to Harriet.

'Look, there's lots of messages between Clary and someone.'

'Who?'

'Someone called Drew Morrison.'

Harriet gasped. 'Isn't that...?'

Finn nodded glumly; his heart dropping like a stone.

He wondered why his brother-in-law was listed in the contacts as Avocado and had sent the last message to Jimmy.

See you at the usual place, same time. Drew

Their lunch arrived and they ate, Finn's mind full of questions about his brother-in-law and his association with Jimmy Clary. Drew had arranged to meet him the day before he was shot. Had they argued about something? Did that make him the murderer? He shuddered at the thought.

Chapter 15

Hattie arrived at The Marsden Hotel at 9.58 am, just in time for her ten o'clock appointment with Jake. Indecision had meant that she had pulled out the entire contents of her wardrobe in an attempt to find the perfect outfit, only to decide on the first dress she had tried on. She ran into the foyer and explained that she was meeting Jake Delamare. As it turned out, she needn't have rushed. After she'd drunk two leisurely coffees in the lounge, he finally walked in at 10.40 flanked by a bald headed man and Tracey, looking anxious and holding a clipboard.

'Sorry we're late,' said Tracey, 'we got held up.' There were no apologies from Jake, Harriet noted sourly.

Jake, wearing another white shirt and tight jeans, was staring at Hattie so hard she wondered if she'd got her dress on inside out or something. He sat down without breaking eye contact.

'You look very well, you radiate health. Did you eat the Life balls?'

Hattie was about to explain that Daisy had eaten most of them, she'd just tried one so far, but Jake didn't wait for her reply.

'I knew it, you see how wonderful they are. Now, how can we work together, you and I? I'm thinking a photo shoot, you, me and the jockeys. Can you get me some guinea pig jocks, Hattie, from your connections?'

Hattie stammered. 'Well, I was thinking more of a research project, a controlled trial to see if they could help a variety of sports men and women.' She was thinking of a proper research study, similar to those she had read about in her degree. Her voice petered off when she saw Jake's impatient expression. This didn't seem to be on his agenda at all.

'Not necessary, Hattie. No one does that these days, they use experiential evidence. They work, are you not proof? Am I not proof?' He clicked his fingers. 'I want jockeys, maximum publicity, I'm thinking breakfast TV, radio, and most importantly a race meeting, as soon as possible.' He glanced at Tracey. 'When's the next race meeting round here?'

'I only know national hunt jockeys...' added Hattie. Tracey frowned. 'You know, those who ride over fences, so there are less meetings. Cartmel run hurdle races in the summer.'

Tracey gave her a dismissive look and tapped the keys on her smart 'phone.

'The next meeting at Cartmel is on Friday...'

'Right, Friday it is. If you let me know which jockeys are in, we'll bike the Life balls round to them. I'll see you there, Hattie.' He waved a hand. 'Tracey will sort out the details. Ciao!'

Hattie watched him go and gulped. Indignation pulsed through her, but then he was famous and clearly very busy, and she had promised to find him some volunteers. How? She decided to phone Finn.

'Help. I need a favour...'

When she'd explained that she and Jake wanted volunteer conditional jockeys to try out the protein balls, Finn had been very helpful. He'd passed on the jockeys' phone numbers, the stables they were based at and looked up who was riding at Cartmel.

'There's Sam, Connor and Callum. So, what's the idea, Hattie? Do the lads just use these ball things on race days or what?'

Hattie sighed. 'I think so, yes. I need to find out more. Tracey, Jake's PA will be in touch with them and if they agree, then she'll send over some samples. The idea is that the balls are designed to be very nutritious and filling, so the lads shouldn't feel so hungry. Therefore, they should find it easier to lose weight and it should prevent them having to resort to saunas, jogging with several layers of clothing or whatever...' Hattie was making that last bit up. Actually, she had no idea how the Life balls worked, and Jake hadn't bothered to hang about to explain himself. She had got the distinct impression that Jake wasn't interested in proper trials, but maybe she could persuade him once the first lads were on board. Something systematic and long term would be good. She had never heard of experiential evidence, whatever that was. Anyone could say that a product had helped them, but it needed to be properly tested. She resolved to talk to Tracey, but realised that she couldn't be too pushy, they were Jake's Life balls, and the whole thing was his idea, after all.

'Let me know how you get on handing in the phone. I'm planning to talk to Drew to find out what he knows and warn him that the police might be asking questions.'

'OK. Can you remind him about the Life Balls too? I did text him.'

'Yes. I'm sure he can help you.'

Hattie ended the call, her mind full of questions, not least about the efficacy of Jake's Life balls. She wanted to study them, question him about the contents before she put her name to anything, but Jake had simply ploughed on.

Hattie drove to the police headquarters in York. It was clearly going to be a day for feeling awkward and compromised. All the way she rehearsed what she might say, conversations going round and round her head. It was important to seem nonchalant, she told herself. Not to give away too much information and crucially to act as if they had just found the phone. The offending article was in her pocket in a freezer bag. As Finn had suggested, she'd also phoned ahead as she couldn't stand the idea of hanging around for ages waiting for someone to talk to her. Hopefully she would get the woman she'd spoken to earlier, a DS Wildblood, who'd sounded efficient and not too curious and would be able to leave quickly.

So, Hattie was uncertain how to react when finally the door of the small waiting room swung open and a tall, dark, well dressed man walked in. He was rather good looking she couldn't help but notice. If this was the Inspector Daisy had talked about, she wondered why she had omitted to mention this fact? Probably because she had been too stressed to notice.

'DI Taverner. So Ms Lucas, I gather you've found a phone which you believe belonged to James Clary?'

Hattie took a deep breath as he sat down and indicated that she should do the same. She found a pair of dark brown eyes considering her, head on one side as she passed him the freezer bag. If he found this way of preserving evidence unconventional, he gave no sign.

'I found the phone in The Blacksmith's Arms pub. I went for lunch with a colleague and saw it under a bookcase and put two and two together.' She found his calmness unnerving and began rambling on about going to the pub, and how she had happened to see the phone, which she believed might be important in a crime investigation. It was a version of events that she'd rehearsed with Finn yesterday.

'I heard that there was an argument between Neil and Jimmy in the pub and happened to be in there the other day. I dropped some coins and bent down to pick them up and saw it under a bookcase...'

DI Taverner nodded and looked amused, then curious.

'Lucas, you say, are you any relation to DS Will Lucas?'

Hattie smiled. 'Yep, he's my eldest brother. You've met Will then?'

The DI gave a slow smile. 'Mmm, he's a good copper by all accounts. So, your father must be the legendary Bob Lucas. I've heard a lot about him from DCI Sykes.'

Hattie began to relax, deciding she liked DI Taverner. He looked like the sort of person who you could trust and had lovely manners and a soothing, well modulated voice.

'Yes, that's him.'

Taverner glanced at the phone. 'So, you've not looked through the contacts or messages then?'

Hattie tried to control her blushes and shook her head earnestly.

'No, of course not.'

'Not even out of curiosity?' Taverner raised an eyebrow.

Hattie stammered, 'No, but I know how important phones are in investigations from my Dad…'

Taverner smiled and his eyes crinkled up at the sides. 'OK, just checking. I will get the tech people to take all the data from it and I'm sure it will give us vital intel. So, Ms Lucas, thank you very much for your help. We may need to speak to you in due course, could you leave me your contact details, phone number and so on?' Harriet stumbled through the details feeling rather flustered.

Hattie got up and as Taverner held open the door for her, she felt curiously transparent in front of him. She was sure that he knew exactly why she and Finn had gone to The Blacksmith's Arms and clearly suspected that they had looked at the phone too. She found him still staring at her as she climbed into her car. He was clearly not convinced about the story they had rehearsed, and the thought gnawed away at her.

Chapter 16

Gabriel glowered at DC Haworth, that was after he had roundly bollocked him for not prioritising the search for Clary's phone.

'Honestly, guv, I just got carried away with my other inquiries and didn't get around to it. Sorry.'

Gabriel noted that his officer did seem genuinely contrite. Haworth seemed to follow his own nose in inquiries and tended to skate over tasks he thought were a waste of time.

'Honestly, we're relying on bloody amateurs to help us now! It's not good enough!'

Haworth looked pained. 'If the phone is with the tech guys, they'll hopefully find something useful, but in the meantime Clary's business accounts look very interesting. That was what I was looking at. I got carried away.' Haworth flicked through a wad of printouts.

Gabriel looked on with interest. 'This had better be good.'

'It is, Sir. The business was doing so badly, I'd say that Clary was barely making ends meet, never mind having the means to entertain his many lady friends.' Haworth paused for effect. Gabriel recognised the slightly smug look on his face as disguised triumph. 'Seemed like our victim had some other sources of income.'

'Go on.'

'Well, for starters we found bags and bags of budget supermarket vegetables discarded in his shed....'

Gabriel contemplated this. 'Ah, I see. So, he was passing off shop bought vegetables complete with pesticides and God knows what else, as home grown organic vegetables at inflated prices?'

'He was.'

He brought out his phone and showed Gabriel what looked like a production line of shop bought vegetables decanted into trendy brown paper bags, complete with the Clary label printed on the side. He pointed to a bucket.

'What's in that?'

Haworth's eyes gleamed. 'It was full of soil. My guess was he dipped them in there to give them that authentic organic look.'

Gabriel shook his head. 'The crafty sod.'

'And that's not all. Look what we found hidden in his polytunnels.'

Gabriel was presented with photos of what was a small but professional cannabis farm, complete with lamps and a rudimentary sprinkler system. The plants were growing beautifully and were thriving amongst normal vegetables.

'Bloody hell!'

Gabriel was pleased at this breakthrough and felt that Haworth had redeemed himself a little, but he couldn't help but think it also laid the case wide open. There would be even more suspects. Cultivating and selling cannabis was going to cause problems with other drug dealers. At least it was something concrete, after last night's little trip down memory lane when he heard from Reg all about Jimmy's extraordinary riding skills and how he grew too big to be a jockey. Hearing about someone's blighted sporting career made Taverner rueful and sympathetic. After all it had happened to him too, albeit in another sport. But that was another story and not one he wanted to dwell on too much. Taverner now had a thick head and was twenty quid worse off after he'd plied Reg with whisky, just in case he gleaned a juicy nugget of information. Passing ordinary vegetables off as organic was hardly going to endear Jimmy to his clean eating clientele either, especially when they realised he was ripping them off too. At that moment DS Wildblood and DC Ballantyne walked in.

He gave them an inquiring look.

Wildblood opened her notebook. 'That Wolf character has no alibi for his whereabouts on the morning of the shooting. Seems all the protesters camped out and didn't get up until midday, the lazy lot. The demo was out at Marchmoor about twenty miles away. Something to do with felling Marchmoor Woods for a housing development. He definitely had time to drive back to Walton, bump off Jimmy and then get back there without being seen.'

'Does he drive?'

DS Wildblood nodded. 'Yes. There was a police presence and our lads confirm that he was there some of the time, leading the chanting from high up in a tree, something along the lines of '1,2,3, save our tree."

'Best place for him, you don't want to get downwind of our Tarquin Montague, he reeks like nobody's business, like he hasn't washed in months…' observed Haworth.

Taverner recalled the statement that Haworth had taken from Wolf. It was not often that words like 'antediluvian' and 'garrulous' were used. Still, he shouldn't be surprised as from their research, Tarquin had been educated at Eton before being expelled. He still got the grades to study medicine at Cambridge but had his sights set on saving the world. Taverner admired his beliefs. His Sergeant had other concerns, however.

'I wanted to take a pair of scissors to his dreadlocked hair,' said Wildblood. 'It looked bloody awful. If my boys turned out like him, I'd…'

'They wouldn't dare, Anna,' laughed Haworth, 'you'd chop their bloody balls off.'

Gabriel drummed his fingers on the table, his team gazing on expectantly. Ballantyne gave a slight belch and stopped chewing his greasy sausage roll.

'Right, if that's all, we'll resume tomorrow. Ballantyne, I want you in town finding out all you can about the food scene in Walton, who supplies who, all that. See if there were any whispers that Clary was cheating about his organic credentials. If someone found out that Jimmy was passing off shop bought veg as organic, then he would have made a lot of enemies, you know how passionate these environmentalists are.'

'Jammy sod,' said Haworth, 'but don't spend all day sampling food, you greedy git.'

Ballantyne flicked a good natured 'V' sign at his fellow officer.

'Right, Patel, you get on to the tech guys to hurry the checks on that phone and find out about all the drug dealers within the local area and see if we have any informants. Let's see what the word is from the local dealers about our victim. Right Anna, you come with me and we'll see what Tarquin Montague aka Wolf has to say for himself this time.'

'Right, boss.'

Taverner hesitated. 'Any questions?'

Anna raised her hand. 'What's DCI Sykes thinking? Does he still think Horton's in the frame?'

Taverner sighed and gave a stock response. 'He's open minded but he reminded me to tell you that it's been nearly a week since we found Clary. He's pressing for a result asap.' And by the way, I hear that old Lord Montague died a couple of days ago, so we need to be mindful of that.'

'Blimey,' muttered Haworth. 'That makes Wolf, Lord Montague, who'd have thought it?'

Wildblood raised an eyebrow. 'Natural causes?'

Taverner nodded. 'Died in his sleep, he was 92, so he had a good innings.'

The team nodded as they took this in. The old man had not been seen around for several years and had been pretty much housebound, but the locals would still feel it. The English feudal system still counted for something in rural areas and he would certainly be mourned.

As the team left, DI Taverner recalled that DCI Sykes had been a lot more outspoken than that. He recalled the conversation.

'Christ almighty man, get a move on, will you? Wrap this up pronto or I'll have to start cutting overtime and withdrawing extra funds. If the bloody press start, I'll have to bring in a replacement, got it Taverner? And don't get too carried away with this nonsense about Tarquin Montague. In case you hadn't heard, his father died last night, so he is now Lord Montague, so you do need to tread carefully.'

A more unlikely Lord than Tarquin he couldn't imagine but Sykes was right. He would have to do everything by the book as far as Wolf was concerned. He knew from experience that rich people were all interconnected and stood together to smooth the way for each other. The old school network was still very much alive and kicking in England and Tarquin would no doubt have top class barristers at his disposal, at the click of his fingers. He was determined to do a thorough job and not let any suspects off the hook and that included Tarquin Montague. Taverner had placated Sykes for now but the uneasy truce would not last long. He hoped fervently that the leads from Jimmy's phone would help solve the case and he was still angry with Haworth for not prioritising the search for it. It made him think back to what the landlord of The Blacksmith's Arms had said about McCarthy. He had felt embarrassed when the striking red haired friend of his had brought it in instead. It made them look sloppy and amateurish. Never mind, Haworth had worked hard in other areas. He mentally ran through the list of suspects and their likely motives. Clary had undoubtedly been a tricky customer with no shortage of enemies, but which one killed him? Gabriel reached for his coat, anticipation mounting. He could almost taste success, it was just within their grasp and he was determined to grab it with both hands.

Chapter 17

'So, have you thought any more about taking the case?'

'I have, but I'm afraid the answer is still the same. I can't take it on, I'm sorry. It doesn't directly relate to racing, so I'm afraid I can't help you.'

Vince nodded grimly. 'Well, fair enough.' He looked at Finn consideringly. 'Look, it's not that I think that Neil is guilty, nothing like that, it's just that any sniff of scandal and I think that the new Lord Montague, Tarquin, will get his brother to take his horses elsewhere. I suppose you heard that the old man died in his sleep a couple of days ago? So now the title will go to Tarquin. I'm not sure what sort of Lord he will make as it's Guy we have dealings with. I just don't want them to have an excuse to remove their horses. You know what it's like when rumours start to fly round...'

Finn sympathised, he really did. He was pretty useless at lying but couldn't very well tell all and sundry that the BHA had asked him to look into the murder, just in case it did involve racing. Everyone would suddenly clam up and they'd find out nothing.

'Does Guy Montague have any decent horses?'

'Oh yes. Fort William is entered in the Group Race, The Bollinger, at York. He's a cracking horse and bound to be placed, but I'm hoping for better actually. Guy Montague is building up their stud and they have some great stallions, so it's really looking positive and Fort William could help them make their name. There are loads of trainers Guy could send his horses to and he chose us, and he sponsors Neil too. Let me show you Fort William, see what you think of him.'

Vince ambled up to a stable where a bay horse flicked his ears back and forth at the sound of them approaching. Vince muttered to the horse and undid the bolts on the door. He put the horse's head collar on and removed the animal's stable rug so Finn could examine him. The horse shivered, his ears still moving back and forwards.

'He's just a wee bit sensitive, that's all.'

Finn spoke soothingly to the horse and went into the stable to examine him. He ran his hands over the horse's legs and studied his outline. He was muscled to perfection, gleaming and his conformation was perfect. Fort William was starting to relax and started to push his muzzle into Finn's pockets searching for treats.

'Well, he's a fine type. I presume he's by King William? Is the mare any good?'

'Oh yes,' explained Vince. 'She won several races as a two-year-old, some of them pretty good, before a pulled tendon ruined her career. She was then retired for breeding.'

'Hmm. I hope he does well for you. Does Guy Montague have others like him?'

'Some good quality horses. But he is the best. You must come and see him work. I'd like your opinion, actually.'

Finn nodded. 'OK, I'd like to. Listen, if Neil is innocent then I'm sure you won't have anything to fear from the police. After all, you know Neil well. That has to count for something, doesn't it?'

Vince eyed him grimly. 'Well, I do know him, of course, but not as well as I'd like. Daisy just turned up with him, I know very little about his background and he doesn't say much. All the local folk know each other, we knew their parents and grandparents, I suppose, that's all. We're a small community. But I can't believe he would be capable of murder…'

The sentence was left hanging, almost as though Vince thought Neil was capable of everything else. This wasn't quite the robust defence he'd have expected for a man who dated Vince's daughter, rented their stables and had a position of trust within the yard. It was clear that Vince was not as confident of Neil's innocence as he first appeared. Now that was interesting, very interesting indeed. It made him feel slightly better about the fact that he had a relative who was potentially implicated in Clary's murder too.

Drew's possible involvement had rocked him to the core but then when he had rationalised it, it was no surprise that Drew knew Jimmy Clary. He was into organic food and Clary could well have been his supplier or they could have known each other as they had similar business interests, but the last text message really worried him as it appeared that they had arranged to meet on the day before Clary was shot. Did that put Drew in the frame? It was certainly possible. Finn thought of his little nieces and his sister. The thought of them suffering as a result of Drew's actions was heartbreaking. He knew he would do anything to prevent any harm coming to them. He was suddenly brought back down to earth by Vince speaking.

'Right then Finn, just keep us in the loop, will you?'

'Oh yes, of course. Bye.'

Finn wondered how best to play it with Drew. He decided not to overreact, but just talk to him man to man over a pint in the pub. That should provide a relaxed atmosphere and no doubt Drew would be able to account for his actions, he should have a cast iron alibi, and all would be well. He wondered whether to invite Hattie, as after all, he would have liked to have her opinion on whether Drew was being truthful. In the end he decided against it.

They met in a small village pub called The Bull's Head on the outskirts of York. The place had had something of a makeover. It was an old stone building with beams, and had trendy lights on each table, which on closer inspection were fairy lights in glass jars and the bar staff looked like extras from a 50s movie. He picked up a menu which boasted 25 different sorts of gin, anything from Bathtub to Tanqueray and settled on a pint of Guinness. Drew arrived a couple of minutes later and they sat down in a quiet corner.

'So, is everything OK?' asked Drew after a few pleasantries. 'Are you having any trouble with the new girlfriend?'

'No, nothing like that, it's a bit delicate actually…'

Drew immediately put his hand in his pocket to pull out his wallet. Finn appreciated the gesture but had to correct the misunderstanding.

'No, that's not why I'm here.' He took a deep breath. 'It's just that I've heard about Jimmy Clary's death and some information has been given to me that I need to clarify with you without Jenny knowing.'

Drew nodded. 'Sounds bad. He was the man who was found murdered in the layby? Yes, I heard about that. I used to get some of my supplies from him.' Drew's eyes narrowed. 'How did you come by the information? Surely the police are investigating the murder?'

'Never mind about that.'

'OK, but what has that to do with me?' Drew frowned. 'I'm starting to get a bit freaked out to be honest.'

Finn studied his brother-in-law, noticed that he was slightly ruffled and tried to quell his feelings of unease. 'Well, it's just that a little bird told me that you knew Clary well and that you were going to meet him on the day before he was shot.'

Drew paled and stared at Finn.

'What exactly are you implying here? Am I under suspicion, is that what you're saying?'

Finn sighed. 'No, of course not, it's just that if you know something, I need to know. The police will very likely interview you.' For some strange reason Finn didn't want to reveal that he had looked at Jimmy's phone, partly because it was unprofessional, but also because he wanted to know what Drew had to say and whether or not he would mention the text. That was the deal breaker for him. He held his breath.

Drew took a sip of beer. 'It's fine, Finn. I have nothing to hide. I knew Clary, of course I did. He used to provide my organic ingredients and I had texted Jimmy to see if we could meet to discuss pricing and whether I could have a discount now I was expanding. We had arranged to meet at The Blacksmith's. I went and Jimmy was clear that he was struggling financially and couldn't give me any further discounts. He explained about his margins and I accepted that. His prices were high, but you have to pay more for organic stuff as there's more wastage. So, we parted amicably, that's it.'

'It's just something I heard. So, what time did you leave the pub?'

Drew frowned. 'God, you sound more and more like a copper. About half eight, I think. Yes, that was right because the girls were in bed when I got back home.'

Finn realised that he had been holding his breath but was relieved by what he was hearing.

'Did you see Jimmy get into a fight a few days before?'

Drew shook his head. 'No, nothing like that.'

'OK. You must tell the police everything you know.'

Drew took a sip of beer but seemed perfectly relaxed.

'Fine. Look, I have nothing to hide. How did you find out anyway? Come on, I'm curious.'

'Well, I work in the area, I speak to all sorts of people and they talk, you know how it is. I just wanted to check out what I'd heard with you, that's all.'

Drew gave him a speculative look. 'By all accounts Jimmy was a bit of a rum lad, liked the ladies and probably liked to live dangerously, but I liked him though, he was a laugh, reliable as a supplier and knew a thing or two about the horses.'

'Yes, he was found near the gallops in Walton. I've often wondered if that was significant actually.'

Drew nodded. 'Maybe, but all Irishmen like racing, don't they?'

Finn had to admit they usually did. He settled down to drink his pint, content in the knowledge that Drew would be ruled out by the police, as he listened to Drew's thoughts on the victim.

He rang Hattie later to discuss what he had found out. She listened intently.

'So, do you reckon he's telling the truth?'

'Yes, I think so. I didn't mention the text message and he volunteered it, so I don't think he has anything to hide and he was pretty relaxed.'

'So, what do we need to do next?'

'I need to think. We probably need to get together to talk things through.' They arranged a time to meet in Walton before travelling to Cartmel.

'Some of the lads said they would try the Life balls, so that will help.' Hattie sounded pleased. They talked through possible suspects and said their goodbyes. Then he rang Kimberley and chatted about how her week was going. There was no mistaking her mood.

'Are you OK, only you sound a bit down?'

'Well, I heard about the acting job. I didn't get it,' she explained.

He spent the next five minutes or so consoling her.

'Don't worry. Something else will come up, I'm sure of it.' It seemed to work as she sounded a little more cheerful after a while.

'There is something else in the offing according to Damien, but I've no idea what it is.'

'Well, give it your best shot, just keep buggering on.'

The Churchillian quote seemed to work as she began to perk up and they arranged to meet later in the week after he had seen Hattie. He went to bed, tired, relieved about Drew, yet still going through the facts. Neil was still the number one suspect due to having openly threatened and fought Jimmy in full view of the whole pub. He was intrigued by Vince's attitude too, but Drew's comments made him realise that they needed to widen their inquiries. What was the phrase Drew had used? He had said that Jimmy was a 'rum lad' who liked to live dangerously. That single one phrase opened the field of potential suspects wide open. They needed to find out about every aspect of Jimmy Clary's life in order to discover who had murdered him and he knew just where to start. Clary's Farm Foods.

Chapter 18

Finn picked Hattie up from outside The Blacksmith's Arms in Walton the following morning. She had two takeaway coffees waiting. Finn grabbed his enthusiastically.

'Cheers.'

'OK. Have you had any thoughts?'

'Maybe we should take a little trip to see Jimmy's place. Have you been before?'

Hattie shook head. 'No, the only time I used them, they didn't deliver, and it was arranged by phone.' She was suddenly pensive. 'It was the day Jimmy died though, so we can forgive him for that.'

Finn nodded. 'Mmm, I thought a quick visit pretending you might be ordering from them more regularly for your cooking demonstrations. Might give us a chance to ask a few questions.'

Harriet pointed at the paper she was carrying.

'Look, did you hear that old Lord Montague died in his sleep, so Wolf will become the new Lord.'

Finn strained to look. 'Hmm. Did he die of old age?'

'I presume so. He was 92. People don't seem to think that Tarquin will adjust to being a Lord, from what I have heard.'

'Maybe the responsibility is what he needs.'

'Perhaps…'

The farm looked a little run down. There were several cars parked outside and as they approached the side door Hattie could see the curved shapes of two long polytunnels. A woman with dirty blonde hair in a plait answered the door. She was heavily pregnant and seemed weary and depressed. She listened to their introductions and then said with a sigh, 'Wolf, will you show these two around?'

A tall man with pale skin and startling red dreadlocks, dressed in khaki shorts and a grubby singlet appeared from inside the house. As he passed the woman, he gave her shoulder a tender squeeze. The woman looked dazed and hardly seemed to notice he was there.

Wolf was a good guide and seemed knowledgeable about the business showing them the raised beds full of lettuces and tomatoes. Several staff were picking tomatoes and putting them in crates. Then he indicated the field planted with parsnips, cabbages and swede. A couple of the polytunnels, furthest away from the house, had police tape around them, Finn noticed.

'So, have you taken over the business?' asked Finn.

'No. I'm helping Perdita out for now. She and the baby need some support.' He looked embarrassed. 'I'm Tarquin Montague, actually Lord Montague since my father died.'

Hattie was surprised at his voice, well spoken and modulated, not the gruff type she was expecting. His eyes were full of concern for Perdita. He was definitely in love with her, that much was abundantly clear. His gaze kept flickering to her. Harriet thought that condolences were in order.

'Oh, I'm sorry to hear about your father.'

'Thank you. He was very ill, so in a way it was a blessing. I will need to sort out lots of stuff.' Again, Wolf looked faintly embarrassed. 'But that can wait. Perdita is bereaved too and in desperate need of help.'

'Yes, we heard about Jimmy.'

Wolf rolled his eyes.

'Yeah. Believe me he's no loss to society.' His expression had hardened, and it was easy to see that he had not thought much of the late Jimmy Clary.

'Why was that?'

Wolf gave Finn an appraising sort of a look, his eyes narrowing.

'Who did you say you were again? You're not the bloody police are you, because I've just about had about enough of the boys in blue!'

Finn withdrew his BHA ID.

'I'm Finn McCarthy. I work for the BHA as a jockey coach, but Harriet here is a dietician.'

Harriet smiled. 'That's right, I am doing some demonstrations for jockeys so want to see if you could supply my produce. I'm passionate about healthy eating, you see.'

Wolf pursed his lips. 'OK. Things are a bit difficult here at the moment as you can imagine, but I'm sure we can come up with some arrangement. We have a whole range of organic produce.' He pointed at the rows of neatly planted vegetables.

'What's in those far polytunnels?' asked Finn, pointing at the ones circled in blue and white police tape.

Wolf frowned. 'Something that shouldn't be there, but it's nothing to do with Perdita, so don't worry about it. We can only sell the organic stuff, had to chuck the rest away and I had to persuade the police to let Perdita continue to trade.'

'Cannabis?' asked Hattie.

Wolf sighed. 'Word gets around fast. I have had to fight tooth and nail to keep the place open for Perdita's sake. Jimmy certainly had some dodgy friends too.'

'Who?' The words were out of Finn's mouth before he realised.

'I'm not sure. I used to stick around just to keep an eye on Perdita you see, to make sure she was alright.'

Finn nodded. 'Who do you think murdered Jimmy?'

Wolf frowned, weighing up whether or not to say anything. He appeared to come to a decision.

'It could be any number of people. Women loved him, though God knows why. You see, me and Perdita were an item a few years ago until Jimmy bloody Clary arrived and charmed the pants off her.

And there have been lots of other women, not to mention dodgy dealings including the cannabis.' He nodded at a series of black bins bags near the path. 'I'm helping Perdita clear up his stuff and hoping to expunge every trace of him. Besides, I was out at the demo in Marchmoor, so I can prove it wasn't me. I camped out with loads of them. They're all from the Green Warriors, the usual gang.'

Finn nodded. 'OK.' He dug in his pocket for a spare business card.

'Listen, if any of this relates to my conditional jockeys, then I need to know. I coach all the conditionals in the area including Jimmy's brother.' He handed one of his business cards to Wolf.

Wolf shrugged. 'Alright, do you reckon Jimmy's death was something to do with racing then?'

'I'm not sure but he was found near a layby near the gallops and the BHA will certainly want to know if anything reflects badly on their industry.'

Wolf nodded and pocketed the card. He was beginning to look suspicious. 'What about the vegetables then?'

Harriet smiled. 'Right, if you could just give me a price list, I'll do the maths and get back to you.'

Wolf nodded and pulled a piece of paper out from his pocket and handed it to Harriet.

'Great. I'll be in touch.'

Finn followed Harriet up the path. The sky was blue, the birds were singing, but Harriet felt her mood dipping. They passed waste bins with rubbish spilling over everywhere. Finn lagged behind.

'Well, that didn't tell us much,' muttered Harriet when Finn had caught up with her.

'Hmm. Not necessarily.' He pulled a piece of cardboard out of his pocket and showed it to her. 'I found this in the bin.'

'Owl CCTV camera,' Harriet read. 'I'm not sure that that helps, does it?'

Finn shrugged. 'It shows that Jimmy was worried about security. Look, it's a CCTV camera hidden in a fake owl. It suggests that he was really hoping to grow his cannabis business and was interested in protecting it.'

'If that's the case then maybe he was killed because of his intention to grow more of the stuff.'

They drove away in silence.

Harriet turned to Finn. 'Do you think we got away with it?'

Finn shrugged. 'Maybe, but he was starting to get suspicious.'

'God that poor woman. Jimmy got her pregnant then goes after Kerry and he has an ex wife with a little girl! What a waster! Then all the other stuff. He adores her, doesn't he? Enough to kill Jimmy, do you think? She could become the next Lady Montague. What did you make of it?'

'Hate to speak ill of the dead, but you're right. So many people must have had gripes with Clary. Wolf seemed alright, decent actually. I think he knows more than he's letting on though.'

'Yeah. I liked him, he seemed sincere. What the hell did any of those women see in Clary, what did he have, is what I'd like to know?'

'Charm, I suppose. A little goes a long way.'

Hattie remembered the photo of the murdered man she had seen in the local paper reporting about his death. He exuded energy even from a photo, was quite nice looking too, with a touch of the Irish rover about him with his curling dark hair and blue eyes. He was certainly a thorough 'wrong 'un' as her father would say. They drove to Cartmel deep in thought. Hattie hoped Finn would have some inspiration because from where she was looking any number of people would have had a motive to kill Jimmy Clary, so where were they to start?

'So, we need to rule out Neil and Drew first.'

Finn was silent for a while. He turned and smiled at her. 'The police will be looking for the gun that was used, depending on the type used they could find lots of stuff out. If it's a shotgun, then it'll be much harder to identify the gun, and half the farmers locally will have one. Someone must know something, though. We need to check Wolf's alibi too.' He frowned. 'God knows. If Clary was growing cannabis, then he would have been annoying the other local dealers who could have cut up rough. Will might know something about the drugs scene locally. Could you ask?'

'OK, I will.'

Hattie couldn't help thinking how well Finn looked. His hair had grown a little and he was wearing a denim shirt and black jeans. Not for the first time the thought of him with Kimberley came into her head. What on earth did he see in her, she wondered? OK, Kim was good looking, but it was in a very careful, well groomed way. Hattie was willing to bet that she looked rough without any makeup on. Also, as far as she could tell they had almost nothing in common, Kimberley hated animals and only liked the races for the glamour. Still who knew how these things worked? If you'd asked her now how she herself had got involved with her coach, Dale, she would not have been able to explain it. Suddenly the hope of seeing Jake came into her head. Tracey had emailed her to say that he'd be at the races.

'Jake has sent some of his Life balls round to the jockeys, I think to Sam and Connor...'

Finn could barely disguise his scepticism. 'What'll that do for them then?'

'Fill them up, keep them strong, some people think you lose weight if you eat more protein and fewer carbs so it should help them regulate their weight, they might even lose some...'

He laughed. 'Better than eating a few jellybeans for lunch like I used to then?'

'I don't know really; he makes great claims. He's easy on the eye too.'

Finn glanced at her. 'You're not blushing are you, don't tell me the open shirts and pop star clothes have worked on you?'

Hattie hit him playfully on the shoulder. 'No, of course not. Anyway, how's Kim?'

'Fine, a bit disappointed not to get that role she auditioned for. She should be arriving at the races after the third race. She couldn't get here before, but don't change the subject Ms Lucas.'

She felt her cheeks grow pink but whether it was from embarrassment about her attraction to Jake or her annoyance that Kim was going to be there, it was hard to say. She was looking forward to seeing Jake, but her heart sank when she realised that Kim was also going to be with them. Luckily for

Hattie they turned into the racecourse at that moment and she was saved from answering by having to look out for the right car park and ask directions, so no more was said.

'I've suggested that Gavin Clary go back to Ireland for a bit, so he can spend some time grieving with his family and we don't know when the body can be released. It must be so hard for him especially with Neil being interviewed by the police.'

'Poor lad. It must be pretty awful, all these rumours and speculation about Jimmy.'

Finn shrugged. 'The funny thing is that he didn't seem to think that Neil was involved at all. I'll have to ask him why he is so sure when he comes back.'

'Maybe he does know more than he's letting on. Listen, catch you later.'

Finn nodded, raising his hand as Hattie strode off. He was on his way to catch up with some of his conditionals.

Hattie had a look around the racecourse. It was very picturesque, an undulating track surrounded by hills and trees and was close to the historic town. She hadn't been before and understood it only held meetings in the summer, jumping only. Hattie had agreed to meet Tracey before the first race by the parade ring. The PA was there with her clip board looking official and anxious. Without preamble she said,

'I sent several sets of protein balls out. Some to the names you gave me. All we need is one of the young jocks to ride well, preferably win and we can get an interview.'

Hattie wondered where Jake was, but couldn't quite bring herself to ask. They watched the crowds go by and Hattie feeling anxious with this tense woman, was happy to listen to snatches of conversation, looking at the groups of people and speculate who was who. That woman was surely with a relative, a sister maybe and that distinguished man in a tweed hat had to be someone important, a steward perhaps? She was just enjoying the familiar rhythm and routine of the parade ring, when she thought she saw someone familiar. Heck the woman in the red dress looked a lot like Kimberley. Perhaps, she had managed to make it in time after all? But Finn had said she wouldn't be here till later, so maybe it was someone who looked like her. The woman was striding about in front of the bookies' pitches staring at the odds. Eventually she selected a bookie and spoke furtively to him, handing over what looked like a thick wad of cash wrapped in a newspaper. The Kimberley lookalike's actions seemed to set off a chain reaction. Hattie watched, fascinated, as the bookies nudged each other. A man next to her flicked through his racecard and circled number 9 in the 7th race, Tea Time, excitedly, presumably the horse the woman had backed. Harriet took a quick photo of the woman on her camera phone and quickly turned away, her mind in turmoil as she tried to process what she had just seen. Perhaps Kim had a doppelganger or had been given a great tip or maybe she had a whacking great gambling addiction? None of these explanations sat comfortably. She pondered over whether to tell Finn and decided that she couldn't. She watched the race deep in thought and made a mental note to look at Tea Time's odds by the time the gossips had done their worst.

Hattie was delighted to win in the first race as she had backed Sam Foster, who won on the third favourite, Montellimar. It was a strange race and Sam's horse won by several lengths after the two favourites collided and fell at the second last. As Sam and Montellimar reached the winner's enclosure, something happened suddenly. In a slick move, Tim Ryedale appeared, and Tracey whispered urgently, 'Quick get into the ring…' Then she remembered what Tracey had said about the protein balls.

She felt herself pushed forwards and suddenly her hand was grabbed by none other than Jake Delamare himself. His hair was tousled as usual and he wore a voluminous white shirt, which had only two buttons fastened, so that the rest of it hung off the shoulders. He smelled of pine and musk and he exuded sex appeal. The crowd gasped and several women surged towards the ring amid cries of, 'Oh look, Jake from 'Cooking up a Storm's' here!'

'Where's Natalia?' shouted one woman.

'Darling, come on let's have a chat with Timbo and get the publicity rolling,' Jake whispered in Hattie's ear and she followed unquestioningly.

'So, well ridden Sam,' said Tim into the microphone with his pleasantly modulated voice. 'Now a little bird tells me that you have tried a new approach to keeping the weight off.'

Sam, happy and grinning, slid off the horse and looked a little confused until Tracey brandished an A3 banner, which showed a pouting Jake holding the protein balls and read, 'Try my Life Protein balls. Life doesn't get better than this!'

The comprehension showed in Sam's face and he grinned even more broadly. 'Yeah, I got some of those. I had one for lunch.'

'And do you think it helped you? Maybe to ride a great finish?'

'Well, yeah I s'pose, I won, didn't I? I felt well…'

Hattie had noticed that Sam had won easily, but she was uncertain at the implication that this was in any way due to the Life balls, yet she didn't say anything.

'That'll be the natural, simple and honest ingredients all working to give you a nutritional boost of energy to ride that fantastic race,' gushed Jake, 'and they can work for you all…' He waved his hand around the ring.

'Very impressive,' said Tim with a nervous guffaw, 'can I have some please?'

'I going to be giving out freebies and then me and this gorgeous nutritional expert, Harriet Lucas, are going to be writing a book together which will reveal some of our recipes. Meanwhile, here's some samples.' He gave Harriet a long lingering stare and then Jake began throwing small silver foil packets into the crowd which were caught with shouts and cheers.

Moments later the interview was over, and Jake strode away, stopping periodically to hug the odd woman and sign autographs. Tracey shoved a huge bag of the protein balls into Hattie's hands and said, 'Give these out will you,' before following him. Hattie watched the disappearing crowds wondering what had just happened. It had been like watching a surreal example of a sleek PR stunt, which she supposed it was.

'God there's something about that man that grates,' said Finn, appearing at her shoulder. He held up the silver packet. 'What's actually in these bloody things? Does anyone actually know? Poor Sam look completely bemused. How the hell does Delamare know that the bloody things helped Sam win? It's utterly ridiculous!' He squinted at the minute list of ingredients, far too small for anyone to actually read.

'I think he's cool,' said Hattie, remembering the intense stare. 'And the balls contain healthy proteins from nuts, fruit and seeds. They taste amazing too.' She handed the last of them to a gaggle of excited young women.

'Have you asked Jake what's in them?'

Harriet shrugged. 'He seems a bit secretive about it actually.' She squinted at the small writing on the packet. 'And it's very hard to read the entire contents.'

'Hmm. Drew will help with that, I'm sure. He'll soon tell you.'

'Yes, I did text him. Anyway, is Kimberley here yet?' asked Hattie innocently.

Finn shook his head. 'No. She's just texted to say she's on her way.'

Then why, thought Hattie, have I just seen her putting on a huge bet?

Finn fished in his pocket for his phone. Presumably, it was Kim telling him that she had just arrived.

Finn read the message and showed it to Harriet.

'Interesting. Wolf wants to meet us at his house. Perhaps, he has some information for us?'

Harriet was glad of the distraction from her worrying thoughts about Kimberley and what she had witnessed earlier.

'Hmm. Maybe he'll find it easier to talk about Jimmy without Perdita being around.'

The following day, she was just finishing off her dissertation and struggling to concentrate when her phone rang. A low voice greeted her. Jake.

'Darling, listen I've got some time today, would you be free to talk about our project?'

'Sure. When and where?' Damn, why didn't she at least say she had to consult her diary, she thought.

Jake laughed. 'Just my kind of gel, The Marston at eleven?'

'Great.'

This time Jake was not only ready and waiting in the hotel foyer, he had also organised coffee in one of the meeting rooms. He enveloped Hattie in a hug and led her to an armchair in front of a fireplace which had flowers in the grate.

'Look at you, you look great, 'he said, his eyes wandering over her. Hattie had made a great deal of effort in the hour she'd had to get ready, putting on her best pale green, linen summer dress which had white daisies embroidered along the bottom. She wore flat strappy sandals and carried a large bag with a notepad in it. Her hair was gathered in a low bun to one side of her neck and she'd sprayed copious amounts of Chanel's 'Gabrielle' on her pulse points.

As ever, Jake wore tight jeans, a huge white shirt, but his hair was held back in place by a band, rather like a footballer. With his tanned skin, he too looked to be bursting with energy and wellbeing. A testimony to his Life balls, maybe? Today, without his secretary, he seemed calmer and more focused.

'So, tell me what ideas do you have for our book? I take it you are still interested in doing one?'

'Oh yes, definitely.' Hattie tried and failed not to sound too keen. But what a boost to her career it would be to write a book with Jake. It would surely lead onto other things and do her job prospects no harm at all.

'I've got some ideas and I jotted them down here,' she added, trying to sound as though she had just thrown some recipes together, scribbled on the back of an envelope.

Over coffee they exchanged ideas. Jake wanted to produce a book which was about healthy recipes, low carbohydrate and delicious food.

'Basically, I want to get the English away from stodgy food, especially processed convenience rubbish. I want every man, woman and child to be able to rustle up something that tastes great and is healthy too. I want them all lean and whippet thin like these jockeys.'

Hattie nodded wondering if this was going to be a diet book. Jake seemed to read her mind.

'Not a weight loss manual as such, but an alternative lifestyle choice. By the way the sales of my Life balls have grown dramatically. And with this book I see radio, TV appearances, maybe even a series. We could help change the health of a nation, imagine that? Together, we should make a great team. What do you think?'

Hattie smiled at that. Jake seemed much more genuine and measured without Tracey's influence. She felt as though she could really talk to him and wanted to know where his interest in nutrition and cooking had come from.

'So, Jake what got you so interested in cooking? You seem so passionate about it all.'

Jake looked downcast. 'My mother, God rest her soul, was a major inspiration, a fabulous cook and society hostess. But she died not long ago, before her time.'

Hattie gasped. 'Oh, how dreadful, I'm so sorry…' Hattie had read the interviews about Jake's privileged background on an estate in the country. She imagined a slender woman, the sort who wore classic clothes, shirtwaisters in floral prints, Burberry macs and cooked for house parties and made picnics for point to point races and grouse shoots.

'My work is my tribute to her and there's no time to lose. So, I need the first twenty recipes by next week. All your healthy favourites, organic, veg and vegan options too. Once we've built up a list, we'll start the photo shoots. I have an expert food snapper in mind, so then we go, go, go. It would be marvellous to improve the health of the nation, don't you agree?'

'Absolutely, it is vitally important work,' she replied, thinking it was rather an ambitious aim.

Jake grinned. 'You see, I just knew we'd work well together, we share the same values, have the same outlook…

The moment was interrupted by her phone ringing.

'I'll ring you back,' she told him. 'That was just Finn,' she said by way of explanation.

Jake nodded and raised a quizzical eyebrow.

'You and Finn seem to spend a lot of time together. Are you an item?' Hattie noted his off-hand manner and was keen to explain.

Harriet flushed in confusion. 'Oh, no, of course not. We're just good friends. We're working on something together, that's all.'

Jake smiled and looked somewhat mollified.

'What?'

'Oh, Finn works for the British Horseracing Authority and I help out too from time to time…'

Jake's eyes searched hers, his manner inviting confidences.

'How intriguing, what are you helping him with exactly?'

'Oh, just making sure everything is above board in Walton, you know, between you and me. You heard about that recent shooting? Someone called Jimmy Clary was murdered, well it's about that, but it won't interfere with the book.' She wondered whether she had said too much.

Jake gazed at her for what seemed an age. He seemed to come to a decision.

'Good, because I need your full commitment to this project. I need someone as passionate about food and good nutrition as I am. I could work with anyone, but I chose you, Harriet, so don't let me down, will you?' His gaze was intense, almost blistering.

'Of course not. I really want to work with you too.'

Jake suddenly smiled broadly. 'Good. I'll be in touch as soon as the arrangements are firmed up. Ciao.'

Chapter 19

Seven pairs of eyes studied DI Taverner, as he took a deep breath.

'Right team. We are reaching a crucial part of the investigation. He pointed at the links board. It had Jimmy at the centre with pictures of the various suspects arranged around him, with post-it notes dotted here and there, outlining the progress of various investigations.

'As you may be aware, turning over Jimmy's place led to some interesting findings. Haworth found that Jimmy was not only passing off vegetables from budget supermarkets as organic when he'd run out of stock, he also had a little sideline in two of his polytunnels. He was growing cannabis. Now as you can imagine this widens the investigation right out. It goes without saying that the local drug dealers are not going to be thrilled about a newcomer peddling weed and probably worse, the clean eaters are going to be livid when they discover that the vegetables they were eating were not organic, but that they had paid organic prices for them.'

DC Haworth grinned. 'He even dipped them in soil to give them that dirty organic look.'

'Right. Neil Horton was overheard rowing with Jimmy, got into a fight and threatened him just the day before, allegedly over his attentions to his groom. So, he's definitely a person of interest. Is there any further information that has come to light?' Taverner surveyed the room.

DS Wildblood rifled through her papers. 'From our information no one had sight of Horton at all times. He was seen on the yard but could have driven the five minutes or so to the gallops, shot Clary and then arrived back before anyone noticed. There are several pockets of time when this could have been possible, especially early on when the staff were still rubbing the sleep out of their eyes. However, he is in a relationship with Vince Hunt's daughter, Daisy. There is no evidence to suggest that he was having an affair with Kerry though, which might have given him a stronger motive to kill Clary. He claims to have been planning to travel abroad with his show jumpers and wanted Kerry to accompany him as she is an excellent and reliable groom, hence his desire to keep Clary away. We have requested his phone records to see if we can link Kerry and Neil romantically. Seems Neil could be sponsored by Guy Montague. He is the younger brother of Tarquin, now Lord Montague, since his father's death. So, Neil is still very much in the frame.'

Gabriel nodded. 'Thank you, Anna. Now that brings us nicely onto Wolf, as you said aka Tarquin Montague, the eldest son and now Lord Montague. He was in a relationship with Perdita Brittain, Jimmy's latest girlfriend. He was devastated when they broke up and hated Jimmy Clary, so he might well be a suspect. Plus, he's an eco-warrior and likely to be into organic food too.'

'Maybe he discovered Clary's little sideline, and this pushed him over the edge. A crime of passion and of vegetables. An interesting combination, a sort of hot potato,' added DC Haworth, wryly.

There was a collective groan from the group.

'And we have Clary's phone which was handed in by a concerned member of the public.' Taverner could not resist frowning at Haworth at this point. Haworth had the good grace to look a little shamefaced. 'It is with the Tech guys. Have they found anything of interest so far?'

Patel nodded. 'We have texts from a Drew Morrison, a local chef, who arranged to meet Jimmy the night before his death. Drew runs a mobile organic food business by the name of Avocado. My guess is that he wouldn't be too pleased if he found out Clary was ripping him off with bargain basement stuff and passing it off as organic, so he is someone we need to speak to. We are also looking at other frequent contacts to try and establish any interesting patterns.'

Gabriel nodded thoughtfully. 'And by the way, Cullen, have we chased up any contacts from Drugs? Any intel on Clary from them? Was he making a name for himself, turning into a big hitter?'

Cullen shrugged. 'The local snouts haven't heard of him and so he hasn't registered any interest from the local drugs barons. He hadn't even begun to harvest his crop by all accounts, which fits with what Perdita told us that she had no idea about what was in the third and fourth polytunnels and that they were only put up a few months ago. Course, we have disposed of the stuff now.'

'Maybe he decided to undercut his supplier by growing his own stuff? Or maybe it's a crime of passion or something to do with horses perhaps?'

Ballantyne frowned. 'I suppose but no one has mentioned anything to do with racing. Maybe he had the odd bet, but it could just be another get rich quick scheme.'

Gabriel thought about this. 'Perhaps, but we mustn't rule anything out and he was found in the layby near the local gallops. His brother is also a conditional jockey at Hunt's yard, don't forget. Was there anything found at the house that suggested horses or betting could be a motive?'

Ballantyne shrugged. 'No, nothing.'

'OK. Ballistics are telling us that the murder weapon is a shotgun, but we already knew that. They are, however, easily obtainable.' He stared at the links board again. 'Which leaves us with little progress until we find the weapon.' He pointed at the board. 'His ex-partner, Caroline Clary, seemed fairly positive about her ex and was at home with their six-year-old daughter. It's possible that she rose early before school and shot her husband, but they separated seven years ago so why would she wait all that time before killing him?'

Ballantyne nodded at the board. 'So that leaves Neil Horton, Wolf, Lord Montague now, as the main suspects and now this Drew character?' Ballantyne frowned. 'Fancy Wolf becoming a Lord! Some people have all the luck, don't they?'

'Not necessarily. Bet the Hall will be a bloody millstone round his neck. Anyway, my money is on that Neil,' muttered Haworth.

'Yes. Neil may have been involved with Kerry. He won't admit this as he relies on Daisy's father for his stables and so on. But Wolf was previously in a relationship with Perdita Brittain and was by all accounts gutted when she left him for Clary. Maybe Perdita told him how Clary treated her, or he heard about him flirting with other women. He could have driven from Marchmoor to Walton, shot Clary and then returned before his fellow protesters even so much as unzipped their tents. He's into organic foods too, so maybe he knew about the vegetable fraud and it tipped him over the edge, so the motives are stacking up. Or maybe several clients Clary supplied, realised he was giving them fake organic stuff and took their revenge?'

There was a silence as the assembled staff took this in.

'What did I tell you, hot potato,' added Haworth.

Wolf was bristling with hostility when Taverner and Wildblood went to see him. Haworth and Ballantyne had been dispatched to question Kerry about her relationship with Neil, and Gabriel had chosen to see the other prime suspect. Wolf wasn't at his cottage on the Montague estate and a housekeeper at Montague Hall explained that Lord Montague was 'helping out' a close friend whose partner had recently died.

'No prizes for guessing who that is,' grumbled Wildblood. Shall we go straight to Clary's place?' She glanced at Gabriel who seemed miles away.

He was jolted out of his reverie. 'What? Course. Let's go to the farm.'

He didn't miss the curious glance from Wildblood.

'I've told you lot before, I was at Marchmoor and came back the day after the shooting. How many more times do I have to tell you? Ask anyone from the group.'

'Would that be the Green Warriors?' asked DC Wildblood.

'Yeah.' Wolf scowled, catching her disdainful expression. 'Despite what you may think, we do some really good work stopping developments on pastures and raising awareness of climate change. Unlike some, WE put our money where our mouth is.'

Wolf had been found at Clary's place with Perdita, tending some of the plants in the green house. His was in the process of weeding a long stretch of what seemed to be carrots, his tall form bent over as he plunged the trowel into the soil.

'So, what are you doing here?'

'What does it look like? I'm trying to keep Perdita's head above water and before you ask, I don't know anything about the shop bought veg or the cannabis Jimmy was growing. I told the other officers. Neither does Perdita. It's what any friend would do. Perdita's about to give birth and needs all the support she can get.'

Taverner nodded. 'So, I presume Clary left her the business, did he?'

'Perdita had put some money into the business, so it was a joint venture. She wants to carry on with it.'

Taverner had already been appraised of this in discussions with Perdita. It was hard to imagine that she hadn't known about the cannabis and the shop bought vegetables, but then she had not had a good pregnancy and the last few months she had withdrawn from physical work in the business due to ill health. She had expressed surprise and dismay at the state of the accounts. It seemed that Clary had tried to shield her from the fact that the business was in a lot of trouble. But the inescapable truth was that Clary's death seemed to have enabled Wolf to prop up Perdita and cast himself in the role of hero at the same time. This would be even more accentuated when the baby was born. It had all fallen into place, so much so, it was almost as though he had planned it. Had he? Gabriel was struggling to concentrate. He decided to get to the point.

'OK. We have checked with the members of the Green Warriors group and they confirm that you were at the protest at Marchmoor and did camp out there overnight. However, your tent was a little away from the others, meaning that they didn't have sight of you at all times. It is entirely possible that you made the 40 minute journey back to Walton, shot Clary and then went back to the camp, as though nothing had happened. You are clearly still madly in love with Perdita and maybe you couldn't stand how Clary was treating her. Perhaps you snapped, killed him and are now being cast as the hero, arriving back here to help her in her hour of need. Maybe with Clary out of the way, you could take his place and even bring up his child?'

Gabriel realised that he had hit a nerve. A pulse was going in Wolf's cheek and he had turned rather red, almost the same shade as his hair. He threw the trowel into the corner of the tunnel, his face contorted with rage.

'And I may just be helping out a friend. I hated Clary if you must know, but kill him? Never! I assume you can see yourselves out and next time you'd better come back with some actual evidence, Taverner, instead of this bloody make believe, otherwise I will take the matter up with your superior.'

Taverner was tempted to come back with an angry retort but Wildblood's hand on his arm persuaded him to leave it.

'Thank you for your help. We'll be in touch,' she added in as pleasant a tone as she could muster before turning away.

'Bloody hell. He got really riled up there, Sir. Maybe he really is the murderer.'

Gabriel was still beating himself up for not taking a more softly, softly approach. He had planned to listen, probe gently and draw Wolf out. What on earth had possessed him to go for the jugular?

'I should have been more circumspect.'

Wildblood obviously thought so too but didn't want to say anything.

'Maybe. It's not like you though, sir. Do you want me to lead on questioning Drew? '

'Good idea.' It might give him chance to calm down.

He felt Wildblood's gaze upon him. 'What's going on, Sir? You're distracted, moody and really not yourself. I suppose it's some woman or other?'

The urge to confide in someone was intense. And Wildblood was a likeable, decent, no nonsense sort of woman who would listen, advise and he could trust her not to blab to the whole team. He needed to speak to someone about his hopes and very real fears. He looked at her open friendly face.

'Well, you remember me telling you about my mother, about me being adopted?'

Wildblood nodded. 'Yes, you were going to meet her and then your father had his heart attack…'

'Yes, so I cancelled. Well, the Adoption Agency have written to me again suggesting various dates to meet her.'

Wildblood beamed. 'That's great. Now your father is better, there's no reason not to go, is there?'

Taverner shook his head. 'No, except I have mixed feelings, that's all. Supposing it doesn't work out, we don't get on, or I find out something I don't like?'

'Look, you'll never know unless you go for it. It could be the making of you. And I meant what I said, I'll come with you if you want me to.'

'Thanks. But then I'll have to wait until the investigation is finished.'

Wildblood sighed. 'Gi' over, will you? Just get on wi' it. Don't over think it, Sir. That's my advice.'

Taverner gave a wry smile. It was strange how his Sergeant's accent suddenly became much more Yorkshire when she felt strongly about something. But maybe she was right.

Chapter 20

Finn had woken early and enjoyed a quick breakfast before going to see the lads at the gallops. That way he hoped to see Sam, Connor, Harry and maybe Gavin in action, all in one place. He pondered on what he had learned from their visit to Clary's Farm Foods. Wolf was no fan of Clary's but was that a sufficient motive for murder? The fact that Clary had also started to grow cannabis was interesting too and did open up the list of suspects. Or maybe someone had tried to sabotage his business or had suspicions about his organic credentials, which clearly had been called into question? Perhaps, there was a fight and that's how he met his death? Yet, why was his body found a couple of miles away, near the gallops? None of it made any real sense.

He had enjoyed the races at Cartmel. It was a great little course, very picturesque and charming, but the company less so. Hattie had been distracted by her burgeoning friendship with Jake, who he was instinctively wary of, and even Kimberley had seemed preoccupied and out of sorts after she had arrived late. He had suggested they spend the evening together after racing, but she had claimed to have a headache and had disappeared off home, leaving him feeling a little disappointed and confused. Kim had looked amazing in a tight red dress, with high heels and her hair in an updo but had looked very pale, he conceded. She must have felt ill or she perhaps she had wanted to avoid him. He decided that he needed to be more understanding. He would text her later after he had been to the gallops.

The gallops, even at six in the morning, were a hive of activity. There were horses and work riders from several yards there and he knew that horses from other yards would come later. The gallops were well used with some all-weather tracks, alongside the grass gallops, all going slightly uphill, which were ideal for training. There was an assortment of hurdle fences situated to one side of the field, which comprised a schooling area for National Hunt horses. It was also used as something of a wildlife park and he noticed birds and feeders in trees situated at intervals along the way. He spotted a couple of wood pigeons, what looked like an owl and a couple of magpies and no doubt there were lots of rabbits, foxes and badgers there too. The whole place was well maintained and professional. He noticed Hunt's work riders in their distinctive navy and red silk caps, saw Connor riding and caught sight of Gavin. He nodded at Vince who was sitting in a Land Rover at the top of the hill. He saw Finn and beckoned him over. Finn settled down in the passenger seat next to him.

'So, how are things going? Are you here to see Gavin? He's back from Ireland.'

'Yes, so I saw, and some of the other lads. Is that Fort William?' Finn had spotted the large bay who was on the flat track.

'Yes. Just watch him work. The big race is next week.'

Finn squinted at the rider. 'Who is that riding?'

'A competent work rider but I'm thinking of using Davy Hughes for the race. Do you know him?'

'I've certainly heard of him, but flat jockeys are not my specialism, as you know. I've certainly not heard anything to his detriment though.'

Vince studied Finn. 'Good. He seems a decent sort.' He trained his binoculars at the group of horses who were galloping up the hill. 'Look, Fort William is on the outside, the one with the longer stride. Now just watch him go.'

Finn watched as the bay continued to accelerate away from the other group of horses, keeping up an impressive pace as the others slowed. He appeared to move up a gear and continued to break away easily.

Vince grinned with barely disguised excitement. 'The horse leading the stragglers is a handy miler, so you can see that Fort William has real class.'

'Great. Well, I wish you all the best with him.' Finn thought for a moment. 'Listen, do you all have to contribute to the maintenance of the gallops? They are really well kept.'

Vince looked at him in surprise. 'I'm not entirely sure. The gallops are run by some sort of local organisation. They arrange regular leveling and harrowing. Clary used to do the work. Usually it's done on the afternoons to avoid closure. I just pay the fees and that's it.'

'Jimmy Clary?'

Vince looked at him sharply. 'Yes. He was employed on an ad hoc basis. God, we'll have to get someone else now, I never thought of that!'

Finn processed this information, feeling it was relevant, but he couldn't really think why. Of course, it gave Clary a legitimate reason to be on the gallops, but as it would be when the horses had finished their work, then he couldn't see how that would have helped him at all.

'How is Gavin doing?'

'He is quiet, but it seems to have done him some good going home to Ireland. He's still going to the Catholic Church here in Walton though. He was asking about the funeral arrangements for Clary. When do you think they'll release the body for burial?'

'As soon as the authorities have carried out all their tests, I suppose.'

'Hmm. The sooner the better. Clary's death has cast a shadow over Walton, and we all need to move on.'

'How are Neil and Gavin together? It can't be easy knowing that Neil has been questioned by the police.'

'Gavin seems fine with him. He doesn't think Neil was involved at all, because of course, he wasn't.'

'Well, that's reassuring. Listen, I meant to ask you, do you get spotters round here? Was Clary one?'

'If he was, he was low key about it. He was sometimes here doing his maintenance stuff. I never saw him when the horses were working and if he was on the gallops, he'd need someone with him to identify the horses. With so many horses and trainers using them, working out which horse was which would be quite a feat.'

Finn supposed that was true. 'How about his brother?'

Vince shook his head. 'I doubt he's knows all the horses, though he could have passed on information about our lot, I suppose.'

'How is Gavin shaping up as a rider?'

'Pretty good, great as an all-round work rider. He sits a horse well and has good hands, so I reckon he'll do alright as a conditional.'

'Was he close to his brother?'

Vince considered this. 'Yeah. By all accounts they spent a lot of time together. It's no wonder he's so cut up, poor lad.'

'Mind if I chat to him when he's done and maybe ask him to do a bit of jumping? He is riding a hurdler, isn't he?'

'Yes, no problem.'

They chatted a little about Vince's prospects for the National Hunt season ahead. Then when he spotted Gavin slowing his mount down, Finn took his cue and strode over to meet him.

Gavin was still rather pale but acknowledged Finn with a faint smile. He was riding a dark bay and was patting him gently after a good gallop. The conditionals helped out as work riders until the National Hunt season started properly and as it approached, they would be able to prepare the horses and start to get them really fit.'

'Now then Mr McCarthy, how are you?

'Fine, but more to the point, how are you? How was your trip to Ireland?'

Gavin shrugged. 'Oh, you know, tiring. There were lots of tears, lots of friends and neighbours called in to pay their respects.' He blinked back tears. 'It was sad, but it was good for us all to be together.'

'It must be an emotional time for you and your family, I feel for you.'

Gavin nodded. 'Yeah. Thanks for fixing things with Mr Hunt about the leave. It was a good call. I just want to know when we can bury Jimmy and lay him to rest.'

'Yes, I can imagine. I'll see if I can ring the DI on the case and find out what's going on.' Finn thought he might also be able to get some information about the progress of the case at the same time.

Gavin brightened. 'Grand. If you could do that, t'would be good.'

'So, how's the riding going? Who is this chap?'

'Riding is going well. This is a hurdler who's just getting back into training before the season. He's called Plum Tree. He's a nice sort, so he is.'

'Great, so how do you feel about jumping the flight of hurdles in the distance? I've cleared it with the guvnor.' He pointed at the set of four birch fences.

'Ah well, I could do with some help over me jumping position, so I'll give it a go.'

'Great stuff. Just start with some circles at trot, working up to canter to warm up and the take him over them when you feel ready.'

He watched as Gavin completed a thorough warm up of several circuits and then he turned and jumped the hurdles. He had good control and apart from being left a little behind by the horse who did a huge leap at the first fence, he regained his position over the other three flights. Finn suggested they go again, and this time horse and rider performed excellently.

Finn noticed Robert Johnson's lot advancing towards him and looked out for his conditionals. He saw Sam Foster who raised his hand and steered his mount towards him. Sam's horse was wearing a hood with blinkers, which was unusual on the gallops. The two jockeys eyed each other curiously.

'Sam Foster, Gavin Clary. Have you two met?'

Gavin nodded. 'Yeah, sort of.'

Finn felt at a disadvantage standing between the two men and their mounts. He turned to Gavin.

'Well ridden there. We will need to work on your positioning a little but for pre-season it was pretty good. I'll catch up with you soon and we can arrange to meet up at Vince's.'

'Grand. See you.' He stooped down to adjust his stirrup leathers as Finn addressed Sam.

'So, who's this chap?'

'It's Rocky or Rock of Gibraltar to give him his proper name, I rode him the last time I saw you. He can be unpredictable and has a trick or two up his sleeve, but the hood is still working well. He has a great turn of foot.'

Finn recognised the horse now and remembered that Sam had ridden him before.

'Oh, he was the horse you told me about. You had to borrow a hood off another horse or something.'

'Yeah. The tack shop order finally came through. Saint George has his own hood back but is still just as one paced. Imagine struggling to get hoods in Walton of all places! Rocky is going to be busy. Guvnor is trying to get some more runs in before the handicapper catches up with him since he won his first race at York a couple of weeks ago. He's been entered in loads of races. He'll win loads more on that performance.'

'Brilliant.'

Robert Johnson was aware that Rocky would soon be carrying more weight, the more times he won, so was clearly hoping to get some wins in before this happened. When a horse wins races, the handicappers adjust the weight they are carrying, but it can take several weeks before this happens. The hood had made all the difference. It was surprising just what one small change could make. The hood, in effect, held the horse's blinkers in place. The blinkers limited the horse's peripheral vision, making him concentrate on the job in hand which reduced distractions. With this horse, it had clearly stopped him seeing the other horses he was racing with and stopped him bolting. Gavin still hadn't moved off and appeared to be listening to their conversation as he struggled with re-buckling his stirrup leathers.

'If he's a flat horse then I can't expect you to do some jumping, so you're off the hook, unlike Gavin.'

Finn glanced at the Irish jockey in an attempt to bring him into the conversation. What he saw horrified him. The lad's face was white, his expression a combination of shock and distress. He stared at Rocky and Sam, shaking his head in disbelief and then kicked his horse into a trot in the other direction, without so much as a word.

'Was it something I said?' Sam asked, staring after him.

Finn looked on in surprise. 'Maybe. I suppose grief can strike someone at any time. You see he is the brother of James Clary.'

Sam looked puzzled. 'Who?'

'You know the man who was shot here, just down the road, a couple of weeks ago.'

Understanding dawned. 'Ah, I see. I knew him just as Jimmy. Poor bloke. Must be awful for his family.'

Finn's mind ran through what Gavin must have heard in their brief conversation to warrant such an extreme reaction but was genuinely mystified. He had thought that Gavin had made a lot of progress since his brother was murdered but apparently not.

Finn managed to catch up with Connor and Aiden too. He made arrangements to visit the yards, suggested several training courses he was running on public relations, the press, diet, insurance and working with an agent. The courses were run jointly with the BHA and Professional Jockeys' Association. Hattie had done well with her cooking demonstration and he knew that a position for a dietician was coming up at the PJA, which he thought might interest her, that was if he could tear her away from Jake Delamare and his wretched protein balls. Finn was very doubtful about their nutritional value and even more doubtful about Jake. He just seemed to fancy himself too much for Finn's liking and the stunt he had pulled at Cartmel, was just pure marketing. He was actually very sceptical about the Life balls. Still, if it stopped the lads resorting to more drastic measures to lose weight, than that had to be positive, he conceded.

He texted Kimberley and she texted him straight back to apologise for leaving Cartmel early, her headache had cleared, she was feeling much better and they arranged to meet up later in the week. His mother rang to invite Jenny and him to lunch and suggested he bring Kimberley along. Clearly his sister had updated her on his love life.

Then he gathered up his phone and a notebook he used to jot down information he had found from their investigation so far. He read through his notes and felt utterly baffled. There were several suspects, all with motives to want Jimmy dead. Neil, Drew, Wolf, his ex-wife, not to mention a cast of rival drug dealers and business associates. He wondered why the BHA were interested and remembered that there had been some information from RaceStraight, the anonymous helpline that anyone could ring to report anything potentially fraudulent in racing. He wondered what the information was. He also picked up a voicemail from Tony from the BHA asking him to ring to arrange an appointment to pick up the gun. He messaged him back.

He texted Hattie to let her know he was on his way and drove to her house to pick her up en route to meet Wolf. He wondered briefly what Wolf wanted to tell them. Perhaps he hadn't been able to talk with Perdita in the background? Wolf had admitted to keeping an eye on Jimmy, and so was in a good position to know who he met on a regular basis and it was highly likely that one of these mystery associates had murdered him. He hoped to God that Wolf had some useful information because he had to admit they were in desperate need of a breakthrough.

'So, what do you think Wolf wants?'

'I'm hoping he has remembered someone who Jimmy regularly met who may be able to help us narrow down the list of suspects. Or like you said, he couldn't really say anything with Perdita around, but wants to now.' Finn glanced at Harriet who was scrolling through her phone contacts. 'I meant to say that there is a dietician job coming up with the PJA which might suit you.'

Harriet brightened. 'Great. It's so bloody boring writing a dissertation. I just want a job. Obviously, I have the Racing to School stuff but I'm struggling to fit in many sessions. I need a proper job. Jake says we should write a book together, so that should be good, but it could take ages. How's Kimberley's job hunting going?'

'Fine. No acting jobs as yet, but her admin job is pretty steady.'

'Is she alright? Any particular issues that she needs to discuss?'

Finn glanced at Harriet, noticing her almost cryptic tone. He could cope with polite inquiries after Kimberley, but her manner was solicitous, worried even.

'Fine. Her headache has gone, so that's good. She had thought she was coming down with the 'flu.'

'Anything else?'

'No, should there be?'

Harriet shook her head. 'No, nothing.'

Finn had the impression that Harriet was fishing, either that or she was trying to tell him something, but he didn't have time to quiz her further as they had arrived at the Montague estate.

'Gosh, this looks expensive and very posh,' added Harriet craning her neck beyond the manicured park land to get a glimpse of Montague Hall, but it was obscured by several huge lime trees. They drove through a pair of vast, gilt gates with an impressive coat of arms depicting a deer wearing a crown. The evening was sunny and the surroundings idyllic. There were several fine horses grazing in a paddock opposite, probably Guy Montague's broodmares. What a wonderful place, Finn thought, as they made their way up the driveway which was flanked on each side by huge rhododendrons and yew trees.

'Wolf said to turn left past the first bend,' Finn added. 'He didn't live in the Hall because of tensions with his father and hasn't moved there yet. The old Lord didn't entirely approve of Wolf's antics. Guy Montague seems a much more suitable son to inherit the title but is the younger son, of course.'

'Hmm, at some point I suppose Wolf will step up to the plate and move into the Hall, especially now the old Lord has died.'

They followed the instructions and came across a detached stone cottage with mullioned windows and two impressive chimneys.

'Here we are. It was the Gamekeeper's cottage apparently,' added Finn as his gaze scanned the property, clearly surprised.

'Wow. What a place! It would be worth a fortune nowadays and the setting is amazing. So much for being an outcast.'

'Quite, he can afford to have principles,' Finn replied dryly.

They exited the car, the still summer air reverberating with tension. Their footsteps echoed as they walked up to the front door.

'Shall I do the talking and you the observing?' Finn turned to her, his hand on the huge brass knocker which was fox shaped.

'Fine.'

'You can chip in too, if you think of anything.'

Harriet nodded as he lifted the fox door knocker. The sound of it falling echoed in the still air. They waited for the thud of footsteps on the other side, but none came. Finn lifted the knocker again, listened to it fall and waited, but there was still no response.

'Damn.' Finn glanced at his watch. 'We're on time, he definitely said seven.' He delved into his pocket and fished out his smart phone. 'No messages from him either.' He felt obscurely disappointed. So much for their bloody breakthrough! Finn looked round the perimeter of the property. To one side, there was a new, shiny Land Rover clearly belonging to Wolf.

'He can't have gone far.' Harriet frowned. 'Pretty smart wheels.'

'So much for saving the bloody planet!'

After standing there for some time, Finn tried ringing Wolf but when there was no response, he walked around the side and to the rear of the cottage. Harriet followed. At the back of the house there was a patio and French doors which led to a modern looking kitchen. Finn put his fingers to his lips and tried the patio doors which opened easily. Finn entered as quietly as he could, a sense of foreboding pressing heavily down upon his chest.

His heart stilled as he called out to Tarquin and advanced into the room. All looked lived in, with stuff lying about, but there was no sign of Tarquin.

'Listen, something isn't right. You stay here and I'll look round.'

'Fine,' Harriet shivered. 'Is it OK if I just take some photos?'

'As long as you don't touch anything.'

Finn advanced, misgivings crowding in. He continued into what appeared to be a study. His heart stopped as he spotted an armchair facing the fire with someone sitting in it, the shock of red dreadlocked hair at the back of the head clearly visible, as were the mass of blood, bone and brain scattered all over the chair, ceiling and walls. Finn took a deep breath, smelling the metallic scent of blood and felt the body for a pulse, knowing that it was too late. There was a shotgun thrown near the body and a piece of A4 paper on the desk in front spattered with blood droplets which simply had the word '*Sorry*' scrawled over it. Judging from the position of the gaping wound, it looked like he had shot himself through the mouth. Finn gagged at the horrific scene and ran back to prevent Harriet from entering the room.

'Christ, Harriet. Don't go in there. It's Tarquin, he's dead.' Finn fished into his pocket for his phone and began dialling 999.

Harriet gasped at him as he gave the details of their whereabouts to the police.

'What?'

He gently took her arm. 'Come on, we'd better wait outside whilst the police get here.'

She gulped. 'OK.' She pulled out her phone and began scrolling through her photos. 'Look at this.'

Finn stared at photos of a water bill, a shopping list and a brochure.

'What am I meant to be looking at exactly?'

Finn watched as Harriet scrolled through more photos of everyday items, letters on the sideboard, a coffee cup, plates in the sink and various brochures that were laid out on the kitchen table.

Harriet settled on the right image and pointed to a small shiny object which looked like a silver deer set with tiny diamonds. Finn scrutinised it. On closer inspection it was clearly a cufflink. The design looked vaguely familiar, but he couldn't quite place where he had seen it before.

'I found it in the hallway together with a small piece of fabric. It might be relevant.'

Finn wondered how to phrase the next part.

'It might be. Look, he wasn't murdered, Harriet. He blew his brains out. Now let's get out of here and don't touch anything at all.'

Harriet gasped. 'Are you sure?'

'Yes, there was a sort of suicide note with '*Sorry*' written on it.'

Harriet blinked back tears. 'Christ, do you think he killed Clary and then couldn't live with the guilt?'

Finn frowned. 'Looks like it. Or maybe he couldn't cope with the thought of having to step up to the plate and take over his father's title. Perhaps, it just wasn't what he wanted. Come on, we need to go.'

Just then, they heard the sound of cars approaching, flashing lights came into view as police cars and emergency vehicles flooded into the driveway.

Chapter 21

It was well past dinner time and Hattie's stomach began to rumble. She felt guilty and immediately tried to concentrate on the scene in front of her. She and Finn had been sitting in the back of the police van for what seemed like hours. After the police cars, there was an ambulance, a fleet of what she guessed were officers from SOCO and finally an incongruous little red Fiat 500 arrived. Hattie recognised the handsome detective, DI Taverner, as he unfolded himself from its tiny interior.

A dour looking Scots officer, DC Ballantyne, with a ruddy complexion and kind eyes had told them,

'You'll need to stay here until we can take statements and I think the guv' will want to speak to you too.'

At some point a uniformed police constable had unrolled some silvery sheets of what he described as thermal body wraps,

'Some witnesses go into shock after finding a body and we wouldn't want that, would we?'

Hattie would have liked to point out that it was Finn who'd found the body and she hadn't actually seen it. Thankfully, Finn had shielded her from that horror. There was just the two of them in the van and every so often the force radio in the front beeped and voices could be heard. Hattie sighed and looked at Finn.

'Listen, we'll keep the photos I've taken to ourselves, yeah?'

Finn smiled but looked rather pale. He'd opted not to wear the thermal body wrap like her and she hoped he wasn't going into shock. She remembered that he often seemed to deflect tension with humour.

'You don't need to whisper. I don't think the van will be bugged,' he teased, eyes crinkling, 'but, yes, keep quiet about them...'

'It's just like on the TV isn't it?' Hattie watched the bizarrely surreal scene, which seemed more out of place because of the beautiful, wooded setting. It made the intrusion of the vehicles seem like a desecration somehow. Poor Wolf, thought Hattie, what a waste.

'I wish someone would switch off the ruddy flashing blue lights. I might go and see what's happening if no one comes soon...'

He was saved that task as a pleasant faced woman poked her head into the van. She passed him a huge grey flask.

'Here, there's hot, sweet tea in there. Have a quick drink and I'll be back in five minutes to take your statements.'

She was back in about ten with her notebook open, just as the two witnesses were sharing tea from the cup lid.

'So, I'm DS Wildblood. Right, let me take your names and then tell me what happened from the beginning.'

The Sergeant was direct and looked like she would take no nonsense.

'So, why did the victim ask to see you?'

Finn glanced at Hattie. 'We don't know exactly. Look, Hattie here is a dietician and we think he might have wanted to talk about organic food. She is thinking of using Clary's Farm Foods as suppliers for her cooking demonstrations and we had already spoken to Wolf at the farm. He was helping Perdita after what happened to Jimmy. So, we assumed he had maybe arranged a deal…'

The detective looked from Hattie to Finn and back again, eyes narrowed. 'And what exactly is your relationship again?'

Hattie found herself reddening.

'We're friends. We both work in racing, Finn's a jockey coach, I work in the Racing to School initiative, hoping to work with jockeys and help them with their nutrition when I finish my degree.'

Finn explained more. Hattie watched as the woman smiled, understanding dawning about the racing connection.

'And the guv' says you're the one who found Clary's phone and brought it into the station. How did that come about again?'

Hattie explained about them visiting The Blacksmith's Arms and finding the phone. It sounded rather lame, even to her own ears.

'Right, just wait here a few more mins, I think the boss might like a word…'

They watched as DS Wildblood intercepted the tall figure of Taverner. He had emerged from the tented area set up at the entrance to the cottage. He wore white plastic feet covers, a baggy white suit and a white hat which Hattie thought looked like some sort of mop cap. He pulled these off impatiently, spoke to his colleague and then made his way over.

The inspector nodded at Hattie from the front of the van and surveyed Finn with interest, shooting out his hand.

'DI Taverner. So, Wildblood has taken your statements? Funny how trouble seems to follow you two around. Something about a missing jockey or something last time and a racing fraud, wasn't it?'

Finn shrugged. 'Well, with us working in racing, I guess we just happened upon a few people and one thing led to another.'

Taverner raised an eyebrow and looked at them both carefully, his expression inscrutable. 'And it involved a chase, injuries and heroics from you both, I read the file. And, of course, you found Clary's phone too.'

Hattie looked at Finn, unsure how to play it but Taverner was speaking again, his liquid brown eyes watching their reactions. 'I've come across people like you two, an ex-jockey and athlete, modern pentathlon I believe,' he glanced at Hattie, 'perhaps finding civilian life a trifle dull, deciding to engage in a bit of amateur detection on the side…' He paused as he considered his next words.

'Oh, we're not, 'Hattie assured him, 'it's just a coincidence, mostly.'

'Absolutely,' said Finn with a smile.

A look passed between Finn and Taverner, Hattie wasn't sure quite how to interpret it. Resignation maybe, irritation definitely. The inspector certainly looked exhausted she realised, with dark smudges under his eyes and his chin covered with stubble as if he'd worked late, rushed out early without shaving and hardly slept.

'Whatever,' Taverner shrugged, 'but if you do come across any more coincidences or happen upon anything you think is relevant to these two deaths, I need to know. You could be charged with perverting the course of justice if you don't inform me of anything that might be relevant. We could do without amateurs messing everything up.' He started to climb out of the van. 'That's all for now, you can go, we'll probably catch up with you again soon, when we've got more from forensics.'

'Inspector, can I just ask, was it suicide?' asked Finn.

Taverner looked like he was going to ignore the question until he realised that Finn had probably seen the gun and the suicide note.

'Maybe, but I can't confirm that until further tests are completed, so don't repeat that, for heaven's sake.'

And then he was gone. Hattie watched as the athletic, fluid figure strode away.

Finn dropped her back at her house.

'Do you want to come in for some supper? Mum's bound to have made loads,' she said.

Finn paused and looked tempted. 'No thanks, I was going to meet Kim later. I might just cancel anyway. I don't really feel in the mood. Are you OK?'

Hattie shrugged. 'I dunno. What do you make of Taverner? Seems on the ball at least. Anyway, I should be worrying about you, after you know...'

Finn frowned. Thank God he'd had the presence of mind to stop Harriet going into the room. The scent of death, the blood spatters and the gore from what he had just witnessed would stay with him for a long time. He felt blown off his feet by the memory of the full horror of Wolf's death.

'Sure, never better. Listen, let me think. I'll phone you tomorrow and we can decide what to do next. Bye.'

Hattie let herself in, feeling tired and confused. She'd been sure Wolf had been about to tell them something vital and now they might never know what it was. He was dead. Investigations she acknowledged were exhausting, often frustrating and upsetting too. She was very relieved that Finn had shielded her from seeing Wolf's body. She caught a whiff of garlic and onions but found that her appetite had deserted her.

Chapter 22

Taverner and Wildblood sat in the stuffy interview room listening to Drew Morrison explain himself. Sykes, of course, felt that the case was solved when Wolf aka Lord Montague was found dead, believing it was by his own hand as he hasn't been able to live with the guilt of killing Clary, but Taverner wasn't so sure. Any sudden death resulted in the police attending the scene and, of course, there would have to be a post-mortem, so until then they needed to press on with finding out who killed Clary and not make any assumptions. Still, there was the cloying sense of being grounded whilst they waited for confirmation of the cause of Wolf's death, which hung around the station like a bad smell. Taverner sent everyone out to complete statements, cross check alibis just to keep his team busy and motivated. He and Wildblood had the rather dubious honour of interviewing Drew Morrison, the man who had contacted Clary last before he was murdered.

'So, you were the last person to contact Jimmy on his phone the evening before he was murdered. Did you send this text?'

Taverner referred to the message written on a piece of paper

See you at the usual place, same time. Drew

Drew looked bewildered. 'Yes.'

'And where did you meet him and why?'

'Jimmy used to supply the veg for my business and I contacted him to discuss some of the pricing. I wanted a reduction in costings, if you must know. We met in The Blacksmith's Arms at about 7pm. I had a quick pint and talked to Jimmy who said he wasn't doing well enough to make concessions, and that was that.'

Wildblood frowned. 'So, I presume that the staff at The Blackmith's will confirm you were there?'

'I think so, yes.' Morrison swallowed nervously, so nervously that Taverner decided to push a bit more.

'Were you in the habit of meeting Clary in The Blacksmith's, only the term, 'see you in the usual place', implies that you were?'

'Well, yes. He was often in there and I used to meet him occasionally.'

'And were you happy with his organic produce?' continued Taverner.

'Yes, why do you ask?'

Wildblood showed him the photos of the fake production line where the vegetables were made to look as though they'd just been dug out of the earth.

'What's this?'

'What does it look like?' she asked.

Drew studied the photo carefully and frowned. 'Looks like some idiot is sticking carrots into soil. Wait a minute, I get it. Did you find this at Clary's?'

'Yes, we did,' Wildblood confirmed.

'So that bastard was selling fake organic vegetables, was he? Damned liar!' Drew was staring at the photos, his colour mounting as the implications of what he had seen sunk in.

Taverner was watching him closely. 'Is this first time you were aware that Clary was selling fake organic produce?'

'Yes! Look, I didn't know anything about Jimmy's ruddy shortcuts in his organic stuff. This is the first I've heard about it. I thought he was kosher and that Perdita, she seemed well into the organic ethos, used to go on and on about it. I can't believe it!'

'Are you sure you didn't find out and then take your revenge,' asked Wildblood.

Drew rolled his eyes. 'Is she for real? Look, if you're asking me this sort of shit then I want a solicitor…'

Taverner lifted his hand in an attempt to calm things down.

'Look, you're not under arrest. You're here voluntarily. Now, you say you met Clary in the pub and left at about eight. What time did you get to the food fair the next day?'

'Oh, at about half eight to set up and I was there all day.'

'And what time did you leave home?'

'At about 7.45.'

'Did you do anything before you went to work?'

Drew looked warily from one to the other. 'Yeah, I walked the dog at about six and came back home, got cleaned up and went off.'

Taverner nodded. 'Did anyone see you walk the dog?'

'I don't think so, I suppose someone could have. I just walk round the block from where we live along Green Lane and back. Why?'

Taverner sighed and pushed his chair back.

'Right, we'll take a short break. Do you want a coffee?'

Drew lifted his head. 'Only if it's decent, not like the stuff you gave me earlier…'

Taverner smiled and shook his head. 'Water then?'

Outside in the corridor, Wildblood and Taverner debriefed.

'So, what do you think?'

Anna shrugged. 'He seems alright and his reaction to the photos revealing Clary's scam, was genuine enough. He was furious.'

'Hmm. We need to check that he was in The Blacksmith's and see if anyone saw him walking his dog. How far is it from his house to the layby where Clary was shot?'

Anna rifled through her papers. 'He lives a few miles outside of York, so I suppose he could have driven to the layby in 20 minutes instead of walking the dog. It's unlikely but possible...'

'OK, we'll send an officer round to talk to his wife and check out the pub to see if anyone remembers him being there. His message was sent the day before Clary was found. For all we know, he arranged to meet Clary at the layby. We'll leave him to stew for a while, Anna. DS Lucas is due any minute. Let's see what he has to say.'

Having now met Harriet Lucas, Taverner was struck by the similarities between DS Lucas and his sister. Something in the set of their eyes and they had the same way of looking at you, direct and sharp, taking everything in. Intelligent but socially skilled, he thought. A good combination of qualities in a detective. DS Lucas worked in the Drug Squad in the area.

'Well, off the record there's any number of gangs from Leeds or Bradford that Clary could have pissed off. I've had my contacts asking around. Nothing definite so far though, but for what it's worth I wonder about checking out the Morans. They run a series of clubs in the North and are into drug dealing. I could sniff around and see if they know anything.'

'Thanks, Will.' Taverner sighed and took a sip of thick treacly coffee from the machine. He shuddered and Will laughed.

'Christ, that stuff will rot your guts. Anyway, how's things with Sykes, can't imagine he's happy.' Taverner grimaced. The meeting earlier in the day had been tense.

'Put it this way, Sykes is back tomorrow, and he wants a result by the end of the week otherwise he's going to bring another DI in to help out.'

Or as DCI Sykes had actually said, 'Get your sodding arse in gear Taverner, else you're out! Got it?'

Will frowned. 'I'll get back to you tomorrow then, keep going, you're sure to have a breakthrough soon...'

Will shook his hand and Taverner watched him go thinking about his sister Harriet. He wondered about the relationship between her and McCarthy. Wildblood had said that she and McCarthy were only friends, but he did wonder. They seemed to be very in tune with each other, he couldn't help noticing, and very at ease.

Dr Ives rang up a little later.

'Now then, Taverner, I expect you and your team have been relaxing thinking that Montague committed suicide unable to live with the guilt of killing Jimmy Clary, so case closed?'

'Well, not quite. I presume you are ringing to confirm that Lord Montague's death was suicide, though?' Why doesn't he just spit it out, thought Taverner. He could well do without Ives playing silly buggers.

'Well, I can't confirm that actually. There are some anomalies. I'd like you to pop in so I can discuss them with you.'

Taverner's brain was in a spin. He hadn't realised until that point that he had sort of bought into the idea that Wolf had committed suicide. It neatly tied everything together, but of course, it was never going to be that easy. He held his breath.

'OK, I will. But can you just give me the gist over the phone?'

He heard Ives sigh somewhat theatrically. He clearly hadn't wanted to miss his moment of glory.

'Well, I have examined the gunshot wound, the length of the gun, taken into account Montague's arm length and studied the fingerprints on the trigger.'

'And?'

'Well, the trajectory of the bullet doesn't fit with Montague pulling the trigger. In other words, if he had shot himself, the injury wouldn't have been where it was…'

'Right, and?'

'The fingerprints don't fit either. It looks like the murderer placed Montague's fingers on the gun and trigger, but not in such a way that he could have possibly pulled the trigger. They're in the wrong place altogether.'

'So, are you saying that Lord Montague was murdered too?'

Ives paused for theatrical effect. 'Yes, I am. It seems you have a double murderer on your hands, Inspector.'

Taverner wanted to laugh at the Scottish pronunciation of 'murderer' with the rolling 'r's, but realised it was not at all appropriate. He felt suddenly lightheaded.

'How confident are you?'

'Very confident, in fact I'd bet my house on the fact that Montague was murdered too.'

That was good enough for Gabriel. 'Right, that certainly changes everything. Thanks for the call.'

Taverner replaced the receiver in something of a daze.

At 5 pm Taverner called the team to attention. He tried to sound upbeat, but the mood was sombre. He sensed the team were tired and frustrated. Even the box of Krispy Kreme doughnuts that he'd sent out for, which were now doing the rounds, did little to raise the team's spirits.

'Listen up, I reckon it's time to knock off now. I have just heard from Dr Ives. As you know Wolf aka Lord Montague was found dead, shot through the mouth. It looked like suicide, but it actually wasn't. So, ladies and gentlemen we have a double murderer on our hands, assuming it's the same person of course. Ives has confirmed that the trajectory of the bullet in comparison to the actual wound is all wrong and the fingerprints are in the wrong place too. So, tonight I want you to go home, chill, spend time with the family,' he said looking at Wildblood. 'Team briefing here at 8 sharp, led by DCI Sykes who will be back from the inquiry and I'll need everyone to be on the ball and raring to go.'

There was a palpable intake of breath from the entire team. Even Wildblood was speechless and stood staring at him open mouthed.

'Christ, Sir. Everyone thought it was suicide. Thought that Wolf couldn't cope with having to step up to become Lord Montague, or with the guilt of murdering Clary,' said Haworth, who was expressing what everyone was thinking.

Wildblood sighed. 'It certainly looked like suicide, Sir. Who would want to murder him?' She had turned pale.

'That's what we need to find out.' He and Wildblood had visited Wolf and despite his hostility he was clearly a man of strong beliefs, both had had some respect for the man, after all, he could have had a much easier life as a Lord without being an eco warrior. At least he had some principles. He was very different to their usual clientele.

'Maybe Wolf murdered Clary and someone knew that and murdered Wolf as revenge?' suggested Ballantyne.

Taverner nodded. 'Maybe, maybe not. Anyway, bugger off the lot of you and I'll see you all tomorrow.'

A ripple of laughter ran through the team.

At least the team don't hate me, he told himself on the drive home, crunching the gears of the Fiat in his tiredness. It was some small consolation and he clung to it like a non-swimmer clung to the side of the pool. The task ahead seemed enormous, so much so, he hardly dared to think about it. Maybe Ballantyne was right, but he knew in his heart of hearts that they were looking at a double murderer. He wondered if either of their main suspects, Horton and Morrison, could be in the frame for this one too. If they weren't, it meant that they were way off beam, which depressed him beyond belief.

When he reached the house, he checked his phone. Damn, he only had a voice mail from his ex, Georgia. That was all he needed after a day like he'd had. A familiar feeling of anxiety and dread overtook him. Of course, the relationship hadn't always been like that, it'd been good until the last six months. Stomach lurching, mouth dry he listened to the message, reminding himself that there was nothing worse she could do to him than the stunt she'd already pulled.

Her clipped, drawly voice was familiar and slightly mocking.

'Gabe, it's Georgia. Listen wherever goddam place you are, you can keep the Fiat, sell it or do whatever.' There was a slight laugh. 'I always hated it and I've got the beamer now. Give me a ring when you get a mo and we'll sort out all the paperwork.'

A beamer, of course you've got a bloody beamer, thought Taverner, wearily. And how like her to send him such a fake, impersonal message. She might have been cancelling a hair appointment, he thought bitterly, not talking to someone who she had once agreed to spend her life with, not that they had ever got around to actually getting married, which was probably just as well.

He found it hard to shake off his low mood. With a sigh, he assembled a stilton sandwich and poured himself two fingers of Macallans. Christ, when did that get so near to empty? There was only one drink left. He resolved to save it for later, made a coffee and fired up his iPad for a start on the evening's work. He was dreading Sykes coming back in person, it was bad enough getting words of advice over the bloody phone. It was hard to admit it, but the team had worked their bollocks off for precisely nothing, and it was back to the drawing board now.

He flicked through the files on his iPad and began to sift through the inventory of items found at the crime scene. Of interest were the items they had found in Montague's stone gamekeeper's cottage, near the scene. A silver cufflink with some sort of crest engraved on it, a folded photo of two small boys and an address book open at the page of numbers beginning with DEF. First Taverner enlarged the photo of the cufflink on the screen. Steadily he began to research silver marks. Then he planned to try all the numbers in the phone book starting with those on the open page. Hopefully he would have something useful to report at the briefing tomorrow. It looked like it was going to be a long night. But time was closing in and he would never forgive himself if there was, God forbid, a third murder. Maybe they were looking at a serial killer? Ballistics might be able to help but shotguns were harder to work with as the gun could not be easily identified, unlike those which used bullets and in a rural community, there were loads of shotguns which farmers kept quite legitimately. It had to be one murderer, surely, for such a small place and if so, how were Jimmy and Tarquin's murders related? Both had been in relationships with the same woman, Perdita Brittain. He felt a rush of sympathy for her, pregnant with both her partner and ex-partner dead, how on earth was she going to survive? But maybe, after all, she held the key.

Chapter 23

Finn was feeling frustrated at the lack of progress they were making over Clary's death. He had been so sure that Wolf had some vital information to impart and now he was dead too, he really hoped that the knowledge hadn't died with him. Images of Wolf's lifeless pallid face with the gaping wound where his face should be, kept floating unbidden into his consciousness. The poor man must have been desperate to do himself in. Had he murdered Clary? His phone beeped, jolting him out of his gloomy thoughts. He was surprised to receive a text from Hattie that shocked him to the core.

Hi Finn. The police are now thinking Wolf was murdered too! Will let it slip. Have emailed photos from house. See you soon. x

Christ! Whoever killed Wolf could have known that they were meeting him and decided to kill him before he could pass on the information. But who and how did they know that Wolf had contacted them? Finn re-read the last text that Wolf had sent him. Or perhaps Wolf knew who had murdered Clary and was going to speak to the police. Finn felt annoyed with himself that he hadn't admitted to working for the BHA when the police has spoken to him, but he had been in shock and he wasn't sure who knew. His boss had said they had spoken to the local DCI, so surely Taverner would know? He felt rather depressed about Wolf. He had seemed an ethical, decent bloke if not a little unconventional, a crusader for animal rights and the environment. He had wanted to share vital information, he was sure, but he had the uncomfortable feeling that the whole thing was spiraling out of control. Two murders in such close proximity were very worrying and made him realise that their murderer, if it was the same person, was very dangerous, not to mention, desperate.

He sorted through the photos that Hattie has sent him of the scene. Had the murderer removed something? If so, the photos Harriet had taken might not be very helpful, unless the murderer had left something in the debris by accident. He scrolled through the photos. There were take-away food menus, bills, shopping lists and something that looked like a brochure in one shot. He widened the screen and was just able to pick out the small print.

Dreams Plastic Surgeons, a new you awaits. Expert, confidential service. Facial surgery, rhinoplasty and face lifts a speciality. For a free quote ring ....

How odd! Mind you, perhaps because Wolf was actually Tarquin Montague, Lord Montague, and presumably very rich compared to most, he received a different kind of junk mail to the usual rubbish about double glazing. Finn's mother, who was a well-heeled widow, received hundreds of brochures for holidays, obscure clothing ranges and stair lifts, that infuriated her, so perhaps this was more of the same? It couldn't be relevant, he decided, as Wolf and plastic surgery definitely didn't go together. He was a man passionate about leaving everything as nature intended and presumably that also included the human body. Feeling irritated he scrolled through more photos. These were of the usual household items, bits of toast, crockery, glasses, bulbs, batteries, a vegetarian cookbook and in one corner a photo of two children positioned in front of a middle aged, pleasant looking woman with dark bobbed hair. Presumably it was Tarquin and Guy with their mother. He expanded the picture and was surprised to find that there was another child's arm on the right-hand side, but the picture seemed to have been deliberately folded so that the other child was obscured. He wondered why Wolf had gone to all that trouble. He googled Lady Montague and compared the image with the woman in the photograph. Lady Montague, who died several years before, was slim, rather beautiful in a refined, aristocratic way and immaculately well dressed. Definitely not the smiley woman in the photo. So, who was she? A cook, nanny, perhaps? She looked full of warmth and proud of her charges.

Then he flicked to the photo of the single silver cufflink which was found in the hall. If the police hadn't found the other cufflink then this could have definitely come from the murderer. The cufflink was fashioned in the shape of a deer wearing a crown, so was quite distinctive. If they were Tarquin's, presumably they would have been boxed in a pair, and as Harriet neatly put it, Tarquin wasn't the type to wear the sort of shirt where cufflinks were required. From where it was found, it could easily have been left by Tarquin's assailant especially with the slight piece of fabric it was attached to. It was almost as though the assailant had caught his cuff on something, tearing the shirt at the same time, probably in their haste to get away. All they needed to do was find the other cufflink and then they would find the killer. The cufflink looked unusual but then Finn didn't wear them so who was he to judge? An uncomfortable thought pinged into his brain that Drew certainly did wear cufflinks. He wasn't sure about Neil, but Hattie would know. In the meantime, he was certain that they needed to speak to Guy Montague and Perdita Brittain. He also decided to ring his contact from the BHA about the gun he had asked Tony Murphy for, and arrange a date to meet. He was spooked by another murder and realised that he and Hattie would be placing themselves in great danger if their activities were discovered. Had the murderer found out that Wolf was about to disclose something of vital importance or was the timing of their visit a coincidence? Either way they needed to take precautions.

After visiting Connor Moore at McMahon's yard, he watched the lad undertake some training with a three-year-old gelding that was going to go hurdling in the season, Finn made his way to Beverley racecourse for a flat meeting. He had arranged to pick Kimberley up, but Hattie was busy, no doubt discussing protein balls with Jake or healthy recipes for their book, he thought wryly.

Kimberley looked lovely in a navy and pink dress and was in good spirits.

'So, how are the auditions going?'

'Hmm, so so. I have been heavily pencilled for a part in a costume drama and have picked up a few minor bits and pieces, so not too bad. How about you?'

Finn went on to explain about finding Wolf dead.

'Oh God, that's awful! I remember you saying you were going to see him. Do you think it's anything to do with the layby shooting?'

'I'm not sure.' Finn felt reluctant to talk about the details of the case with Kimberley. He didn't stop to analyse why he felt like this. Maybe it was simply because it was just too sombre a topic for a sunny day. 'Let's just enjoy ourselves, shall we? Hattie won't be joining us today.'

Kimberley frowned but it seemed a little forced Finn decided, wondering if there were some tensions between the pair.

'Never mind.'

The East Riding course was nestled into the countryside just outside the historic town of Beverley and was a lovely course with a good quality card. The day was bright, and it looked like the rain that was forecast later might hold off. Finn bought a couple of racecards as they made their way to one of the restaurants. The place was filling up and Finn enjoyed the familiar sights and sounds, the scent of cigar smoke, the chatter of the race goers dressed in their finery and the scent of grass, mingled with the smell of horses.

At the bar he was greeted by his old friend Melvin Vine. Finn had completely forgotten about the odd betting pattern that Melvin had highlighted but was interested to find out what had happened since. The restaurant was heaving, so Melvin by virtue of his series of eyebrow raises and twitches, managed to order a couple of whiskies and motioned for them to have a confidential chat in a quieter corner, in answer to his query. Finn was about to mention that he was with Kimberley but decided against it as Melvin clearly wanted to speak to him. Perhaps, the queue for food would die down in the meantime.

Melvin pulled out a folded piece of A4 paper with one hand and scrolled through his phone with the other. He looked around him, checking who might be listening.

'This is a list of the races where there has been a bet placed by someone at the course. A different person has been used to lay the bet each time, and it has been done in a very showy manner. And each time they have placed the money on, the horse lost but by putting the money on, other punters followed suit.'

Finn shrugged. 'So, why are you bothered if they and others stupid enough to follow them, lose their shirt? What does it matter to you?'

Melvin shook his head. 'And you an ex-jockey, Finn McCarthy, didn't you learn anything?' He sighed. 'The actual bet is only about £1000, but when it's put on in such an obvious manner, others have followed and it has skewed the odds. Thousands have been put on by other punters who think they're onto a sure thing. The bookies automatically adjust their odds, narrowing the odds on the horse who had just had a lot of money placed on them and lengthening them on the others in the field.' He pointed at the piece of paper he had handed Finn. 'In all cases, a horse with the longer odds came through to win and there was a flurry of bets on this horse placed after the odds changed, but in such small amounts so as to go unnoticed by the bookies at the time. Altogether, these bets amounted to thousands. We only discovered this later when the money had been paid out. If one person orchestrated the bets, then they would have won a tidy sum overall on the outsider, even taking into account the bet placed on the first horse. They must have inside information to make it work, though, so they could correctly back the winner. We could be looking at a sophisticated betting scam. Don't know who's behind it though. It's someone different each time, see? They put the money on early in the meeting and make such a scene about it, other punters follow like sheep.'

Finn nodded. Of course, he should have known that. It was basic book making practice, the odds usually added up to 120, which included the bookmakers' premium or 'vig' as it was known, so narrowing the odds on one horse would naturally lead to longer odds in the rest of the field.

'Of course. Why are you telling me this?'

Melvin studied him intently. 'Because I think you're the sort of man to keep your wits about you. You go to the races, you're well known, popular and people tell you things. See what you can find out.'

Finn pocketed the piece of paper without looking at it.

'OK. I'll keep my eyes and ears open.'

Melvin took a sip of whisky and handed Finn his silver smartphone.

'Scroll left and look at the photos. Each of these individuals has laid the bets we are concerned about.'

Finn scrolled through spotting a range of people, three women and four men, all elegantly dressed in eye catching but smart clothes, each with a newspaper as they hovered near the bookies' pitches, just before they placed their bets. Their attire was designed to draw attention to themselves and therefore to their bets. He spotted the man he had seen at York dressed in a coat with a fur collar and a bow tie. He scrolled to the next photo of an elegant woman wearing a tight red dress, her hair twisted into an elegant bun. Recognition flooded through him. Finn nearly dropped the phone in surprise. It was Kimberley in the clothes she wore at Cartmel. He clutched the edge of the bar and threw back his drink so fast, it burned his throat, his mind in turmoil.

He tried very hard to modulate his voice and give nothing away. His brain processed the possibilities. Supposing Melvin had recognised Kimberley and was trying to ambush him? Maybe Melvin thought he and Kim were in the scam together? He glanced at his companion but found nothing unusual in his expression that indicated he was remotely suspicious.

Finn handed the phone back to Melvin and took a deep breath.

'Well, if I find anything out, I'll let you know.' He attempted a smile. 'It might be useful if you could email me those photos, so I can make some inquiries on the quiet.'

Melvin clapped him on the back and handed him a folded up piece of paper. 'These are the dates and the races that we are concerned about. I'll send you the photos now. If you do find anything out, let me know. I'd be much obliged to you, Finn.'

Finn went back to the table where Kim was waiting. She frowned when she realised he was empty handed.

'God, it's hellishly busy. Let's go somewhere else, shall we?'

She pouted. 'OK.'

He led the way out of the restaurant, his mind full of questions to which he had no answers.

He spent the rest of the afternoon dodging Melvin, being polite and resisting the urge to question Kim closely. She was her usual pleasant self and the afternoon passed without incident. If Kim noticed his reserve, she said nothing until they were on their way home. It had started to rain heavily, and the swipe of the windscreen wipers was the only noise they could hear as their conversation had run dry. The silence was oppressive. He noticed Kim casting him surreptitious glances every now and again as the conversation had begun to stick.

'Is everything OK, Finn, only you've been a bit weird since you met that man at the bar. Hope it wasn't bad news.'

Finn took in her immaculately made up face and creamy skin, feeling annoyance and regret in equal measure. She was so attractive but clearly, she was not who he thought she was. He wondered whether to broach the subject of the betting, decided not to and then changed his mind as anger and curiosity coursed through him.

'Well, you know when we went to Cartmel and you arrived late that afternoon…'

'Yes?'

'That man I met was talking to me about a betting scam where a flamboyantly dressed person places a large sum of money on a horse to alter the odds on the field.' Kim frowned.

'And?'

Finn turned to her. 'Then he showed me photos of several people who had been involved. One was of you, clearly placing a bet on a horse at Cartmel. I just don't know what to make of it. Can you explain what on earth you were doing?'

Kim turned to him, horrified. 'What do you mean?'

Finn sighed. 'I mean I need an explanation because from where I'm sitting you lied to me about being late at Cartmel, so you could place a bet on a horse. It seems to me you're involved in something very dodgy indeed! In fact, I'm beginning to think I don't know you at all!'

Kimberley paled then flushed in confusion. Eventually great fat teardrops began to fall down onto her cheeks.

Finn shook his head, irritated and angry.

'Look, I'm sorry for shouting, but I do think I need to know what is going on,' he added more gently this time.

Kim wiped her eyes and sniffed. 'You're right. I'm sorry.' She paused as if wondering how much she should say. 'It was an acting job, well not an acting job as such, but it came through my agent, Damien Lloyd. Several of us who are on Damien's books have been paid to do the same thing. I mean what harm could it do? We were paid to place a bet on a particular horse, that's all, but to make a show of it, wear noticeable clothing, act confident, all that. Well, we're all actors, so we can do that easily.' She bit her lip. 'I don't know anything about racing or betting, so how would I know it was a scam?'

Finn handed her a tissue, but he was not convinced. 'You really have no idea?'

Kim looked appalled. 'No, why would I? I mean it was just a job, an easy job. Besides the horse lost, so what's the problem?'

Finn took a deep breath, surprised at her naivety. 'The problem is that placing a bet in such a showy manner, caused other punters to back the horse in their droves, distorting the odds on the eventual winner, so the odds were much more favourable. The criminals used lots of different punters to put small amounts on this horse, so small they were unnoticed. The scammers walked away with thousands of pounds, meaning that you have been an accessory to a betting scam. Don't you see, you've been used to shield the person who is behind it!'

Kim's shoulders began to shake as once again tears began to fall.

'I swear I didn't know it was wrong. It was just a job, an easy job, Damien told me. His client wanted complete confidentiality but asked that we put the bet on in a flamboyant sort of way, that's all. Just make it look obvious to anyone watching what we were doing. It was dead easy.' She dabbed at her eyes. 'I didn't say anything because that was part of the job to keep quiet…' She paused. 'You don't think the police will be involved do you?'

'It is possible, but it's vital that you try to find out who paid you to do it. It's really important.'

Kim thought for a moment. 'I know several people on Damien's books did the same job, so I'll ask them.'

'What's your agent's name again?'

'It's Damien Lloyd at Lloyd Agents. He's based in London but has a Northern Office in York.' She passed him a business card. She wrung her hands together and sighed. 'Look, I'm sorry. I didn't realise it was wrong.'

Finn glanced at her. 'OK. I'm sorry too.' He really was.

He dropped Kimberley off. 'I'll call you,' he added, thinking that he was not at all sure he would. He couldn't shake the feeling of utter annoyance and betrayal somehow. He sensed that she was telling the truth, and that she hadn't given any thought to her actions, but surely, she realised it was wrong? It made him wonder what sort of a person she was.

He pulled out the sheet of paper Melvin had given him and checked the horses that had been backed on those occasions to see if there were any patterns. There were seven races in total which corresponded with the seven photos Melvin had sent him of the people who had put the bets on. The racecourses where this had happened varied but were largely in the North and Midlands. The photos had dates and times on them which indicated that the bets had been placed early, either before or just after the first race. The horses were from a wide variety of stables, pretty much all over the UK. He scrolled through the photos that he had been sent. Each person was dressed quite flamboyantly and there was a mixture of ages and sexes. Then he came across the photo of Kimberley and felt horribly low and quite unable to think straight. It was no use; he could not concentrate so he put the papers away in a drawer. He sat brooding as he flicked through the TV channels, finally settling on something light on TV about nature. He poured himself a drink and tried in vain to get into the programme. He was just about to flick through the channels when his mobile rang. It was Harriet.

'Oh God, Finn, we've got to do something. The police have arrested Neil again for the murder of Wolf and Clary. Daisy is in bits. She thinks he might not get bail this time…'

He took a deep breath. 'OK, calm down Harriet. Why has he been arrested again?'

'The police reckon that he has a motive for killing Wolf and they have found some shot cartridges at his home.'

Finn's head was spinning. 'What possible motive could Neil have for murdering Wolf and why does he have shot cartridges?'

There was a pause. 'Well, that's just it. Neil and Wolf go way back when Wolf was involved in the anti-hunting movement and, of course, Neil hunts regularly. It seems that Neil blamed Wolf for ruining one of his good show jumping horses. One of the protestors put a wire in front of a fence, the horse was badly injured and was totally spooked by the whole thing, so much so, he would never jump again. It was one of Neil's best horses apparently.'

Finn took this in. 'Shit. And the cartridges?'

'Neil borrowed Vince's gun for shooting birds and rabbits in his arena.'

Finn felt as though he had been punched in the stomach. How had they missed the connections between Neil and Wolf? He arranged to drive round straightaway and meet her, his heart in his boots. Could things get any worse? If his relationship was in tatters, then his tenuous career as a part of the BHA integrity team was in an even worse state, he realised.

Chapter 24

It was around 8pm when Hattie answered the door to Finn.

'Hi, come in.'

Hattie noticed that he looked tired and seemed a little out of spirits.

Inside, Hattie's parents Bob and Phillipa were in the hall, gathering their things, clearly on their way out.

'Sorry to miss you Finn, but you know how it is, Philippa's dragging me out to a wretched dinner party…' Bob rolled his eyes and adopted an air of martyrdom.

Philippa clattered over, unsteady on kitten heels and gave Finn a brief kiss on the cheek.

'Don't listen to him. There's plenty of food in the fridge, Hattie, do cook him something. There's tons of booze too, so have a nice evening, you two.'

Hattie winced because her mother's comment seemed to hint at some burgeoning romance between the two of them and she had explained about Kimberley, Finn's girlfriend, but her mother had disregarded this.

'Right, food?' said Hattie briskly once they were alone.

'Well, what have you got?'

Over a cheese omelette and salad, washed down with a glass of white wine, Hattie filled Finn in.

'The police searched Neil's house, found the cartridges and took him off at around 6pm. He's definitely been formally arrested…'

Finn frowned. 'And do you think they're the right cartridges? I mean, surely they are pretty standard?'

Hattie speared a cherry tomato. 'Well, Dad says it takes a few days to get ballistic reports, they'd have to match up the two murder scenes. I reckon there's not been time and that they're trying to see if he confesses. Or they might have lots of other information that they haven't yet revealed.'

'Can you see him murdering two people? You know him, Hattie…'

'God, no! I mean, Neil, he's so laid back, the only thing he cares is his horses. And this incident with Wolf, it had to be several years ago, so why wait until now to get even?'

Finn studied her. 'But you do have some doubts?'

Hattie shrugged. 'It's just something Daisy said about not knowing too much about Neil's family, his past and so on. She's never met any of his relatives, he doesn't talk about them, it's just a bit weird. Everyone knows everyone in Walton and he just appeared seemingly from nowhere…'

'And…'

Harriet looked shamefaced. 'It's just that for all that he seems easy going, he does have a temper. I remember when he thought Daisy was still seeing her ex, he did threaten him. I suppose he's a bit macho and could certainly handle himself, but not enough to murder someone.'

Finn took a deep draught of wine. He remembered that Vince had said something similar about Neil's family, but was it relevant? Not everyone had a stable background, but was that necessarily a problem? He wasn't sure.

Hattie pushed away her plate. 'Listen, I had a few ideas, want to hear them?'

They cleared some space on the table and Hattie got out her notepad.

'Right, I've been looking at the photos I took at the scene…'

Finn suddenly grinned. 'Me too. Did you spot the photo of the boys?'

'Yep. Has to be Guy and Wolf as kids, don't you reckon?'

The boys had reddish hair and were unmistakably brothers. Hattie reckoned that the photo was probably taken when they were about seven and five years of age. Cute little lads with impish grins. It had made her unbearably sad to think that one of them was now dead.

'Yeah, but look there's a third arm, another child but the photo's been folded, or the child's been cut out …'

'Well spotted.' Hattie squinted at the photos on her phone. 'So, who's the woman in the middle and who's the other child?'

Finn shrugged. 'A relative? A nanny maybe? And the kid, God knows. I looked up the family in Debrett's. There's a sister but she's five years younger. She'd have been a baby, so it can't be her. She lives abroad now after she married a polo player from Argentina. You know what we're going to have to do, don't you?'

'Go and see Guy?'

'Yep, tomorrow first thing, I reckon.'

'What do we say? Do we go on some pretext or do we just come straight out and tell him what we're up to?'

Finn paused. 'I've ridden for the family, for old Lord Montague at least, so I know them a little. I reckon it's best to be straight, probably best to tell him about the BHA link, at least that is something Guy will know about.'

'And we could ask about the cufflink at the same time.'

Finn nodded. He seemed to be thinking hard. Again, there was a faraway look in his eyes, as if he was lost in a little reverie of his own.

'More wine?'

'No, look I'm driving. A coffee would be good though. Right, did you have any more brainwaves?'

Hattie paused. 'What do you think the killer was after? And you do realise whatever it was, he probably took it with him.'

'Or it could be because of something that Wolf knew, so the murderer had to kill him to silence him. Maybe, they knew he had contacted us, which could be worrying.'

Hattie felt her eyes widen. 'We could be in danger.'

'We could which is why I said that you must step back it there's any danger, promise me?'

'Yeah, yeah,' replied Hattie, a little too quickly. 'When shall we go to Guy's? Do you want to drive or shall I?'

'I'll pick you up at 9. I reckon if we go early, we might catch Guy in.'

Hattie nodded. 'Great, that fits in with me. I'm meeting Jake later to go through some recipes. It really looks as if the book's going to come off, you know.' Hattie could not hide her excitement. 'Hey, listen I've got some Life balls. Want to try one?' For some reason Hattie wanted Finn to be as pleased as she was about the protein snacks. 'He's been sending them out to the jockeys. Sam Foster swears by them, Aidan Collins as well and even Nat Wilson's agreed to try them out!'

Hattie passed Finn a foil package. Nat Wilson was a champion jockey and close friend of Finn's. His involvement would really add some credibility to Jake's marketing. He made a mental note to speak to Nat, as he thought the Life balls were a complete gimmick and the whole thing was getting out of hand. He pocketed the foil square but shook his head.

'Look, I'm bushed. I'll see you tomorrow, Hattie.'

It was as if the shutters had come down on a shop window and suddenly Finn wasn't there at all, so quick was his leave taking. He was clearly deeply preoccupied.

Hattie closed the door, quietly berating herself for her insensitivity. Christ, she thought, I completely forgot to ask him how he was. Poor Finn was the one who'd found Wolf's body. She hadn't even seen it because he'd stopped her going in. He's probably suffering from PTSD, she thought. God, then she'd wittered on about herself and how well the plans for the book were progressing. She supposed that things were not going well with Kimberley. I'll be nicer to him tomorrow, she decided. She wondered if he had somehow found out about Kimberley's betting habits and that was what was bothering him. Should she have said something to him? Sometimes, Finn McCarthy, I don't know what you're bloody thinking at all. He did have the capacity to go all silent and moody on her. A complex man, at times taciturn and hard to read, she thought, concerned that he was not quite himself.

Finn arrived at 9am exactly and when they travelled over to Guy Montague's home, seemed, for now, at least to be back to normal. Although she'd glimpsed Montague Hall a few days earlier, she was unprepared for the grandeur as they approached. It was simply quite stunning, a Jacobean mansion house built in mellow stone with mullioned windows which matched the gamekeeper's cottage. There was an entrance tower with the same coat of arms, a deer wearing a crown over the vast, studded door. Following Finn's lead, Hattie waited as he used the bell pull.

Before it could be answered, a man's voice bellowed from the right, 'Come around to the side.'

Several dogs appeared, a grey wolfhound and two small Yorkshire terriers. Finn made his way towards the voice while Hattie bent to pat the friendly wolfhound. She then made her way over the gravel between its yapping companions.

Guy Montague was every inch the country squire. The reddish curls were cut short, he looked a shade paler, but he was still well dressed, albeit in an old fashioned style. Although, he was only in his thirties, his clothes and whole demeanour seemed to suggest he was middle aged before his time.

'Ah, Finn McCarthy and…'

'Harriet Lucas.' She shook Guy's outstretched hand.

'What can I do for you?'

'Can I just say how sorry we were to hear about your brother, Tarquin,' said Finn.

Guy nodded, looking grim faced. 'I gather you found him. But I presume you haven't come out here just to express your condolences?'

'No. I'd rather this was kept confidential, but I work for the BHA as a jockey coach, but have been asked to look into Jimmy Clary's murder to see if there is any link with racing and then with Tarquin being murdered, we have to see if the murders are connected. You see, it was Tarquin who asked to see us.'

Guy looked sombre. 'Hmm. The BHA Integrity Services, I presume? Why did Tarquin want to see you?'

'We never got to find out. I was hoping you might know something.'

He led them into a vast, cavernous kitchen and gestured to chairs arranged around a long, battered refectory table.

'Right, what do you want to know? Tarquin and I weren't so close latterly, so I have no idea why he contacted you, but I'll try and help if I can.'

Finn was encouraged, and took out his phone, scrolling down to find the pictures.

'We want to know who's in this photo for a start…'

Guy looked from Finn to Hattie, eyes assessing the situation.

'You took these at the scene, with my brother dead in the next room? I'm sure that breaks every rule in the book, tell me why I shouldn't shop you to the police right now?' His cheeks reddened and Hattie gulped. Guy was right of course.

'We didn't know Tarquin was dead at that stage,' muttered Hattie.

'Look, remember that betting fraud case about the man who was exposed as blackmailing people last year?' asked Finn.

Guy nodded.

'We found out about it and helped to get the evidence together,' blurted out Hattie. 'Look, it's just a few questions and then we'll be out of your hair.'

Guy ignored her and stared at Finn. 'I saw you at Hunt's place and you used to ride for my father. He rated you and so does Hunt. As it happens, I think the police are bloody useless, so ask away.'

Finn showed him the photo of the two boys. 'Me, poor Tarquin, of course, and that's Nanny Davies. So?'

'And there was a third child, see this arm, any idea who that might be?'

Guy frowned. 'No, why should I? I was only four or so myself. It could have been anyone, a relative probably, one of Tarquin's friends, a child from the village.' He paused. 'Look, Nanny would know. She's in her eighties now, at St Mary's home in Harrogate. You'll have to ask her. What else?'

Hattie showed him the photo of the cufflink on his phone. Guy narrowed his eyes and then enlarged the photo. 'Hmm, it's very like the ones Tarquin and I were given when we reached twenty-one by our father, but ours have the family crest, the crowned deer with a diamond. As you can see the diamond is missing here. Similar but not the same and not as good quality. I don't know whose it is. Certainly not Tarquin's.' His voice sounded bitter and suddenly full of emotion.

'Would anyone else have any reason to copy the family crest?'

'No, I don't think so.' He looked inquiringly at them. 'Anything else? Only I have a funeral to arrange and I need to consider what to do about my horses.'

'Ah, you have Fort William racing next week in the Bollinger Cup.'

Guy gave a faint smile. 'Yes. The police seem to think that Neil Horton is a suspect for both Clary and Tarquin's murders.' He raised an eyebrow. 'Apparently Tarquin and this Neil clashed about hunting or something.' Guy flushed and wiped away a tear. 'He was always such a headstrong boy, wanted to save the world singlehandedly, but if Horton is guilty then I can't very well leave my horses in the same bloody yard but with Fort William's race so close, I'm not sure what to do.'

'My advice is don't do anything hasty. There are other suspects besides Horton. At least leave it until after the race when you'll know more.' Hattie burst out, hardly unable to contain herself.

Finn gave her a sidelong look. 'I agree. Horses are sensitive creatures and can struggle with change, moving Fort William, could really upset him. And if Horton isn't involved, then you will have moved your animals for no good reason.'

'Hmm.' Guy looked deep in thought. 'Perhaps you're right. Listen, if you find anything out about what happened to Tarquin, then do let me know.'

'Of course. Right then, we'll leave you,' said Finn and they walked away.

They left Guy staring into the middle distance at nothing in particular.

Hattie was sympathetic. 'Poor chap. He doesn't know if he's coming or going, does he?'

Finn shook his head. 'Nice pitch on behalf of Vince, though. Let's just hope Neil isn't involved.'

They were halfway down the drive when they had to pull in to let a red Fiat 500 squeeze past. Hattie ducked as she spotted DI Taverner.

'Thank God he didn't turn up while we were talking to Guy!'

'Right, now we're finally getting somewhere.' At least DCI Sykes was pleased, thought Taverner. 'We have a search warrant for the cottage where Neil Horton and Daisy Hunt live. I'm so glad that we had a look in the outbuildings, otherwise we would never have found the cartridges in the first place and with the ANPR picking up that Horton was in the area of Montague Hall at about the right time, our suspect is looking pretty likely, I'd say.'

Taverner knew he was having a dig at him for not taking Neil seriously as a suspect, but he managed not to rise to it. But self doubt kicked in. Had he been too quick to dismiss concerns about Horton? The again, why would he have allowed them to search the barn if he had anything to hide?

'Taverner and Wildblood, I want you to interview Horton. I want you, Wildblood, to be the soft touch, more empathetic and Taverner to be the raging, 'you've lied to us, we can't believe anything you say', type.'

Good cop, bad cop, Taverner realised, thinking that was just so typical of Sykes. He had the imagination of a fly and was just as irritating.

'What are we looking for?' asked DC Haworth.

'Patel and Cullen are chasing up ballistics and forensics, the rest of you can search the outbuildings of the cottage for any other incriminating evidence. Montague's murder will have caused a huge amount of blood spatter, so the murderer must have had bloody clothing to dispose of and don't forget the cufflink. So, my guess is we're looking for a bloody pair of trousers and shirt, the type with loose cuffs. If we find the other cufflink to the one left behind, or the shirt he was wearing, then we'll have him.'

DC Ballantyne and DC Haworth looked irritated to be missing out on the interview of Neil Horton. After the investigation floundering, finally the team were suffused with energy and determination. Taverner still had misgivings but even he had to admit that the clues were stacking up against Horton.

'And it goes without saying, we need to find anything to link Horton, Clary and Montague.' DCI Sykes was warming to his theme, his face was pink with excitement, his eyes gleaming. 'And we'll have an interruption after a few hours, DC Patel can pop in with some 'new information' and we'll really rattle the bugger.' He grinned at the team. 'We're nearly there everyone, we just need one last push to nail the bastard.'

Taverner nodded unenthusiastically. He wasn't at all sure that Horton was the murderer, there were just too many things that didn't fit. Even if he had a grudge against Wolf for harming his horse, it was years ago, so why would he suddenly murder him after all that time? And they had failed to prove any link between Horton and Clary. There was no evidence to substantiate the theory that Horton was romantically involved with his groom, so it really was down to the forensics. Still, Sykes clearly had his next promotion in his sights, so he had better just get on with it. He just hoped that Sykes wouldn't be proved right, otherwise he'd be unbearable. He caught Wildblood's eye and decided to plan a strategy before they went into the interview room, picking up Horton's statements as he did so. The sooner they got on with it, the sooner they could release Horton and get on and find the real murderer. He was convinced that Guy Montague was the key to finding out who had perpetrated these appalling crimes. He knew the jockey and the dietician had been to the Hall before him, despite them trying to hide from him and he wondered why they had been there. Maybe to pay their respects about Wolf and Lord Montague, he thought.

Neil was looking tired and rather scared. His solicitor had arrived and drew back his shoulders in a belligerent manner, clearly spoiling for a fight.

'My client is ready and willing to answer any questions. He has absolutely nothing to hide, so if we could get on please?'

Taverner glared at him.

He read Horton his rights and began.

'So, as you are aware, we searched your outbuildings with your consent and we found shotgun cartridges similar to those that were used to kill both James Clary and Tarquin Montague.'

Taverner showed Horton iPad photos of the cartridges, scrolling his fingers across the screen.

'So, I take it you admit to using them?'

Neil pulled a face. 'Yeah, I do. I borrowed them and a gun from Vince Hunt. I had a problem with rabbits digging up my arena, so I took pot shots at them.'

'Yes, we did make a search of our gun license records and realised that you weren't listed. But what I'm more interested in is where you were between the hours of one and four yesterday afternoon.'

Neil sighed. 'As I've already told you I was at the yard schooling a couple of youngsters all afternoon.'

'All afternoon? Surely you had a break?'

'Yes, I had a cup of tea about three and then I went to see a man about a horse.'

Taverner looked inquiringly at him.

'I am always on the lookout for promising youngsters, you always need to be planning ahead in the show jumping game, besides I school them and make good money selling them on.'

'How much could you sell a good show jumper for?' Wildblood was certainly warming to her theme as a good cop, Taverner realised, as she batted her eyelids at Neil.

'Oh, anything from twenty to sixty grand, more for a top notch animal.'

Taverner frowned. 'Where did you go to see the horse?'

'To a local yard, Malcolm Jeffries, he's a good guy. Lives out towards Saxby, they live off Walton Road at The Rowans.'

'What time did you get there and how long were you there?'

'Oh, about a couple of hours. I saddled up and rode the gelding for a while and came back about five.'

'And will Mr Jeffries vouch for you?'

'Of course, ring him.'

'We will,' replied Taverner. 'How well did you know Tarquin Montague?'

Horton nodded. 'Fairly well, the Montagues are well known in the area and Tarquin was one of those tree hugger, anti-hunting types.' Taverner noticed the curl of disdain on Neil's face.

'So, you didn't like Montague?'

Horton shrugged. 'That's one way of putting it.'

Wildblood agreed. 'Quite understandable, these protestors are a pain in my book.'

Taverner continued. 'I hear you had some run-ins with Tarquin...'

Neil shrugged. 'If you want my honest opinion, I thought he was an idiot. He was into animal rights, climate change and was anti-hunting. But he was born with a silver spoon his mouth, so he's nothing but a hypocrite jumping on the eco bandwagon. I came across him on the hunting field yelling and screaming. I tried to keep out of his way, as much as possible. And him a bloody Lord too! He should have known better.'

'I have it on good authority that he ruined a horse of yours, a show jumper with a lot of potential, a few years ago by placing wire in front of a fence and injuring the horse out hunting. The horse recovered from his injuries but never jumped again.'

Wildblood smiled. 'It must have been awful for you, your horse being cut by a wire. A good horse at that, they must be very hard to come by.'

Neil shook his head. 'One of the saboteurs did do that a few or so years ago. Laid a load of barbed wire out in front of a hedge. Bastards and they call themselves animal lovers! Sixty sutures that horse had, and he was never the same after that. Ruined him, he was a bag of nerves. I don't think it was actually Wolf that did it, but I did have a go at him about his anti-hunting antics. I was furious, I'll admit, but it was ages ago. I didn't like Montague, he was a rich, over privileged idiot who had too much time on his hands, but I certainly didn't murder him.'

Taverner raised his eyebrows. 'Well, you seem to have a few problems containing your temper, Mr Horton. What with fighting with Jimmy Clary over your groom and then arguing with Tarquin Montague over injuries to your horse. Strange that both of them should wind up dead, isn't it?'

Neil had turned white. 'I had nothing to do with Clary's death as you very well know and the same with Montague. You are clutching at straws, that's all.'

Taverner sat back in his seat and regarded Horton with a scornful expression.

'Well, it's to be hoped that forensics don't find any of your prints on the cartridges found at the murder scenes, then isn't it?"

At that point DC Patel entered the room and thrust a piece of paper at DI Taverner. Taverner pretended to read it as this was what had been agreed. However, it was worth reading. The words suddenly came into focus.

With shotguns, there is no way of telling which gun fired a particular cartridge. Neither cartridge found at the murder scenes had any prints on them which suggests that the murderer was wearing gloves. The cartridges found in Horton's property had fingerprints on them, which match those of Mr Neil Horton. This suggests that he did not intend to conceal his actions. The cartridges found at both the murder scene and at Horton's are a popular make and widely available.

Patel had written in the margin. *Vince Hunt's gun found in his gun cabinet at his property. He confirms that he allowed Horton to use it for the purpose of shooting rabbits.*

He relaxed his posture and passed the report to Wildblood. As expected, the fingerprints on the cartridges found at Horton's had his prints on them but not the ones from the murder scene. Perhaps, Horton was just clever, but it left them with absolutely nothing to go on unless the team had found anything else in their search.

Taverner wrote a message to Patel.

Was anything else significant found at the property?

Patel shook his head. And it was the same several hours later when they'd checked out Horton's version of events. Malcolm Jeffries lived near Montague Hall and had been able to vouch for Horton and nothing of any real relevance had been found in the search of the property he shared with Daisy. The team had seized a computer and were checking banking and phone records, but that would take more than the standard time that they could hold Horton for and there was nothing so far to warrant seeking an extension. Frustrated, it was agreed that the team were no further forward. Eventually, Taverner came to a decision.

'Thank you for coming to talk to us, Mr Horton. You are now free to leave.'

The two officers left the interview room leaving their suspect and their solicitor relieved.

Haworth joined him at that point, his expression gleeful.

'I might just have something to cheer you up, it seems that no one remembers Morrison being at The Blacksmith's on the night he said he was there, and we can't find anyone who saw him walking his dog on the morning of Clary's murder, and digging into his history he'd had one or two scrapes with the law under his previous surname of Morgan.'

'Previous name?'

'Yes, he was known by his mother's surname until she remarried then he took on his step-father's surname of Morrison.'

Taverner paused, his skin prickling. 'What sort of offences?'

Haworth grinned. 'Some car thefts and a couple of assaults, broke another kid's nose and hit a teacher. Seems his step-father got him back on the straight and narrow, but perhaps he has regressed.'

'Right, we'll need to speak to him again.' Taverner was thoughtful. Any youngster committing offences at such an early age was always a concern. Coppers knew that criminal behavior was a habit that was hard to break, especially if it started in a child's formative years, so that's why they needed to take a much closer look at Morrison.

Chapter 26

Finn met Tony Murphy's contact at a derelict farm outside of York. Eddie Jones was dressed casually in trainers, joggers and a cap, but his neat hair and upright bearing made Finn think he was ex-military. He wondered how his boss knew him but guessed that the BHA Integrity Services had lots of useful contacts.

'Do you need to see any ID?' asked Finn fishing in his pocket for his lanyard which he rarely used.

'Nope. I watch a lot of racing. I'd know your face anywhere.'

Finn grinned. It was nice to still be recognised, but bittersweet too, as he realised that those days would never come back again.

'So, what do you have for me?'

Eddie beamed and produced a black holdall, unzipped it carefully, eventually pulling out a grey handgun.

'Right, this is a Glock 17 which is standard issue to police forces in many different countries due to its safety and performance record.' He pulled out a magazine and proceeded to load it. 'It's a 9mm polymer gun, so won't be detected by metal detectors, has a safe locking mechanism and has a range of 50 or so feet, which should be ideal.' He took the magazine out of the gun and handed it to Finn.

'Now you load it.'

Finn copied Eddie's previous actions and handed the gun back to him.

'Right, here is the sight system, so all you do is line it up and release the trigger. Be wary of the recoil, so brace your shoulder as you fire.'

Eddie paused to fish out a pair of protective glasses and ear defenders. He aimed the gun at a paper target sign he must have fixed up earlier, some 35 feet away. He pressed the trigger and fired four times. Each bullet penetrated the red inner circle of the target. Eddie was clearly a crack shot, so no pressure then.

'Right, you give it a go.'

Tentatively Finn took the gun and donned the glasses and ear defenders and tried to copy Eddie's performance. He fired four times, all but one shot, missed the target entirely.

'Not bad, go again.'

After several more tries, Finn was managing to hit the target more reliably and even managed to get two shots into the red inner circle.

'Reckon you'll do,' added Eddie after about 45 minutes. 'From what the boss was saying, the gun is more of a precaution than anything else. Is that right?'

'Yes, definitely,' Finn replied. It really was the last resort as far as he was concerned. 'If I do have to use it, then I want to injure someone, nothing too serious though.'

Eddie nodded. 'In that case, aim for the feet or legs, try to avoid any area above the hips where the vital organs are situated. Avoid the knees too, if you can. They're a bugger to fix.'

With that, Eddie gave him several more magazines, gave him a cheery wave and disappeared into his black Land Rover. Finn held the gun gingerly, then packed it up carefully and hid it in the glove box of his car. He felt more reassured about continuing his investigations, but only marginally. He fervently hoped he would never have to use the damned thing.

The next day, Finn sat with Perdita whilst Harriet made a cup of tea. Perdita was wearing a shapeless, khaki dress which accentuated her swollen belly and a cream cardigan. Her dark hair was twisted up into a bun and her face was pale, with the exception of her eyes, which were red from crying. She had strong features and would have been very attractive in other circumstances, Finn decided. They were sitting in a homely farmhouse kitchen with stripped, pine free-standing cupboards and a stone flagged floor. The dresser was a riot of bright mismatched china, edged with homemade bunting. Colourful and charming.

'Why would anyone kill Wolf, for Christ's sake?' She looked dazed and puzzled.

Harriet came back with three mugs of tea and some biscuits. Finn was rather unnerved by weeping women and he was pleased when Harriet saw him struggling with what to say and pitched in.

'I can't imagine what you're going through, so soon after Jimmy's death. Do you have any family members or anyone who could stay with you?'

Perdita shrugged. 'My sister is on her way. The police suggested a police officer come here after Jimmy, but I refused. Useless buggers, anyway.' She wiped her eyes and looked at Finn. 'Do you think the murders are related?' she asked.

Finn shrugged. 'They could be. The police are looking at Neil Horton as a person of interest.'

Perdita grimaced. 'Idiots. The police don't know their arse from their elbow. Course, Jimmy was a charmer, I knew that, but it was just his way, he meant no harm by it. He liked all women, but he loved me, it was me he came home to.'

Finn realised that Perdita certainly loved Jimmy if she was prepared to put up with his routine philandering. Unless of course, she didn't, and she killed him.

Harriet took a sip of tea. 'So, did Wolf talk about anyone who might want to harm him? Did he ruffle some feathers with all the eco stuff? Did he mention anything?'

Perdita sighed. 'He was preoccupied now you mention it.' She frowned as she thought back. 'God, I was so upset about Jimmy, I could hardly breathe and he was so kind, made me eat, helped with the business.' Tears poured down her face. 'I should have thanked him, but now I'll never get the chance…'

Finn wondered what to say to that.

126

'I'm sure that Wolf knew you were grateful. Sometimes, you don't actually have to say anything,' Harriet said.

Perdita managed a weak smile. 'The police told me he was shot like Jimmy. I suppose it would have been quick…'

They nodded. It was at least some consolation, Finn supposed, thinking back to the horrific scene he had witnessed.

'So, what was worrying Wolf, can you think of anything? It might just help us find the murderer,' asked Finn.

Perdita nodded. 'He was on about his old nanny. He seemed worried yet elated somehow. It's hard to explain. I think nanny Davies lives in an old people's home in Harrogate. He visited her on and off and was going to visit again.'

He wondered what Wolf wanted to speak to her about. Maybe she was ill?

'Did Wolf mention any other concerns, at all? Was he upset about his father dying?'

Perdita frowned. 'No, not unduly. He and his father didn't always get on, but he would have been a good heir. Mind you, he would have done things his own way. He was concerned about me. He spoke to the police who were going to close down the place after finding out about the fake organic veg and the cannabis, he really pulled some strings so we could keep going. He did lots of work, just keeping the place going and now he's gone…'

Perdita began to weep again. Hattie moved to comfort her. Much later, after Perdita's sister had arrived and they were satisfied that Perdita at least had someone to look after her, they made their way back home.

Harriet looked thoughtful. 'I really feel bad for her. What awful timing, two deaths in quick succession just as she's about to give birth!'

'Yeah. I know what you mean. I'm glad her sister is around.'

Harriet studied him for a minute or so. 'You've been a bit down lately, Finn. Is there anything wrong?'

Finn sighed and for a long time did not speak. He didn't want to appear needy, yet on the other hand it would be a relief to talk about what had happened.

'Just that Kim was involved in a betting scam.' He told her about the trip to Cartmel and his encounter with Melvin. 'He had photos of all the people who had put the big bets on and there she was. She didn't get why I was angry either.'

'Who did she say paid her to place the bet?'

'It was her agent, someone called Damien Lloyd. He has an office in York apparently.'

Harriet bit her lip. 'You know I thought I'd seen her earlier, but I wasn't sure, so I didn't say anything. Maybe, she just saw it as an acting job. Did she win a lot of money?'

Finn explained about the betting system.

'Melvin reckons that the single bet placed early on in such a showy way, encouraged others to back the horse and had the effect of lengthening the odds on the other runners, one of which our dodgy punter backed heavily. They must have had inside information to know which horse to back. And then they must have used a series of people to place lots of small bets on to make it worth their while.'

Harriet nodded. 'Right. So, is Damien Lloyd the man behind the scam?'

'Could be. I said I'd keep my eyes and ears open, so I need to follow that up. Do you want to come?'

Harriet seemed surprised at the question. 'Of course.'

Finn grinned. 'We also need to visit Damien and Wolf's nanny. What was the name of the care home again?'

Harriet grinned. 'St Mary's in Harrogate.' She fiddled with her phone. 'It's about an hour away. We could meet in York, go to the agency and go from there to Harrogate.' She studied Finn. 'Look, don't be too hard on Kimberley. She probably didn't even think about the consequences, it was just a role to her. And don't forget that she's just like your conditionals, desperate to succeed in her chosen field and therefore she's quite vulnerable. Listen, why don't you ring her and talk it through?'

Finn nodded. At home his finger hovered over Kimberley's name in the contact list in his phone, but something held him back from ringing her. He just didn't think he could ever fully trust her again and deep down he knew that a lack of trust was no basis for any sort of relationship.

Chapter 27

Harriet spoke to Daisy, who was pleased that Neil had been released after police questioning but was still anxious.

'I suppose the police will just try to find some other evidence to incriminate him. Neil is pretty sure he's being tailed by them and it just never seems to go away. God, supposing I've been wrong about Neil all this time?'

Harriet was appalled. 'You can't really think that Neil murdered Clary and Wolf? I think you'd know if he was capable of murder, surely?'

There was a silence. 'I don't mean the murders, of course he didn't do those, I mean the fight over Kerry. Supposing he really did fancy her?'

Harriet took this in, realising that Daisy was actually quite insecure and looking for reassurance.

'Look, Neil loves you, I think he was genuinely annoyed with Jimmy. Kerry is an excellent groom, so he wouldn't want her distracted by someone who had no real interest in her.' She thought of Perdita and realised that Clary and his Irish charm had a lot to answer for. Then she remembered that Clary was dead, shot through the head, and felt instantly contrite.

Harriet spent some time writing her dissertation. Her attention drifted and she googled Jake Delamare. There were loads of references to the 'Cooking Up A Storm' programme, lots of images of Jake making delicious meals in the show which had brought him to prominence and lots of photos of him and Tatiana Black, the model, he had been in a relationship with for several months following the programme. The pair made a glamorous couple and Harriet found herself entranced by Tatiana's gorgeousness. Her eyes rested on Jake, who was a little less bronzed than he was now, but just as handsome. She also googled the ingredients of the Life balls and studied the contents. Dried dates and apricots, nut butter, vanilla essence, chia seeds, cocoa powder and some preservatives. Nothing particularly unusual but then Jake had hinted at some secret ingredients too, hadn't he? The Life balls were healthy, but she felt disappointed somehow. Whilst wholesome, it was hard to see how they could live up to such dramatic claims about weight loss and improved health, but then she berated herself, she mustn't be so negative. If Jake had found a very healthy snack that could delay hunger, which due to the high protein levels, was entirely possible, then who was she to question him? She needed to keep a clear head when researching them, however, and had to remain objective at all times. She must ask Finn if his brother-in-law had found anything out about them. The thought of what Jake could do to her career combined with his overall sex appeal, made it very hard to remain focused. She thought back to their last encounter and shivered. The attraction was overwhelming and mutual, she was sure of it.

The agency was situated in a Georgian property not far from The Shambles in York and was marked out by a brass plate with 'Damien Lloyd, Agents and Management for Actors' written in italic lettering. Finn peered at the sign.

'So, how are we going to play it?' asked Harriet. 'You can't just march in there and start accusing people. Why don't we have a coffee and a chat about it?' Harriet was concerned that Finn was still furious with this Damien character and might well lose it with him, such was his anger about Kimberley being implicated. Finn flexed and unflexed his fists. He looked around him.

'OK, there's a Starbucks on the corner. Let's have a coffee and a think.'

Once settled inside, they sipped cappuccinos and considered their options.

'I suppose I could pretend to be an actress desperate for work?'

Finn frowned. 'I don't see how that would help. Even if this Damien offers you some work, say for instance, the betting scam job, then he's hardly likely to reveal the name of his employer.'

Harriet took another sip of her drink as she thought hard for ideas.

Finn suddenly brightened. 'How about you cause a diversion, something that empties the place, and then whilst that's going on, I can be on hand to have a quick look round. Can you think of anything?'

Harriet loved a challenge, so she ran through a range of options such as fainting, losing her temper or kicking off because she was owed some money.

'Hmm. Don't worry I've got it…'

The office was on the third floor of the building and smelt of polish. Mr Handley, Damien Lloyd's assistant, beamed behind a large old fashioned desk. He was probably in his forties, balding, and wore a badly fitting navy suit and dirty brown shoes.

'So, Miss Jameson, can I ask what acting experience you have?' His eyes gleamed behind his round glasses as his gaze roved over her body.

'Well, I've had walk on parts in some soaps, I've been an extra in Doctors and Hollyoaks.' Harriet crossed her fingers that he wasn't going to ask for more details.

'Excellent, excellent. Can I ask what sort of roles you are currently looking for?'

'Something in the same vein, I suppose, but I can turn my hand to most things.'

Mr Handley regarded her steadily, clearly wondering what 'most things' might mean. He paused, as though giving the matter a lot of thought.

'There is some work I can put you forward for. Do you like horseracing?'

Harriet nodded, trying not to give too much away. 'Yes, I do, actually.'

His pudgy fingers reached for an old style rolodex file. 'If you wouldn't mind filling in this form, you'll note the paragraph about agency fees.' Harriet pretended to search in her bag for a pen. He presented her with a fountain pen with an exaggerated flourish. Harriet started to cough, on cue, and carried on in a consumptive fashion. Mr Handley began to look concerned.

'Let me get you a glass of water.' Mr Handley rushed off, frowning. Harriet had already observed that the kitchen was on the first floor, giving her time to dash out into the hallway where the fire alarm was. She had noticed it when she came in. She looked around her and seeing that the coast was clear, took a deep breath and broke the glass with the screwdriver Finn had provided. Then she rushed downstairs and out into the street, as the alarm sounded. Staff were pouring out behind her. The cool air nipped at her. She twisted her hair into a messy bun and put on her coat as a sort of disguise. Then she made her way back to Starbucks. There, she ordered chocolate brownies and coffee and waited for Finn to join her.

Twenty minutes or so later, he strolled in.

'So, what did you find?'

Finn felt in his pockets and brought out his phone. He scrolled through several photos.

'I took photos of everything I could find. These photos were of the rolodex and those were from other papers in his desk drawers. Finn frowned. 'This is the page the rolodex was open at. I presume he was talking about a job?'

'Yes, the racing one. What does it say?'

Harriet squinted and moved to get a closer look.

'GP 07764354222? What the hell does that mean? He was talking about some roles but wasn't specific about what they involved.'

'No idea. It looks like a mobile phone number. I suppose it might just be his doctor. I'll pass it on to Melvin and see what he makes of it. I'll check through the other stuff later.'

'OK. We'd better get going to Harrogate then.' Harriet felt obscurely disappointed. All that acting and thinking on her feet had been for nothing. She hoped they would have better luck with the Montague family's nanny in Harrogate.

Saint Mary's was a beautifully appointed nursing home situated in a smart area of Harrogate. It used to be an old convent that had been sympathetically restored, so that many of the old period features had been kept. The whole building was made of honey coloured stone with huge pillars either side of the imposing main doorway.

Finn scanned the building as they pulled up. 'Hmm, I dare say that the Montagues are footing the bill. I don't think a nanny's wage would run to all this.'

Harriet had been thinking the same thing. 'Still, it's good of them. The family must think a lot of her. Do you think she's compos mentis enough to answer a few questions?'

'I think so. Guy said she's a little deaf and crippled with arthritis which affects her mobility, but other than that she's fine.'

'Did you bring the photo?'

Finn patted his shirt pocket. 'Yep, I printed a copy off from the photo I took on my phone, so it's a little larger. Hopefully, she'll be able to shed some light on Guy and Tarquin's childhood friend or at least explain what Tarquin wanted to talk to her about.'

Harriet shrugged. 'I hope so. What else do we need to ask her?'

'What she knew about Tarquin's life I suppose, if he was in touch and if there was anything bothering him. After all, she was probably more like a mother to the boys than their actual birth mother.'

Harriet took this in, then she thought of something.

'What excuse are we giving for the meeting?'

Finn grinned. 'I had a word with Guy, and he phoned ahead to let the staff know we were visiting. Guy told them that we were writing a book about the family and just needed to ask her some questions about her memories of working for them.'

Harriet grinned back. 'Great.'

The smell of polish overlain with fresh flowers greeted them as they walked into the large reception area. There was a vast staircase with a discreet lift in one corner and reception area with a huge vase of pale lilies, hence the delicious smell. A woman in a smart navy uniform approached them with an inquiring expression.

'We're here to see Gladys Davies. I believe Lord Montague telephoned to say that we were coming.' Finn smiled. The woman, who had her hair twisted into a severe bun, instantly smiled when she'd had a proper look at Finn.

'Ah yes. I'm Sarah Cohen, the manager here. Guy Montague rang to explain. You're writing a book on the family, aren't you? Mrs Davies is looking forward to meeting you.'

'Is she well?' Harriet asked.

'Oh yes. She's a total darling, just struggles with mobility, and she has a heart condition, but mentally she's fine. She was very upset about Tarquin Montague's death. Guy Montague came to tell her, so please take that into account.'

'Of course.' The woman could not take her gaze away from Finn. Still, she supposed they didn't get many attractive men visiting a nursing home.

Gladys Davies was a spritely looking 80-year-old. Her thick grey hair was cut into a bob and her bright blue eyes surveyed her visitors with interest. She was clearly the young woman in the photo pictured with both Tarquin and Guy Montague, just older and faded. Her hands were swollen and red around the joints, presumably from the arthritis, but she beamed and said she was quite happy to speak to Finn and Harriet on her own. She waved her hand as an invitation for them to sit on some hardbacked chairs.

'Now I know you had to give them some guff about doing some research on the family, but Guy says you want to know about Tarquin and any recent contact I'd had with him?'

Finn smiled. 'Yes. I'm very sorry about Tarquin. I found him you know…'

Gladys regarded him for a minute, her face softening. She wiped away a tear. 'I know. I also know that you are a famous ex-jockey and you,' she turned her gaze to Harriet, 'are a plucky young gel. Guy seems to think you two are more likely to find out who killed dear Tarquin than the police, so I'm quite happy to tell you what I know.' She dabbed at her eyes with a lacey handkerchief. 'His Lordship has died and now Tarquin, it's terrible...' She managed to compose herself after a few moments.

Finn smiled and told her about Jimmy Clary's death and how they had spoken to Wolf, aka Tarquin. He had then got in touch and arranged to meet them.

'It was then that we found him dead. Perdita, his ex-girlfriend, said he was sort of elated before he died and that he had been to visit you.'

Gladys pursed her lips. 'Yes, that's right. Tarquin used to come most months. He was such a sweet boy; all that animal rights and environmental stuff, was not who he was. As a boy, he was quiet and sensitive, a kind, decent person. He came to see me last week. He was troubled about the murder of Perdita's partner and really tried to help her. He adored her, you know. Anyway, he had got something into his head about a boy he and Guy used to play with. Gary, someone or other. You see, it was something of a scandal.' She paused. 'I don't suppose it will do any harm to tell you now. All the parties are dead anyway, even Tarquin.'

Harriet smiled encouragingly, willing the old lady to continue.

'Lord Montague, Guy and Tarquin's father, was a bit of a ladies' man. He had many affairs and did little to hide them from Lady Montague. He even employed one of his women, Martha, as a cook, and she was allowed to bring her little boy to the house. Lord Montague encouraged him to mix with his own sons even. Lord Montague had a stud farm and allowed this boy to play down there with Guy and Tarquin, taught him about horses, betting and breeding. He really brought the boy up as his own son. Lady Montague turned a blind eye, but it must have been very humiliating. I think Lord Montague even made promises to the lad about paying for his education and setting him up in business. Anyway, that all stopped when Lord Montague went abroad to finalise some business agreements. He was gone for about two months. Lady Montague had Martha turned out of the house for stealing. She said that she found some of her priceless jewellery in Martha's room, made out she'd stolen them. So, without Lord Montague around to protect her, Martha and the boy were turned out without a penny. I suspect that her Ladyship had planted the jewellery and took full advantage of her husband's absence.'

'Why was Tarquin asking you about this boy?'

'I'm not sure. He just kept asking where the pair of them had gone, did I know anything about them, did they keep in touch, that sort of thing.' Gladys sighed. 'It was years ago, and I believe they went to live with a relative near the North Yorkshire coast, I seem to remember. Martha would have found work, she was actually a reasonable cook, but the boy was a slight, sickly thing, not at all like Tarquin and Guy.'

'How did Tarquin and Guy get on with him?'

133

'To begin with, before they could understand what was happening, they got on very well, especially him and Tarquin. He was older than Guy, nearer to Tarquin's age. The Montague boys must have realised what had actually happened when they got older, but before then, they got on well.'

Finn bit his lip. 'Do you think that the boy was Lord Montague's illegitimate son and that's why Tarquin wanted to know about him?'

Gladys thought for a moment. 'I suppose it's possible. He was nothing like the others in looks, he had dark hair and was slight, but it could be the case, I suppose. Martha came here with him when he was about four, but she could have known Lord Montague beforehand.'

'What was the boy's name? Gary, did you say?'

The old lady nodded. Finn pulled the copy of the photo out of his pocket and showed it to Gladys.

'We found this photo at Tarquin's place.' He pointed at the homely looking woman. 'I presume this is you with Tarquin and Guy. As you can see, there is another child in the picture, but the photo was folded over. Could the third child be Gary?'

The old lady peered at the photo of the two Montague boys and the arm of the third child.

'Hard to say, but it could have been. He was often there, but I can't remember that photo being taken. Perhaps, they took him out of the picture because they realised who he was. It must have been very difficult for them too, especially Tarquin, who must have put two and two together.'

'Can you remember his surname?'

The old lady frowned. 'Gary, and his mother was called Martha. I can't just think of their last name. Damn, it's gone.'

Finn stood up to leave. 'Well, thank you so much for your time. If you remember the boy's surname could you ring me?'

Gladys took the card Finn had offered her. 'Does that help you?'

Finn shook his head. 'I'm not sure but thank you for your time, anyway.'

Gladys smiled. 'I do hope you can help put whoever shot Tarquin behind bars, for all our sakes. He deserves justice, he really does.'

Harriet stood up. 'Thank you. It was lovely to meet you.'

They walked down the vast staircase and out into the bright sunshine.

Finn looked at Harriet. 'I can't think any of that has anything to do with why Tarquin was murdered, or Clary for that matter. What a waste of time. Mind you, it's a great story and Gary would have good reason to hate Tarquin and Guy. But I don't think it helps us, do you? Anyway, fancy a pub lunch to cheer us up?'

Harriet nodded. 'Great. She was lovely, but it sounds like Tarquin was just having an attack of conscience to me, about a childhood friend who could also have been a half-brother, nothing else. Listen, I noticed that there was a nice pub on the way down, The White Hart. Shall we go there?'

Harriet was starving and in need of some reviving. She felt utterly deflated. They had come all that way for nothing. She'd had such high hopes that had now been completely dashed. Her gloomy thoughts were interrupted as Finn's phone began to ring.

'Hello. Yes?' There was a pause as Finn's expression changed. 'Right. I'll meet you tomorrow for lunch.'

Harriet looked at him inquiringly.

'It was Kimberley. We are meeting up tomorrow.'

'Good.' Harriet was pleased for them. Finn had been very subdued for days after their argument.

'She has remembered something that the other actors said, the others who were involved in the betting job.'

Harriet gave him a meaningful look. 'Good. Listen, you need to talk to her and sort all this out.'

Finn's expression was unreadable. 'I know, I know.'

Taverner and Wildblood were about to give another briefing when Sykes called him into his office. Sykes was furious that the cartridges found at both murder scenes yielded no fingerprint matches, and that Hunt's gun had been found in situ at home, locked in a cupboard. Hunt was clear that Horton had handed the gun back before both murders, so unless Horton had a key to the cupboard, or Hunt was lying, he wasn't the murderer. So, they had no evidence.

'Well, what other lines of inquiry are you pursuing?' Sykes demanded.

Taverner was irritated that his boss took no responsibility for being blinkered and fixated on Horton as the murderer. This had quite possibly skewed the whole investigation. It was always a mistake to zone in on one suspect unless you had a lot of evidence, in his experience. Still, it was no use arguing. He took a deep breath.

'We are looking into Clary's business dealings and also at the links between Clary and Montague, assuming there is one murderer. We have his accounts and his computer is with the Tech team, door to door inquiries are ongoing and SOCO are presently at the murder scene. On the face of it, I wonder how Clary survived financially. His business was in a terrible state, so he must have had another source of income. And we're looking at a business associate of Clary's, Drew Morrison. He runs an organic cookery business and bought his produce off Clary. He also texted him, arranging to meet before Clary died. It is possible that he found out about the dodgy organic stuff, or maybe he was involved in the cannabis business and things turned nasty. We are looking at his computer and bank accounts in more detail.'

'Hmm. Well, it goes without saying that we must not leave any stone unturned with either one or two murderers on the loose. I have drafted in two experienced DC's from other areas of York, but we need results and fast! And don't rule out Horton.' He glowered, then waved his hand in the air. 'Now get on with it.'

Sykes had to get that last bit in about Horton, Taverner realised. He couldn't bear to be proved wrong. At least, he wasn't being replaced as DI. He could do with the extra manpower to talk to the Green Warrior community and find out more about Wolf and his activities. Some of these Green groups had very extreme ideas about national protests and he wanted to know what else the organisation had planned. But it was very hard to find a motive that linked both crimes. The men seemed to be total opposites. Wolf appeared to be a committed eco warrior, whereas Clary was clearly a total fraud with absolutely no green credentials. Maybe there wasn't a common thread and there were two murderers? Montague could have killed Clary and one of Clary's associates, his partner or ex-wife could have killed Montague? Trouble was, he couldn't see Montague killing anyone. He actually seemed a decent enough guy. He hoped to God that they would start to make some progress, but at the moment they were clutching at straws.

The two new officers, DC Buxton and DC Major were already in place when he addressed his team. DS Wildblood had been busy adding photos to the links board and was waiting patiently for Taverner to pull it all together. No pressure then. He looked at the expectant sea of faces and begun.

'So, welcome to our two new officers who are on attachment. I hope you're settling in OK?'

The two officers grinned and nodded.

'Great. So, SOCO/ Forensics have gathered lots of samples from our second murder scene. The cartridges found at the scene of both murders were the same but clean in that they had no fingerprints on them, so the murderer used gloves and was careful. The shotgun found at Horton's had his fingerprints and Hunt's as expected. As you know, shotguns do not give us much information, so Horton is still a suspect in Clary's death. We are also looking at Clary's business associates, namely Drew Morrison. He is a suspect as he arranged to meet Clary and has a motive and the opportunity to murder him. He may have discovered the fake organic vegetable scam, which wouldn't have gone down well.'

'Like I said, hot potato, 'muttered Haworth.

There was a ripple of laughter but that quickly dissipated as they turned their attention back to the boss.

'Obviously, we are investigating Montague's murder and looking at possible links. He was shot through the mouth, but Montague's death was made to look like a suicide and the killer even left a note. However, the pathologist ruled this out because the trajectory of the shot was all wrong, as was the position of the fingerprints. We have a time of death at between 10 and 4pm. He was found by Finn McCarthy and Harriet Lucas at 4.30 pm.' He looked at the two new officers. 'They are an ex jockey and student who had success in investigating a betting scam and appear to be interested in Clary's murder. I suppose it's because McCarthy mentors Gavin Clary, Jimmy's brother. He's a conditional jockey. What is interesting is that Tarquin asked to see them, so it maybe that he had information to give them.'

DC Buxton put up his hand. 'Are they suspects? Do you think a betting fraud is going on here?'

'No, but we can't rule it out. We have interviewed them both but neither have motives, so they are not suspects, at present. Harriet's father and brother are both policemen. Will is still serving and DI Lucas retired last year.'

There was a murmur of understanding as they realised who Harriet was related to.

DC Ballantyne rolled his eyes. 'That's all we need bloody amateurs!'

Taverner ignored him but he didn't disagree with the sentiment. He just hoped that the pair didn't get in the way. Still, they needed to focus and do their job.

'We have Tarquin's mobile and laptop so that might be useful. DC's Buxton and Major can work on Wolf's murder. You could interview the people Tarquin was close to, like the Green Warriors, see what protests were planned, if anyone had any beef with him. Some of the movement are into animal rights, so may have had links with more extreme groups. Also look for links to Clary. It may be possible that Drew Morrison was involved in Clary's murder and could have been involved in Wolf's too, so look for connections between Morrison and Wolf. It could be worth talking to Clary's brother, Gavin. He is a jockey at Vince Hunt's place. I wonder how he and our other suspect, Horton, get on? Now that might be very interesting.'

DC Ballantyne put up his hand. 'Do you think that Wolf murdered Clary because of the way he was treating Perdita and one of Clary's lady friends realised and killed Wolf?'

Taverner shook his head. 'It's possible but women rarely use guns as a murder method. We could have two murderers or one.' Taverner paused as the group took this in. 'If McCarthy and Lucas are telling the truth, and we've no reason to disbelieve them, they were seeing Wolf about some vegetable orders. Lucas is running some sort of cooking demonstrations apparently. Wolf may have confided his concerns to someone else, his brother, Perdita, friends, so we need to be really thorough. So, you all know what you need to do, we'll reconvene the minute we have any update from forensics. OK?'

DC Patel burst into the room. 'Sir, you need to see this.'

Taverner read the piece of paper he was handed.

'We need to get down to the hospital. Gavin Clary is in intensive care, suspected suicide. But we can't rule out murder at this stage.'

Or perhaps he is the murderer, thought Taverner, shivering. He had thought that Walton was a sleepy backwater where nothing much happened. How wrong he was.

Chapter 29

Finn heard about Gavin's suicide attempt and went straight round to Hunt's place. The mood of the yard was rather low, despite the fact that Guy Montague had a runner, Fort William, in the Group 2 race at York in a few days, and preparation was well underway for that. Seemingly, Harriet's pitch to Guy to leave his horses with Hunt had worked, at least until after the big race. The press had been full of Fort William's chances and Guy Montague was really hoping for a good win. Vince Hunt shoved his hands in his pockets and sighed.

'Well, I don't mind telling you, this thing with Gavin has completely thrown me. I know he was low after Jimmy's death but to try and hang himself, well! I feel very bad for the lad, it couldn't have come at a
worse time with the stuff about Neil, Wolf and the big race for Montague coming up.'

'Hanging?' Finn shivered and felt a spasm of guilt. He was Gavin's mentor and he should have been able to help him. Gavin was probably kicking his heels over the summer, with fewer National Hunt meetings and less race riding. All the more time to brood about Jimmy.

'Yep. One of the lads found him in the barn. It's cordoned off whilst the police take a look.' For the first time, Finn noticed the police tape and forensics van. Finn's brain was whirring through the possibilities. Was it suicide or had someone tried to murder him too? He knew that the police would be at the hospital, waiting to interview Gavin, so at least he would be safe for now.

'Which lad found him? Is he close to anyone in particular here?'

'He was found by Matt Simpson, a stable lad. He talks to Becky a lot. She's one of the stable staff and took him under her wing after his brother died.' He regarded Finn steadily. 'God, what the hell is going on? Two murders and an attempted suicide in Walton of all places? And the murderer is still on the loose. Do you have any clues?'

'Well, the police are no doubt doing a thorough investigation.'

Vince looked far from impressed.

He was saved from further questioning by a smart Range Rover arriving in the yard.

'Best get going. Guy's come to see Fort William work out. You'll find Matt in the stables.'

'OK.'

Finn located Matt Simpson mucking out. He knew the man by sight and had seen him several times at the yard. He was a short man in his thirties with a crew cut, pointed features and pale, watery eyes.

'Bad business about Gavin. It must have been awful finding him like that. Had he been particularly down?'

Matt shook his head. 'It shocked me, I can tell you. I just came around the corner and there he was, strung up. Shook me to the core, it did.' Matt wiped his eyes. 'As to his mood, he seemed better when he came back from Ireland. He's been spending some time at the Catholic Church seeing the priest and seemed alright, but then he had a call and it seemed to set him back like.'

Finn took this in. 'Really? Who was it from?'

Matt sighed. 'I don't rightly know.' He scratched his head uncertainly.

Finn felt he knew more than he was letting on.

'Look, if you do know something then it needs to be passed on.' Finn fished in his pocket and pulled out a twenty pound note. 'I work for the BHA and if this involves racing then they will certainly want to know.'

Matt took the note eagerly.

'Well, it's just gossip, that's all. You see Jimmy was thought to be involved in passing info about the horses to someone. Funny thing was he was never seen up at the gallops, so I thought it was just a rumour, but now I wonder if Gavin was involved too?'

Finn felt his skin prickle with anticipation. OK, so it was just talk. Yards were full of it, thrived on it in fact, but just sometimes there might be a grain of truth in it and the lads who had been there longer, seen the comings and goings over the years were far better placed to know what was really going on. Because it was gossip, then it was the sort of information that wasn't likely to be passed on to the police. Finn's brain sifted through the possibilities.

'So, did he meet this person perhaps, and maybe was under pressure to continue where Jimmy left off?'

Matt shrugged. 'Could be. Becky might know more or the priest. Look, it's just talk, that's all. Jimmy liked a bet, maybe he was just trying to get an edge to help himself.'

'Do you know how he did it? It would be quite hard to identify all the horses from different places.'

Matt scratched his head. 'No. Gavin's quiet. He knows about our horses, we all do, but not about the horses from other yards.'

Finn nodded, noting Matt's backsliding. It made him more convinced that Jimmy had been passing information onto a third party. God, he had been so blind! It was obvious, Clary had even been found near the entrance to the gallops. He must have hidden somewhere on the gallops, watched the horses and passed the information on. Finn wracked his brain as to the layout of the place, but there wasn't anywhere he could have hidden without someone seeing him.

'OK. Do you know where Gavin's phone is?'

Matt shrugged. 'Could be in his locker. Guv doesn't like us using our phones when we're on the yard. He's had a crackdown recently, so he'd have put it in there.' He led Finn into the tack room where there was a row of grey lockers. Matt pointed at one to the left. 'That's Gavin's.'

'Do you happen to have a key?'

Matt fumbled in his pocket. 'I have the master key as the lads are always losing theirs. Guvnor gave it to me rather than keep pestering him.' He unlocked the door with one swift movement. Finn put on some woollen gloves and peeped inside. There was a plastic carrier bag inside. Finn gently opened it. It contained spare breeches, gloves and a waistcoat but no phone. He delved in deeper and pulled out what looked like a receipt. It was a scrap of paper, torn from a larger sheet. There were two phone numbers scribbled on it. Finn quickly took a photo of it with his phone and put everything back.

Matt was at his shoulder. 'Any good?'

Finn shook his head. 'There's no phone but no worries. Was there any news on how Gavin was doing?'

Matt shrugged. 'I think we pulled him down just in time, bloody hope so, anyway.'

Finn thanked him and rounded off with a chat about Fort William's chances in the big race.

'Should win, he's the favourite,' commented Matt. 'God knows, we need some bloody luck after everything that's happened.'

Finn agreed and wished him well, deciding he would check the photos later. Maybe several lads were involved and paid off to give information to someone about the horses in their yard?

He drove to York, his head full of questions. He was dreading lunch with Kimberley for personal reasons, but he was also fearful of what she might reveal. Kimberley was dressed in her smart but casual work wear and was already waiting for him in the coffee shop, sipping a cappuccino. Finn was unsure whether or not to kiss her but decided against it under the circumstances.

'So, how are you?'

Kimberley smiled tightly. He noticed that she was desperately pale.

'OK.'

After they had ordered food, Finn knew it was time to grasp the nettle.

'So, what information did you have?'

Kim swallowed nervously. 'When I spoke to the others who had done the betting job, they said that no one wants to do it now because the man involved is really violent and aggressive. He'd employed a lot of them to go around putting on small bets, going from betting shop to shop too. They put on loads of money in dribs and drabs. And no one's been paid for the last few jobs.'

'How many people?'

'At least ten.'

'Any ideas who this person might be? Is it Handley?'

Kimberley rolled her eyes. 'God, no. It's someone close to Damien, though. Damien talks to him and he tells Damien what he wants us to do.'

Finn bit into a piece of pie. 'OK. Has anyone seen this mystery person? Are there any clues as to his or her identity?'

Kimberley shook her head. 'Archie thought he'd seen him. But the man was really annoyed about a betting scam that went wrong a few weeks ago. He rang Archie, the actor who put the money on and shouted at him. Archie said he did what he was asked, and the man checked which horse he had put the money on. When Archie explained that he had put the money on the right horse, as asked, he went quiet and rang off. Archie reckoned that someone was for it though. We have all been talking and have decided not to do any of this sort of work again.'

Finn thought it was a little too late for that.

'When was this incident, when Archie put the bet on?'

Kimberley pouted. 'Oh, about three weeks or so ago, I'd say. Archie thought that someone must have inside information about the horses, then changed his mind when the horse he backed ran down the field. I mean who puts money on a horse that loses?'

Finn's brain was whirring with activity. Yet another horse that had been heavily backed had run down the field, so whoever was involved was not very successful at predicting winners. Then he remembered what Melvin Vine had said about a heavy bet manipulating the odds on the rest of the horses. With sudden clarity, he realised that he had been looking at the wrong thing all along. He shouldn't have looked at the horses that the actors had been paid to back, instead he should have studied the horses who had won in those races. If he did, a pattern might very well emerge. He was more and more convinced that Clary's death was related to betting after all. Was this person pressuring Gavin to carry on where Jimmy had left off and had that prompted Gavin's suicide attempt?

Finn sat in his car and pulled out the piece of paper Melvin had given him. He considered the list of races that Melvin Vine had highlighted and hastily went through the list to find out which horse had eventually won. It was easy enough to find the results. He then crosschecked who the trainer was and then the final odds. The racecourses were mainly in the North with some notable exceptions such as Chelmsford and Windsor. He wrote the names of the horses down and then the trainers, experiencing a prickle of alarm when he realised that of the seven races, every horse that had won was from Walton. Five of them had odds of over 10-1, some as much as 20-1. One name stood out, though. Rock of Gibraltar had won at York some three weeks ago at odds of 33-1. Then it came to him. He felt a rush of realisation and adrenalin. Of course! That was a couple of days prior to Clary's death. Pieces of information began to settle down into one inescapable conclusion. He thought of Gavin's reaction to Sam Foster's remarks that day on the gallops. Sam had explained that Rocky had won at York and had been much better when he was tried in the hood. Clary must have noticed the improvement on the gallops and asked who the horse was, but the horse had been identified wrongly as St George, because he was the horse that usually wore the hood. So, when Rocky won at such long odds, the murderer had missed out as they had backed St George instead. Judging by the look on Gavin's face, he knew that too! It proved categorically that Clary was murdered because of his role in passing information about the horses onto a third party. But who?

He turned on his car engine and roared off to see DI Taverner. He just hoped that someone had a police officer outside Gavin's hospital door, as the murderer might come back to finish the job. Then he would systematically go through the information he had gathered and try and make some sense of it. He felt that the answers were within reach. He really needed to speak to Gavin as he was sure he knew something that could assist them further. He had to know who Jimmy was working for. Then his phone rang. It was Jenny. Her voice was barely recognisable, high pitched from anxiety.

'God, Finn. The police have asked Drew to go into the station again about that murder...'

'Right. I think it's probably just routine. Clary supplied Drew's organic produce, so they know each other.' There was a pause as Jenny composed her thoughts.

'The thing is that I've been going through the books and there are some anomalies.'

Finn's brain was in overdrive.

'Anomalies. What do you mean? What does Drew say? Have you asked him? I mean it's probably just a mistake.'

'No. I wondered if you would actually. And he has been behaving strangely too. Oh God, Finn, supposing he is caught up in this murder?'

'Listen, take a deep breath and try not to worry.'

He heard Jenny exhale in an attempt to calm herself down. He hadn't been able to give her any other reassurances, because he had begun to wonder just how well he knew his brother-in-law after all.

Chapter 30

Harriet was shocked to hear about Gavin but encouraged when Daisy telephoned to say that he was doing well and sitting up and talking. His family from Ireland had been contacted and his sister was on her way over.

'God, Jimmy and now Gavin. It's been miserable here since Jimmy was shot. Everything has gone wrong. Dad has Guy's horse running in the Group race at York this week, so he could do without the distractions. Fingers crossed Fort William will win. Dad's got Davy Hughes riding. He's even had Jake Delamare contact him about his protein balls. He's going to try them to see if he can lose those excess pounds.'

Harriet was pleased as Davy was a local flat jockey and was down to attend her cooking demonstrations. He was on the tall side for a flat jockey, hence the need for the Life balls. He'd had a brilliant season on the flat and was really doing well.

'Great. I did mention him to Jake, and Davy was really happy to give them a go. How are things?'

Harriet could almost see the frown down the phone line. 'Oh, you know. Neil feels he's still under suspicion and the fact that he can't prove his innocence about things doesn't help. He still has a cloud hanging over him.'

Harriet heard the stress in her voice. 'I know. The police are doing their best, I'm sure.'

Daisy tutted. 'Meanwhile the real murderer is still at large.' She tried to rally. 'But even if Neil and I are hardly talking to each other, it doesn't mean I don't want to hear about you and Jake. What's happening there?'

Harriet felt a flurry of nerves. She was like a child on Christmas Eve and could barely keep the excitement out of her voice.

'Well, I'm meeting him later to go through the recipes for our new book. I've spent ages devising healthy and nutritious meals, which are accessible to everyone. You know, no weird ingredients that you can't get hold of, just wholesome and low calorie, so I can't wait.' Harriet suddenly felt worried about her outfit, what makeup to apply and how to behave.

'God, I have no idea what to wear. I'm thinking something smart, yet not like I've made an effort, you know the sort of thing.'

'Hmm, in fact, I have something that would suit you. Do you remember that dress I wore when we went out for that girls' night out?'

Harriet thought back. Daisy had worn a fabulous black dress decorated with huge, vibrant flowers. Hattie had admired it. That would be just the job for such an occasion.

'That would be perfect. Can I borrow it?'

'Course. You will look great in it. I'll leave it in the kitchen so help yourself if I'm out. I've got to teach at a Pony Club rally, but Neil will be around to sort you out.' There was a pause as Daisy's spirits dropped again. 'Listen, do you have any ideas about who murdered Clary and Wolf, has Will said anything, only I'm starting to get really worried.'

Harriet heard the strain in her voice that she was trying so hard to hide and felt that she ought to offer some reassurance.

'No, but they are all hard at it. I'm sure they'll be arresting someone else soon.'

'God, I hope so. Walton had been hell recently. These murders have made everyone suspicious of each other. I do hope they catch the swine.'

Harriet laughed as she recognised the effort it took Daisy NOT to ask more. Her spirits lifted as she anticipated the evening ahead.

Harriet showered, pleased that she had decided on what to wear. She conditioned and tried to style her red curls and thought about the case. She hoped Gavin was recovering and suspected that Finn's visit to him might shed some light on his state of mind.

She had a coffee with her mother and chatted about the forthcoming school play. Her mother had taught at the school for several years, but she had never seen her quite so anxious. It was the first performance and her mother had to be back in school to supervise her young charges. The dress rehearsal had been a disaster, so her mother really hoped the children would be able to put in a good first performance.

'Honestly, when I said it was bad, it was actually a lot worse.' She began to go through the errors, but Harriet was distracted by her phone beeping. It was a message from Drew.

Hi, it's Drew Morrison here. Finn asked me to look at the Life balls. Have had a look. Are you free to meet up today at 3?

Harriet looked at the address Drew had texted. It wasn't too far away. She had been planning a more leisurely day where she could spend a couple of hours preparing herself for the meeting with Jake at 7pm. Still, she was intrigued about what Drew had to say and it would be helpful to have the information before her meeting with Jake. He had been dreadfully vague about the recipe for his Life balls and she needed to be certain that they were the real deal before she committed to working with him, let alone writing a book together. If she was honest, she was doubtful about his claims that they helped people lose weight and didn't want to put her name to anything that didn't live up to the hype, so it would be a really good idea to have something to put to Jake. She tried to think like a businesswoman. What were they all going on about in Dragon's Den? Patents or something that would make the Life balls difficult to copy. She really ought to check them out beforehand. She raked her fingers through her hair as she tried to factor a visit to York into her schedule. Her day was fast slipping away from her.

Her mother realised she had tuned out. 'Everything OK?'

'Yes, of course.' Harriet texted Drew back and went to put on her coat.

'Where are you off to?'

'Well, I've got to see a man about a recipe, then pop to Daisy's and then I'm meeting Jake Delamare later.'

Her mother raised her eyebrows at this. 'OK darling. I hope you have a good time.'

Harriet grinned and suddenly felt guilty about dashing off and being distracted when her mother was so worried.

'Listen, don't worry about the play, mum. It will be alright on the night, as they say. See you later.'

Chapter 31

Taverner listened intently to DC Haworth.

'So, no-one remembers Drew Morrison being at The Blacksmith's Arms when he said he was there meeting Clary. Now that's interesting. Suppose he wasn't there at all?'

Wildblood nodded. 'He does not specify a time or date in his text, so he could have met him in the morning, maybe things got heated and he came back and shot him?'

DC Ballantyne thrust some papers in Taverner's eye line.

'Guv, look. Morrison has a bit of form as a youngster and get this, his old man used to have a shotgun, so what's the betting our man knows his way round a firearm.'

DC Patel nodded. 'And I have just come off the phone to the bank. Morrison is in debt, but there are some strange payments. From his profile, it looks as though he's been augmenting his income somehow.' He wafted copies of Morrison's bank statements which had some transactions highlighted. 'There are several cash payments into the account and then a recent large withdrawal which leaves him in considerable debt.'

Taverner stared at the cash payments. There was six over the last three months and then a withdrawal of twenty thousand pounds a few days before Clary's death.

'Hmm. Where was he getting that sort of money, what the hell has he done with it and what is the link to Clary?'

'Could be from drug deals and then maybe he owed money, maybe to Clary.'

Taverner was checking the dates of the transactions and typing them into his phone. Several pairs of eyes watched as he pursed his lips and thought. An idea was beginning to form in his mind, a theory about why Morrison could have a motive for murdering Clary.

'Right, when he comes in, I want the wife to be spoken to at the same time.'

DC Haworth joined them. 'Listen, I've just had a call from a witness who will testify that on the day of Montague's death, she saw Horton near Montague Hall, driving from there at some pace, so we can't rule him out either.'

Taverner grinned. He had been hoping and praying for some sort of breakthrough and now he had two. Bloody typical!

'You and Ballantyne can bring Horton in again and question him about his alibi. Anything else?'

'We're chasing up the cufflink that was found at Montague's and have narrowed down some jewellers who may have made it. Seems like it was a one-off piece, so it shouldn't be too hard to find out who commissioned it. We're also scrutinising Montague's laptop. He had some strange searches, look.'

Taverner scanned the list of recent internet searches that Montague had made before his death.

'The 'Cooking Up A Storm' website, 'A New You', plastic surgery website, a search for Gary Pedley and Jake Delamare many times by the look of things. Is there anything that could link to Clary?'

'Not really but we'll keep looking.'

'Check his bank accounts and see if there's any unusual activity that might point to a connection between him and Morrison.'

It was always like this, he realised. He had been searching for vital clues for days on end without result and now within the space of an hour he had several. The problem was that instead of narrowing down his suspects it had blown the whole case wide open.

Gavin Clary looked pale and still, apart from the livid red marks around his neck. His arm was attached to a drip. He opened his eyes which were fringed with long lashes, which fluttered as Finn approached. He noticed the police officer outside, he'd had to give his name to him and show his ID, so at least they were protecting him which was something.

'Are you up for a little chat?'

Gavin had been sedated and tried to say something but sagged down into the pillows.

'Don't keep him long and certainly don't upset him,' added the ward sister with a frown.

Finn nodded and sat down besides the bed. He noticed a large range of 'Get Well Soon' cards and several bouquets lined up on a table next to the bed.

'How are you, mate?'

Gavin tried to nod and gave a half smile.

'Listen, I don't know if you can help me but the BHA have asked me to keep my ear to the ground about your brother's death. What I suspect is that your brother was murdered because he was passing on information to the murderer about which horses to back. I think he gained the information from observing horses on the gallops and identified the horses from his contacts in the yards.' Finn pursed his lips. 'He needed to identify the horses and I think he used his contacts, even you, to help him.'

Gavin's eye lids fluttered and there was an almost imperceptible nod.

He opened his mouth to speak but it was clearly an effort. His voice was barely audible.

'I didn't know what he was up to, I swear. He asked me in passing, just chatting, that's all...'

Finn could believe it. Clary seemed to have been socially skilled enough to do that, just ask something very casually, in normal conversation. At least, Gavin wasn't in on it. Finn was willing to bet that the first time he heard about it was on the gallops that time with Sam Foster. No one could have feigned such shock as Gavin had displayed. Guilt at his hand in his brother's death had clearly caused him to try to end his life.

'So, what I need to know is who was involved and what are the links to Tarquin Montague? Who is behind the scam, Gavin? Help me out here. We need to stop whoever it is, so he won't kill again!'

Gavin shook his head, his voice barely audible.

'I don't know.'

'Can you tell me anything about him? Are there any clues to his identity? Did Jimmy say anything that might indicate who he is?'

Gavin shook his head.

'Anything at all,' Finn persisted. 'Did Jimmy give you any information, did he seem scared? Did he let slip his name, any clue about this person's age, accent?'

Gavin sighed. 'No. Nothing.'

'Are you at risk?'

Gavin shook his head. That was something at least. Finn's mind was in overdrive. He remembered going through the races that Melvin had highlighted. Finn was certain that the misidentification of Rocky or Rock of Gibraltar, which had lost the murderer a huge amount of money, had cost Clary his life. Presumably, the murderer had bet a lot of money on St George, lost his shirt and was gutted to have lost out on a 33-1 winner. So, who was behind the scam? It had to be the same person that had paid the actors to back the horses. He thought about their trip to the Damien Lloyd agency which had given them precious little information. They must be missing something, but what?

Deep in thought, he made his way to Jenny's in York. She grinned as soon as she saw her brother and popped another chop under the grill. Finn noticed that she was very pale and sensed that she was holding in her emotions and putting on a brave face. He was greeted by his nieces, Ava and Lola, who flung themselves at him before being asked to play in the garden whilst 'the grown ups' talked about boring stuff.

'So, did you manage to ask Drew about the anomalies in the accounts?'

Jenny frowned, stress evident by the dark smudges under her eyes. She looked like she had hardly had any sleep.

'Well, I asked him, and he gave me an explanation about suppliers, but I'm not at all sure I believe him. I mean there's no proper receipts from them, so it can't be true, can it? But Drew says that the receipts might not come through because the man died, you know, the man that was murdered in Walton, he used to supply Drew's organic vegetables and eggs.'

'Hmm, well I suppose that does make sense. Have you got the bank statements handy?'

Jenny fetched them out of a drawer. She had highlighted the transactions she was concerned about.

'Look, there's five thousand paid in there, nearly eight thousand here and ten thousand, with no reference where the money came from. And look here, there's twenty thousand drawn out here and it is never paid back. I can't believe Drew spent twenty thousand on bloody vegetables!'

Finn checked the date of the transaction and wondered. He suddenly felt very sick. He could think of another explanation for the pattern. Betting. The date was not lost on him either. It was two days before Rocky's race. He tried to quell his rising panic and hoped he was wrong. Maybe it was just a co-incidence, but deep down he was really worried.

'When is Drew back?'

149

'Not until late. He's catering for a party, so I'm not expecting him back until midnight.' Jenny suddenly looked anguished. 'God, what on earth has he got himself involved in?'

Finn shook his head hardly daring to say anything. He really needed to speak to Drew to find out what was going on. He could sense that Jenny was on the verge of hysteria, so he tried to keep his voice low and calm.

'Where is the party?'

'Out at Thornaby, I think.'

'How did he seem?'

Jenny swallowed hard. 'OK, a bit stressed but then he had lots to do. Why?'

'Did he say anything, something usual, out of the ordinary?'

'Now you're scaring me, Finn. Like what?' She sighed. 'Now you mention it, he was going on about someone he knew from college.'

'What?'

Now was not the time to be chasing old acquaintances, Finn thought crossly. What the hell was going on?

'Yeah, it was someone who he recognised, someone from college who had done quite well for himself. I suppose he feels that he's falling behind and that's why he keeps pushing himself to provide for us all. You know how keen he is to open his own restaurant. Honestly, I just want to know what's going on...'

Finn gave her a hug. 'Look, I'll talk to him, man to man. Don't worry. It will all sort itself out.'

Jenny, his usually confident sister, felt fragile and slight in his arms as he hugged her. He felt a desperate need to protect her. He only hoped his assurances were not just empty words.

Chapter 32

Finn drove off, determined to find out what his brother-in-law was involved in. He rang Drew a couple of times but wasn't able to get through to him, so left messages. He tried to quell his feelings of unease. Still, if Drew was working flat out then he wouldn't have his phone on, would he? He thought back to the bank statements his sister had shown him. An excellent and hardworking chef, Drew was untidy and disorganised with paperwork, so maybe the anomalies were symptomatic of that and nothing more. He certainly hoped so. He thought back to his initial conversation with Drew, when he realised that he'd met Jimmy Clary the night before he was murdered. Had he missed something? Drew had seemed calm and reasonable, there was no sign of him being shifty or awkward, but it was clear that he knew Clary well, very well. Had Jimmy passed betting tips on to him? Was his own brother-in-law the Mr Big behind the betting operation? Had he murdered Clary? Jesus Christ, he needed a drink.

He fixed himself a whisky, his favourite brand Jura, when he got in and tried to straighten out his thoughts. He glanced at the clock. It was 11.30 and there was still no response from Drew. He checked through his emails and found a couple from Tony Murphy inquiring how the investigation was going, which he decided to leave unanswered for now. 'Don't ask,' was the easiest answer, at this present moment. Then he came across one from a Madeleine Simpson, a nurse at St Mary's nursing home.

I work with Gladys Davies and am just passing on a message from her. She was most anxious to contact you about a name she has remembered. It is Gary PEDLEY. I hope this means something to you as although elderly, Gladys, is of sound mind, so this must be important.

So, that was the surname of the young boy who played with Tarquin and Guy Montague when they were kids. Gary could even be Lord Montague's illegitimate son, though quite what that had to do with anything, he had no idea. He desperately wanted to pass this on to Hattie as he felt it was bound to be significant somehow. He sent her a quick text, took another sip of whisky and savored the delicate taste, as he typed Gary Pedley into Google. It certainly took his mind off his brother-in-law, Drew, as he could see no possible link between this man and the murders in Walton. He worked well into the night. Something nagged away at his brain. The odds on there being two murderers in Walton must be very long indeed, so assuming there was one murderer then how were the murders of Clary and Tarquin connected? If he could work that out, then he would be halfway to working out who the murderer was. He also felt that it was high time he called the police to pass on what Kimberley had told him about the actors. Whoever instructed them and employed Clary, had to be their murderer.

Unbeknown to him, Taverner was similarly engaged, sipping Macallan whisky and leafing through evidence on his iPad. He preferred actual paper reports but due to security issues around

151

working from home, had been offered an iPad which stored all the reports and kept them safe. He worked well into the night without result. They were missing something, he was sure of it.

Chapter 33

Unable to sleep and frustrated about the progress of the case, Taverner found himself driving to the scene of the crime where it had all started, from his cottage in Langdale. It was 6.30 am and the sky was gloriously blue and the sun bathed the scene with its rays. He had no real idea what he hoped to find, but the drive out amongst the verdant scenery at least lifted his spirits. He pulled in at the layby Clary had been found in and noticed that the undergrowth pretty much obscured any view of the horses at work from that position. What was Clary doing there? Apart from the gate, which was situated some thirty or so metres further down the road that led to the gallops, there didn't appear to be any worn pathways that led from the layby to the gallops. His staff had checked out the area at the time and they had found nothing either. He locked up his car and enjoyed the feeling of the early morning sunshine, as he walked up to the gallops. At this time of the morning, the place was teaming with activity. He walked on taking in the groups of horses, the bays, chestnuts and greys, watching as they galloped up the hill and beyond, ridden by lads and lasses. There were various vehicles, all 4x4's, at the top of a wide lane and a range of hurdles with several horses jumping them, looping back to complete another circuit. He heard the thundering sound of hooves, the chatter from the lads, which gave him an insight into a fascinating, vibrant world. There were still more horses arriving and some leaving, as the yards waited their turn to work their charges. He noticed Vince Hunt and nodded briefly at him.

'Just having an early morning walk,' he called, letting the trainer know that he wasn't coming to interview him. Hunt visibly relaxed and lifted his hand in greeting. Ignoring the curious glances of the staff, Taverner took out his phone and took a range of photos of the area. He photographed the gallops at various places. Then, he walked back down to the road feeling a little foolish. He had no idea what he had wanted to achieve, but at least he felt physically refreshed. He quickly scanned through the photos, saw nothing of interest and drove to the office.

DI Taverner called the briefing to order. He'd wanted to delay the briefing until later in the day but was feeling the pressure. DCI Sykes was wanting them to focus on Morrison as the prime suspect, but Gabriel wasn't ready to close in on him just yet. He needed more time, but his boss had been on the warpath again this morning and had left saying, '48 hours Taverner and then I get someone else in to help, someone with more experience. Got it?'

As a motivator it was right up there with, 'Solve this today or else it's curtains for your career.' At least that's how he interpreted it. He glanced around his team and began.

'So, I don't need to tell you that time is marching on and we really need a result. It is time to pull out all the stops and work together. Right, any news on the cufflink?'

Ballantyne stood up. 'We showed it to Guy Montague, guv, and he reckoned it was a very poor copy of their family crest. Look, he showed me his own pair of cufflinks given to him by his father.'

153

Taverner peered at the proffered phone screen. 'Yeah, see what he means, the copy is poorly defined. The real crest is a deer wearing a crown and is clearly visible on Guy's cufflinks, on this one the crown looks like a blob. Mmm, is it another titled family's cufflink or something? Maybe a relative's family crest?'

Wildblood took over. 'No guv, we checked with a heraldry website. It is poor quality, but it is silver.'

'Can we find out where it was made from the hallmarks, maybe? Or ring round some jewellers, someone must have commissioned it.'

'Yep guv, onto it...'

Yet why would someone go to all the trouble of replicating a cufflink to look like the Montague crest? If it had come from the murderer, which seemed highly likely, then it was a question that might prove crucial.

Taverner looked around the room. 'Any more updates anyone?'

Cullen raised her hand. 'Got the data off Tarquin Montague's laptop. It's a bit weird but he was looking up plastic surgery websites mostly. Oh, and he seemed interested in Jake Delamare and his time on 'Cooking up a Storm".

There was a titter which ran around the room.

'Maybe he was thinking of having a nose job?' said Haworth but stopped when Taverner glared at him.

'Have some respect. The guy's dead...'

'Sorry guv, but perhaps he was trying to see what was possible, you never know with these posh gits, public school makes 'em all weird if you ask me...'

Patel cleared his throat. 'There's quite a lot about celebs too, especially those who had had 'work." Patel made his fingers into quotation marks when he said work.

'Probably most of them,' said Wildblood.

'Perhaps he was going to have a makeover, woo Perdita, he certainly had the hots for her...'

'Good looking woman...' said Haworth and received a fierce glare from Wildblood.

'He'd also looked up someone called Gary Pedley, not sure why, seemed to be trying to locate him for some reason.'

'Mmm, right.' Taverner sighed. He really wasn't sure how significant this was. Gabriel knew he had to make some quick decisions.

'Right, I want Patel and Ballantyne to stay here and follow up the Montague leads and the rest of you need to be on standby for when Drew Morrison comes in. Me and Wildblood will interview Drew, Haworth and DC Buxton, are to interview his wife. We have a warrant to search the premises, so the rest of you can get on with that.'

The desk sergeant poked his head around the door. 'A Mr McCarthy for you guv, he says it's urgent. He's waiting downstairs.'

'I meant to say that Drew Morrison and Finn McCarthy are related. They are brother-in-laws, just so you know,' added Haworth pointedly. 'Perhaps, he's come to plead Morrison's case?'

'Maybe. I'd better go and find out what he wants then. Now the rest of you, scram.'

Finn McCarthy was pacing up and down in the waiting room clearly anxious.

'Hi, listen DI Taverner. Look, two things. Firstly, I found out from the Montague's old nanny that there was a boy who was brought up with Guy and Tarquin, Gary Pedley...'

'Sit down, please,' said Taverner, ears pricking at the mention of the same name he'd heard a few minutes ago. He was momentarily wrongfooted and has been expecting McCarthy to have some information about his brother-in-law, something in mitigation perhaps, as Haworth has suggested. 'And the other thing?

'I was wondering about Clary's murder. I think Clary was providing racing tips to someone and he made a mistake over the identity of a horse and this person lost an awful lot of money. He could have been murdered because of it.' He went on to explain about Kimberley and the betting scams highlighted by Melvin Vine.

Taverner listened intently and took down the details of the Actors' Agency. He raised an eyebrow as Finn described how Harriet had gone in there posing as an actress and noticed the phone number details of 'GP' on the rolodex file. Finn omitted the fact that Harriet had hit the fire alarm button to allow him to search for it. He didn't want a lecture on wasting the time of the emergency services.

'So, that was all that she could see on the file. The initials GP and a phone number. I don't know if that helps.'

Taverner nodded, his mind in overdrive. He was thinking about his interview with Drew Morrison. McCarthy didn't appear to know his brother-in-law was a suspect, and he didn't want him to tip Morrison off. He needed to keep McCarthy occupied whilst they conducted the interviews.

'Hmm. I have to be somewhere. Let me ask one of my team to take a statement from you, if you don't mind waiting. Do you want a tea or coffee?'

'Coffee, please, just milk.'

Taverner passed the information onto DC Patel and DC Ballantyne. Everyone else was on standby to pick up Morrison and his wife and conduct a search of the property on the basis of his contact with Clary, their meeting before his death and the irregularities in the bank statements. Wildblood had gone with them and would either interview Jenny Morrison or come back and interview her husband, depending on the situation. Taverner had a very high regard for her people skills and thought if she developed some empathy with Jenny, she should stay there as she might be able to get more information from her.

'Patel, can you look into McCarthy's information?' He passed him his notebook. 'Ballantyne, can you go and finish off and take a statement from him and make him a coffee? I don't want him to leave until we have Morrison in. If they're related, even by marriage, I don't want McCarthy talking to Morrison. He seems to know an awful lot about the investigation, and I don't want this to compromise our interviews. Got it?'

Ballantyne nodded mournfully. 'Right, guv.'

In the time it had taken for Taverner to go upstairs to relay this information, Finn had become increasingly more agitated. He glanced wildly at Ballantyne when he came in with his drink.

'I've just come off the phone to Harriet Lucas's mother. Apparently, she did not come home last night and she's not answering her phone.'

Ballantyne scratched his head. 'She is an adult, though, isn't she? She's probably met a mate, stayed at her boyfriend's, I bet she'll turn up right as rain. When did her mother last see her?'

Finn looked ashen. 'Apparently, her mother saw her yesterday afternoon. She was on her way to see Neil Horton, Drew Morrison and then Jake Delamare.'

Ballantyne baulked at the mention of the two suspects they were investigating. 'Busy lassie,' he added dryly.

Finn frowned. 'You see, the BHA asked me and her to investigate Clary's murder, just to make sure that it wasn't anything to do with horse racing.'

'The BHA?'

'The British Horse Racing Authority and I was trying to tell your inspector that I know why Clary was killed...'

Ballantyne nodded gravely. 'I think you'd better tell me all about it...'

After about an hour, Taverner burst into the room and motioned for Ballantyne to follow him. Once Ballantyne was out of the room, he hissed,

'Morrison has gone AWOL, so we have pinged his phone and found a location just outside of Walton. I need you to come with me and check it out. Everyone else is at the house or interviewing his wife.'

Ballantyne sighed and indicated the statement he had painstakingly taken from Finn.

'Guv, listen. McCarthy and Lucas have been asked by the BHA to investigate Clary's death.'

'Christ, that's all we need!' He was sure he had heard of the organisation before, but he couldn't remember where from. 'Remind me, what is the bloody BHA, anyway?'

'The British Horseracing Authority, sir. They monitor racing and were worried that Clary's death might be related.'

'Now they bloody tell us! You just wait until I get my hands on the bloody BHA idiots. If they have buggered up the investigation, then there will be hell to pay. Now, we've got a suspect to find.'

Ballantyne put his hands out. 'Hold on sir, I think we ought to listen to McCarthy. He's canny and he's on to something and besides Harriet Lucas might well be with Drew Morrison.'

'What?'

Ballantyne shrugged. 'She went to see him about Life balls or something. That was after she called in to see Neil Horton and she hasn't been seen since.'

'Jesus Christ!' Taverner flushed with sheer unadulterated rage. He made to go into the room where Finn was waiting, then turned back to face Ballantyne. 'Does he know that his bloody brother-in-law is in the frame for the murders?'

'He knows we spoke to Drew and has already spoken to his sister about the anomalies in the bank statements, apparently.'

Taverner strode up and down the corridor. 'Right, we need to check Morrison's phone again and run an ANPR check on his vehicle, fast and make sure he hasn't moved. Harriet is in grave danger if she is with him!'

Ballantyne blinked. 'Mind you, I hear she is a spirited girl, a fighter, so let's hope she'll be OK.'

'Hmm.' Taverner wasn't convinced. 'We'd better get cracking.' He idly flicked through the photos he had taken that morning in the layby and the gallops. It was a time filling exercise, designed to give him something useful to do as he waited for the confirmation about Morrison's whereabouts to come back. He flicked backwards and forwards through the photos, admiring the greenery and how well kept the gallops were. There was a photo of a tractor with farm equipment attached and miles of well-kept gallops, some ascending, marked out with hundreds of white plastic railings similar to those he has seen on racecourses. He had also taken shots of the trees as there were several beautiful oaks and lime trees. The horses looked spectacular galloping this way and that. It was then that he noticed something strange. The trees had birds in them, a couple of magpies, rooks and wood pigeons but when he scrolled back and forwards, the birds were still there in the same place. But the strange thing was they had not moved at all, not an inch! Realisation gripped him and he enlarged one of the photos and studied the bird in the photo in greater detail. The bird's eye looked unnatural close up, suspiciously glassy, almost manmade. Then it came to him, that was because it was! It was a bloody camera and as he scrolled through the other images, the wood pigeon, the magpie and the rook, all had the same artificial appearance. This added considerable weight to McCarthy's theory that Clary was gathering information about the horses and selling it. But who put him up to it? He thought back to Drew Morrison's accounts, the gains and then the large withdrawal and what McCarthy had said about the massive loss due to Clary mixing two horses up. It all fitted. Was Morrison the brains behind the scam?

Twenty minutes later, Ballantyne, Finn, Wildblood and Taverner were hurtling down a country road on their way to the location where Drew's phone was last used at around 11 am that morning. Taverner had been unsure about bringing McCarthy along because of his relationship to the suspect but thought on balance it was better to have him where he could see him. Taverner had insisted that Finn drive and had asked him to send a text to Hattie's phone asking her to text back before he took the wheel.

'Why did you ask me to send her a text?' Finn glared at Taverner. The tension was palpable between the pair. Wildblood was sitting in the back and was quite glad she was out of their way. Ballantyne followed with a police van full of coppers, with armed response and helicopters on standby.

'You, my friend, are bait. If Morrison knows Hattie is onto him then, he'll sure as hell, know you are too. If he replies, we'll track the phone's location, as he could have moved again.'

Finn raised an eyebrow. 'Listen, I've been thinking about that. Drew probably took tips off Clary, may have got himself into debt but I don't think he's your man. He is my brother-in-law, you know, and I just can't see it…'

Taverner gave him a sidelong look. 'With respect, I think you're too close to him to form an objective view. Besides, I think I have worked out how Clary managed to pass him the information. You see what puzzled me was that everyone thought Clary was watching the horses on the gallops and selling the information, but no one had actually seen him there, but look.' He scrolled through the range of photos he had taken earlier. 'If you look carefully, there are several birds in key positions that haven't moved at all and do you know why?'

Finn was concentrating on driving, so couldn't see what Taverner was pointing to.

'No, why?'

'Because they are fake with tiny cameras inserted into the eyes. Technology is so good these days, Clary could have recorded what was going on at the gallops and watched it later, so he could work out which horses to back.'

Finn took this in. Damn. He had seen that bird camera at Clary's too. He had obviously bought a job lot. Still, it was hard to see Drew as the Mr Big in the operation, unless he had been living a lie all these years. Then he remembered something else.

'Oh God, that makes sense. Clary used to do the maintenance on the gallops, so he would have had the perfect opportunity to put the bird cameras there in the first place.'

'Hmm. Perhaps, he moved them around from time to time too, to avoid detection? So, it seems like Morrison is behind the scam, from what we know.'

Finn shook his head. 'Look, I'm still not at all sure Drew's behind it, I'm really not…'

Taverner merely gave him a knowing look.

Wildblood had her phone to her ear, taking directions from DC Patel. 'Looks like we're here,' she said, pointing at a white building which was a rural pub. Finn pulled into the car park.

Finn scanned the place. 'Look. That's Drew's van there.' Taverner looked at the white van with 'Avocado Organic Food' printed on the side in fancy lettering.

Taverner leapt out. 'Come on. First we'll check the van then the pub.'

Chapter 34

Hattie tried to stretch out but was unable to fully. Damn, her hands and feet were tightly bound, and a blindfold was stretched over her eyes. Her hands felt some soft fabric underneath her. She thought she was lying on her side on a bed, her knees bent. The rope ties tore into her skin, making her wince in pain. Fragments of information danced round her brain, but it was impossible to make any sense of it. Her head ached, she felt woozy, and different coloured lights streamed past her eyes, lighting up the darkness. It was impossible to hold onto any thoughts or ideas, they all escaped before she could process them. She was completely and utterly disorientated.

She listened intently, her brain trying to connect to her senses. What the hell was going on? She remembered feeling happy, full of anticipation and then feeling drowsy, had a vague sensation of being carried, rocking backwards and forwards in a vehicle she supposed, and then this. It was warm, the air smelt stale but whether this was the sweat from her own body she couldn't tell. Occasionally, she could hear the soft hum of a vehicle and something louder, altogether more insistent. Then she realised what it was. Seagulls squealing outside. She was momentarily confused. It was a sound she associated with the seaside, family holidays, the scent of sun cream, buckets and spades and going crabbing as a child. She remembered being in the back of the family car with her brothers, all craning their necks to get that first, delicious glance of the sea, seagulls wheeling overhead. It was a glorious sound, but now it was a sound that heralded disorientation and fear. Her whole body ached, and she was losing the battle to keep her eyelids open. Then she felt herself succumb to sleep once more.

Chapter 35

After a search of the van proved fruitless, they found Drew slumped in the bar, drunk as a skunk and tearful. He was incredulous as Taverner instructed Wildblood to cuff him. Finn looked on and shook his head.

'Surely there's no need for that! Can't you see that he's absolutely bladdered,' he muttered crossly.

Wildblood looked at Taverner, who nodded in agreement.

Drew looked at him in desperation. 'What's going on, Finn?'

'Look, just answer the Inspector's questions and it will all be sorted out. They think you murdered Clary and that you have Harriet Lucas held hostage somewhere, so you've got some explaining to do.'

'Wha...' Drew looked from Finn to Taverner, belched and then began to wail. 'I've been sussh a fool, Finn. Don't desherve Jen, just wanted to make some doshhh, that's all...'

Drew's eyes were blood shot and he was having great difficulty standing up. He hiccupped loudly.

'What exactly was your relationship with Clary?' asked Taverner.

Drew opened a red rimmed eye. 'Bought me veg off him, then tips. Man is a genius with the geegees, made some money, then it all went wrong, lost me shirt...'

'Which horse did you lose your money on?' asked Finn.

'Clary told me one horse was gonna win, got given duff info...'

Finn's brain was in overdrive. So, he had been right, after all.

'He didn't tell you to back St George and Rock of Gibraltar won instead?'

Drew looked at him open mouthed. 'How did you know? Losh twenty bloody grand, I did, twenty bloody grand! Jen'll go mad...' He gave Finn an imploring look. 'Shhe'll divorce me, she will when she finds out...'

'No, she won't,' Finn assured him.

Taverner looked from Finn to Drew and back again. 'Never mind all this. Look, what have you done with Harriet Lucas, we need to know where she is!'

'Come on, this is serious,' added Wildblood. 'She could be at risk.'

Drew's mouth hung open. 'Who?'

'You know, Hattie, the girl you were going to talk to about the Life balls. Did you see her?' Finn was becoming exasperated.

'Ah, yeah. She came yesterday, made her some of the Life thingies, she said they were just like the real deal. Told her it were real easy, a cinch, to make.' Drew's head lolled alarmingly as he rested his arm on the bar to prevent him from falling over. Finn stifled his annoyance.

'Where did she go after she met you, Drew? Think, it's important.'

Drew blinked furiously. 'Said she were meeting up with that posh git, wi' the Life balls, Jake Whatsit…'

'Jake Delamare. Did she say where she was meeting him?'

'Posh hotel or summat. He looks just like me old mate, he does from college… can't think of his name…'

Drew put his head in his hands, as though remembering the name of his friend was uppermost in his mind. His timing was terrible.

'Never mind that now! We need to know where Harriet is!' grumbled Taverner.

'I have seen him in Walton, wi' Jimmy a time or two. He could be the double of him, can't think of his bloody name…'

Finn gave Drew a sympathetic smile. 'I'm sure the name will come to you, mate. But Hattie could be in danger, so we really need to know where she went. It's urgent.'

Drew nodded. 'Hmm. She looked at her watch, said she was going to pick up something, a dress first…'

'Where from?'

'Her mate's…'

Finn looked at Taverner, a terrible sense of foreboding washing over him.

Wildblood had paled. 'What was her friend's name?'

'Hmm. Daisy, that was it.'

Taverner swallowed hard. 'Right, we need to get to Hunt's place pronto.'

'Shall we just leave him, guv?'

Taverner nodded.

Finn slammed a ten pound note on the bar and shouted to the barmaid. 'Get him a couple of strong black coffees, won't you?'

'And for God's sake, don't let him drive!' added Wildblood. Then she turned to Drew. 'If you think of the name of the man you were at college with, then ring us.'

Taverner raised an eyebrow at this.

'Think about it, it might be important,' she added.

They sped off in Finn's car, leaving Drew and the barmaid gaping at the clouds of dust that fanned out behind Finn's Audi.

Whilst Finn had been sure about Drew's innocence, he could not say the same for Neil Horton. He barely knew the man, but the evidence was certainly pointing to him. He'd had an argument with Clary, ostensibly about his groom, but supposing that was a smoke screen and it was really about the mix up of the horses? Neil would certainly be in a position to know which horse was which and could easily find out about horses from other yards. He chewed over Vince's comments. What was it he had said, something about Neil just arriving in Walton, no one knowing anything about him? Was that suspicious? It certainly seemed like it now.

Finn swore as he was forced to slow down behind a tractor, his fingers drumming on the steering wheel in irritation. After what felt like an age, the tractor turned off, stuttering alarmingly. At last the road was clear.

'Drive! Just go! Don't worry about speeding. I'll vouch for you. It's an emergency,' yelled Taverner clutching his seat with white knuckles as Finn jammed his foot down on the accelerator. Wildblood rolled her eyes and held on tight.

Chapter 36

The man glanced at the sleeping girl and watched her movements for a minute, trying to gauge how alert she was. He decided that the dose he had given her would keep her knocked out for a few hours more, she would be groggy when she woke up and unable to move, so he would have a few hours to play with. He checked the ties he had put in place on her hands and ankles, secured them and moved an auburn lock of hair from her face, almost tenderly. It was such a shame but then he had to cover his tracks. He sent a quick text to lay his trap and arranged to meet later. Satisfied, he gave sleeping beauty one last look, locked the doors and set another part of his plan in motion.

Daisy was in the yard, hay net on shoulder. She lifted her hand as soon as she saw Finn, then her smile slipped when she noticed his expression and saw Taverner unfolding himself from the car accompanied by Wildblood. The place was a hive of activity, as a series of horses' heads popped out of their stable doors to peer at the strangers.

'Is everything OK?' she asked.

Finn shook his head. 'Listen, where is Neil, we need to speak to him.'

Daisy looked suspiciously at the police officers. 'In the arena schooling, why what's going on?'

Finn and Taverner made their way to the arena leaving Daisy jogging to catch up with Wildblood.

Wildblood explained. 'It's Harriet. She's gone missing. We believe she came here yesterday, and she hasn't been seen since. We just need to speak to Neil, that's all.'

Daisy's face was a picture.

They found themselves in front of the arena, watching Neil trotting in increasingly small circles, on a dark bay horse with practiced ease, Finn couldn't help but notice.

Various expressions flitted over Neil's face as he saw the two officers and Finn approaching.

Daisy climbed onto the fence that edged the arena. 'Neil, just tell them about Hattie, will you? Here, I'll hold Nelson.'

Neil dismounted, removed his helmet and handed the horse's reins to Daisy. Dressed in a polo shirt, jodhpurs and riding boots, he looked tired, sweaty and more than a bit wary.

'What's up?'

'It's Hattie, Neil. She's gone missing,' explained Finn.

Taverner took over, looking alert as though he might spring into action and arrest Horton at any minute.

'We believe that she came here last night to pick up a dress.'

Horton nodded. 'Yeah, that's right. She borrowed one of Daisy's, had a hot date or something, I think.'

Daisy walked up to them leading the horse. 'Yes, she was going to meet Jake Delamare,' said she didn't know what to wear and I had just the thing.'

'Were you here when she arrived?' Taverner asked Daisy.

'No, I was out teaching but I left the dress in a bag in the kitchen, Neil was here when she came, weren't you?'

Neil nodded. 'Yep. I was schooling when she came at about half five. I had a brief chat with her over the fence and told her to let herself into the house. She helped herself to the dress and drove off.'

Daisy took up the story. 'She was really excited. Don't blame her, though, meeting that Jake. I texted her later to wish her luck and she texted me back just before she went out saying the dress fitted fine and she was looking forward to her date.'

Taverner and Wildblood exchanged glances. 'Do you have your phone on you?' asked Wildblood.

Daisy fished it out of her pocket and fiddled with the buttons before handing it over to Wildblood, frowning. 'I did text her this morning actually, to get all the gen about how the evening had gone, you know, but she never rang back. I just thought I'd catch her later.'

Wildblood handed the phone to Taverner, who checked the messages.

'She replied at 7.35pm, so she was fine then. Can you remember where she was meeting this Jake Delamare?'

'Oh, somewhere fancy. Think it was The Marsden in York, yes that was it.'

'Are you sure?' Taverner clarified.

'Yes, I'm sure,' Daisy's face fell. 'Listen, do you think she's OK?'

Taverner fished out his phone and rang the station, sending officers to The Marsden Hotel. Finn managed a half smile at Daisy, but his heart wasn't in it.

'Listen, it's just a precaution that's all.'

Daisy looked sceptical. 'Finn, it's not anything to do with the murders, is it?'

Taverner motioned for them to leave.

'I'd better go. Try not to worry,' Finn replied.

If only he could follow his own advice.

'Christ, this is turning into a real farce. Right, we need to get to The Marsden, I've sent a unit up there ahead of us,' muttered Taverner. 'That text was clearly genuine, so we know she was fine before she went to see this man, so it looks like Horton and Morrison are off the hook. What do you know about Jake Delamare?'

Finn swerved to avoid a cyclist. 'He was on some celebrity chef programme or other and is a bit of a prat if you ask me. He's trying to sell some bloody protein balls, he calls them Life balls but is marketing them as a slimming aid, he was trying to get Hattie to help him. Gave her some guff about the

164

pair of them writing a cookery book together. My guess is he needed Hattie to give his product some credibility. She's about to qualify as a dietician, you see.'

'You didn't like him?' Wildblood asked.

'No, not at all. But I can't see why he would abduct Hattie...'

Taverner sighed. 'She could just be spending time with him romantically, he's not on the suspect list at all, so we could just be on a wild goose chase.'

Just then Finn's phone rang.

'Answer it, will you?'

Wildblood did so. 'It's Drew. I'll put it on loudspeaker.'

After a while Drew's disembodied voice crackled out of the receiver. He sounded like he'd sobered up, Finn was glad to hear. The barmaid had clearly followed Finn's advice and given him copious amounts of coffee.

'Finn. That friend of mine who looks like Jake, with a makeover, it's someone called Gary Pedley. Met him on the chef's course. Saw him wi' Clary near the gallops. Might be important that's all...'

'Thanks,' called Finn sharing a look with Taverner.

Then Wildblood's phone rang. She answered it and listened carefully, her expression grave.

'Sir, that was Patel. They've found out who commissioned the cufflinks from a jewellers in York. They were commissioned by someone called Gary Pedley!'

Finn took this in. Gary who looked like Jake Delamare, who had been seen with Jimmy in Walton, who had been the Montague's childhood friend. What if…

'Supposing Jake Delamare is Pedley? Maybe he slightly altered his appearance, had a bit of plastic surgery. If he is the brains behind the scam, that would give him a motive to kill Montague and Clary...'

Taverner looked thoughtful. He turned to Wildblood who was still holding Finn's phone. 'Has Finn had a response to his text to Hattie?'

Wildblood fiddled with Finn's phone. 'Yep. *'Meet me at 3pm in York in The White Horse. Have lots to tell you x'*'

Taverner rang Patel back. 'We need a GPS trace on this telephone number urgently.'

Wildblood showed him the message.

Taverner frowned then read out the telephone number it had been sent from. Then he turned to glare at Finn.

'Right, Mr McCarthy, you have a lot of explaining to do. I distinctly told you to inform me of anything you found out during your investigations, but it seems you have been holding out on me.'

Finn shrugged. 'I did ring you. Check your phone. I left you several voicemails and your other officer has my statement, it's all in there.'

Wildblood looked from one to the other. 'This really isn't getting us anywhere. We should pull up and wait for Patel's trace. I doubt that Delamare is holding Hattie in York, he's bound to have moved her somewhere more remote, surely?'

The radio crackled again. It was Patel with Hattie's last GPS location. If Delamare had Harriet's phone, then it was Delamare's location too.

'His last call was from a place on the coast. It's near Whitby, a place called Robin Hood's Bay.'

Finn pulled up the car. Several pieces of information settled down in Finn's brain and suddenly began to make sense.

'Listen, hear me out. I think that Jake will try to stop Guy Montague's horse, Fort William winning in the 7.50 at York this evening. It's a group race and he is hellbent on humiliating Guy and will no doubt have a hefty bet or two into the bargain. He aims to cause a distraction by hiding Harriet, maybe in Robin Hood's Bay. I think his mother, Martha, used to have a house there.'

Taverner scowled. 'Then we need to split up. Wildblood and Ballantyne need to go to York and me and McCarthy to Robin Hood's Bay. How exactly does he intend to stop this Fort William winning the race, do you think?'

Finn's head was spinning. 'I think it's something to do with the Life balls. He asked Hattie to give them to the jockeys. It was some weight loss gimmick. I think she said Fort William's jockey, Davy Hughes, had been sent them. Jake could have injected the LIFE balls with some sort of drug, enough to knock the jockey off his stride. You need to check to make sure Davy Hughes hasn't eaten them and check on the horse. I have Davy's mobile number here. I'll send it to you.' He glanced at his watch. 'The horsebox won't set off until about 3 pm so you need to check the horse. The trainer is Vince Hunt. And listen, Delamare may try to harm Guy Montague too.'

Taverner looked puzzled. 'Why?'

It was all starting to make sense to Finn at long last. 'Because, he believes he is Lord Montague's illegitimate son and the rightful heir to the Montague title. Pedley may have started with the betting scams, he killed Clary for mixing two horses up but then he realised that Tarquin was on to him. When Lord Montague died, he killed Tarquin to stop him revealing who he was, but he realised that he was one step nearer to becoming Lord. He tried to make Tarquin's death look like suicide. He will see Guy as the only person standing in his way now.'

Taverner began speaking frantically into his phone. Wildblood joined Ballantyne, who had followed them in the police van, and sped off to Hunt's yard. Taverner turned to Finn.

'Right, we'll set off to Robin Hood's Bay to the last GPS location and you can explain everything you know on the way.'

166

Chapter 37

Harriet woke up less groggy. She realised that her hands and feet were bound and that she was wearing a blindfold. She remembered seeing Jake, her excitement at the prospect of writing a cookbook with him, how kind he'd been, how they'd toasted their partnership with Veuve Cliquot champagne and then how she'd started to feel sleepy, she could barely keep her eyes open. God, he must have drugged her. Fear coursed through her as she realised the implications of what had happened. Christ, Jake was the murderer! Fear at the situation she was in gave way to anger that she had been so taken in. She was horribly aware that if he had murdered two people, he would not baulk at killing a third. She listened intently for any sign of life, but the house was silent. Where was he? How long before he came back? She tensed her muscles and thought hard. Well, if she was going to die then she'd not go down without a fight. Years before, she had trained to become a modern pentathlete and had even made the British Junior team. She had trained in all five disciplines of show jumping, shooting, swimming, running and fencing. Although she hadn't kept it up, apart from a few Keep Fit activities, she knew she was still well-conditioned, strong and supple. She thought about what to do and suddenly had a brainwave. She could do this

She manoeuvred herself around on the bed and lifted her arms up towards her shoulder blades and bent her head back. Her blindfold had been tied tightly but the ends were long and just within her grasp. If she could just reach them, she may be able to pull the blindfold off. After lots of moving and stretching, she managed to bend her neck back as far as she could and push her hands up, so she just reached the end of the tie. She grasped it with her fingertips and pulled with all her might. The blindfold moved almost imperceptibly. She tried it again and the blindfold slipped down, so the room was revealed. Euphoria coursed through her. She was in a darkened room, lying on a single bed, there was a blind at the window with daylight flickering around the edges, the floor was wooden and rough looking, the walls painted magnolia. The light was so bright it must be coming up to midday. There were no personal belongings. It had the neglected look of a spare room. There was a door to one side which she longed to get to, but first things first.

She flipped her legs backwards behind her and studied the rope and the knots on her ankles. She raised herself up on her knees and directed her free fingers tied behind her back, to where the knots were located on her ankles. The rope was tight, so she pulled at the knots trying to loosen them. It was going to be a hard job, but she kept going, trying to find any piece of rope that she could loosen. Her thighs began to burn, unused to the strained position. She sank down onto her heels for a rest. Come on, come on, she could do this. The thought of Jake's face, his smug manner and the way he had humiliated her, spurred her on.

She rested for the count of ten and set off again raising her thighs and using her free fingers to pluck at the rope on her ankles again and again. She listened out for her captor and then tried again. She had to do this now and had to make a run for it before he came back. When he did, it could be a different story, one she didn't want to imagine. She repeated the pattern of pulling at the knots and resting then hoisting herself up, several more times. There was precious little give in the knots but there was some, she told herself, willing herself to carry on. She knew her parents, her brother and Finn would all be looking for her and she hoped and prayed that she would come out of this alright. Three more goes and suddenly her sore fingers pulled the knots into a loop. She looked back from her kneeling position and almost cheered. A few deft movements later and her feet were untied. All she had to do now was free her hands. She looked round the room for something that she might be able to wedge between the ropes and noticed a nail sticking out above the bed where a picture had once hung. She climbed back onto the bed and backed onto the wall, hoping and praying that the nail was not too high. Standing on her tip toes she could just about manoeuvre the knot onto the nail head. She almost overbalanced as she raised herself onto her tip toes and lifted her arms a little so she could manoeuvre the knot towards the nail. All she had to do now was try and find a gap, even a narrow one that she could wedge the head of the nail into it and undo the knot. Outside she could hear the distant buzz of traffic and hear the sound of what she assumed were holiday makers arriving to make the most of the sunny afternoon. People meant safety. Her mood lifted and she set to work stretching up onto her toes once more, telling herself to never give up.

Chapter 38

Finn was trying very hard not to panic but given that Jake was a double murderer, it was not hard to imagine what he might do to Harriet. He willed himself to concentrate on the road ahead and overtook every car he could at 100 mph.

'So, tell me everything again?' Taverner had lost his angry look and seemed curious. 'Who is this Jake Delamare/ Gary Pedley character?'

'He obviously trained with Drew as a chef, but prior to that according to Tarquin's nanny, he spent a lot of time with Tarquin and Guy growing up. It seems that the old Lord was something of a ladies' man and it was suggested he had been having an affair with Gary's mother, who worked as a cook. The affair could have been going on a while, so maybe Gary was Lord Montague's son. Lady Montague saw them off when her husband was out of the country on business. Gary used to go to the stud farm with Lord Montague and he may have even mentioned about paying for his education, so when you think about it, it's not surprising that Gary has delusions of grandeur. He then became a chef and became famous from the 'Cooking up a Storm' programme. '

Taverner glanced at his watch. 'Of course, I think I caught some of that. How will Hattie cope with being held captive, do you think?'

'Well, she used to be an athlete, so she's fit and healthy. She's also very upbeat, so she should cope. Probably, better than most, I'd say.' He gave Taverner a side long look as they sped down a country road towards Scarborough. The scenery was breath taking but he didn't have time to admire it. 'So, if my theory's correct, he could be on his way to York for Fort William's race. Do you think Gary will have someone guarding her?'

'Maybe he's drugged her or…'

Taverner left the sentence hanging. They both looked at each other, not wanting to acknowledge what exactly Gary might have done to Harriet. After all, all the evidence pointed to the fact that he was a coldblooded murderer. Finn felt a spasm of alarm course through him, as he stepped on the accelerator and overtook several more cars.

He nodded towards the glove box. 'The BHA gave me a gun, but you might be able to handle it better than I can.'

Taverner opened the glove box and unwrapped the Glock 17.

'Fine. I have done my firearms training. So, I presume the BHA Integrity Unit liaised with the police about all this?'

'Yes, I think so. I believe, it was all agreed with your DCI. My boss said he'd arranged it.'

Taverner nodded grimly wondering why the hell no one had told him.

Then his phone rang out. 'Right, OK, Patel. So where is that then?'

Finn looked expectantly at him as he slowed down for a tractor.

'Jake is on the move, but he could be on his way back to Robin's Hood Bay.' He googled the GPS position. 'He used his phone a few minutes ago and he was twenty minutes away from Robin Hood's Bay when he made a call, but we don't know if he's leaving there or coming back.'

Taverner glanced at the satnav in Finn's Audi. They were now forty minutes from Robin Hood's Bay, but as it was a sunny day the traffic was worsening. Everyone wanted to go to the seaside today, it seemed. Finn hit the accelerator and swerved around a white van, praying they would be in time, whilst Taverner sorted through the gun's holdall to count the ammunition.

Meanwhile Hattie continued with her efforts to remove the ties around her wrists. She persisted with her back to the wall, to manoeuvre the rope onto the nail head so that she could prise the knot apart. Her arms were aching from the effort of straining to reach the nail in the wall. It was absolutely exhausting and there was limited progress. She rested for a minute or two then decided to try the door. She clambered off the bed and backed up to the door and tried to turn the handle with her fingers. Of course, it was locked as she expected. Damn. She quelled the rising panic. Then she saw the window and edged towards the window blind and bent down to reach the rope at the side. She opened her mouth to bite the toggle at the end of the lead and pulled it by moving away from the window. The bright sunlight caused her to blink as the scene outside came slowly into view. Wow. She gazed at the idyllic scene. The house was situated in a narrow road with cottages either side. Outside there were people in summer clothes walking towards the sea carrying beach towels, bags, buckets and spades. The sky was azure blue and over the pantile roof tops, she glimpsed the harbour and heard seagulls as they circled above her. She saw a young woman in a floaty dress with a little girl of about three clutching her hand pass beneath her. They were so close she could see the excitement on the little girl's face, the expectation. She was about to shout out to them when she heard a bang from downstairs. What the hell was that? Was Jake back? She considered rushing back to the bed as the blind fell shut. Then she changed her mind. She had to be positive. In one deft movement, she hid behind the bedroom door. She tried to think of a plan, knowing it would have to be a good one. Her life depended on it.

As the key was inserted into the lock, she made up her mind what to do and waited until the door opened and Jake was partially inside, then she kicked against the door with as much strength as she could muster. Jake was taken by surprise and she heard him cry out as he fell backwards. Then she slammed the door into his body again for good measure, heard him groan in pain and stepped over his body and ran down the stairs to freedom. Downstairs she backed up to the front door, turned the handle and opened the door. Sun light flooded in almost blinding her.

'Help,' she shouted, before she heard heavy breathing behind her and felt her arms and shoulders being yanked backwards. She felt powerful arms engulf her and the thud as the door was slammed shut.

Jake pushed his hair out of his eyes and hauled her kicking and screaming up the stairs. He slammed her head into the wall.

'Shut up, you stupid bitch, or I'll do it again!'

He hauled her back into the bedroom and roughly tied her feet and surveyed her before digging into his pocket and pulling out a roll of gaffer tape. He tore a length off and pressed it over her mouth.

'That'll shut you up,' he muttered a look of satisfaction on his face. 'Any more trouble out of you and you'll get this, understand?' he muttered, waving his fist in her face. Hattie glowered at him, willing herself to not show fear. She would not let him beat her.

Chapter 39

By the time Taverner and Finn had arrived at the narrow street, a small crowd had begun to form in a narrow road that led down to Robin Hood's Bay. Above the seagulls circled and day trippers were arriving in brightly coloured short and tops, wearing flip flops and carrying beach towels as they made their way down to the sea.

Finn walked up the cobbled walkway to where several people were standing in front of a stone cottage with a long driveway and a blue door. A young woman was bending down to talk to a little girl.

'What's going on?' asked Finn.

'My little girl says she saw a woman trying to escape from that house and a man dragged her back.' The woman pointed at the cottage with the blue door.

Finn knelt down. 'Hello, what's your name?'

'Milly,' replied the little girl. Her blue eyes were huge and her expression sombre.

'Now Milly, can you be a really big girl and tell me and my friend what you saw?'

The little girl looked uncertainly at her mother who nodded.

'The lady looked scared and she shouted, 'Help', then the man got hold of her and pulled her.'

Taverner joined them. 'What did the lady look like?'

Milly bit her lip as she thought for a moment. 'Her hair was all wavy and red and she had a nice dress with flowers on it.' Milly frowned. 'She looked scared and her hands were behind her back.'

Finn winced at the accurate description of his friend. It sounded like she had been tied up. At least she was still alive though. Please let her be OK.

'Thank you, Milly. Me and my friend will go and check that she's alright.'

An older woman dressed in cream shorts and a black shirt approached them. 'The kid's right, I heard the woman scream too, but when I turned around there was no one there. She definitely shouted 'Help' and sounded terrified.' She frowned. 'Bloody domestic, I suppose. I have just rung the police, though, as it sounded serious.'

Taverner flashed his warrant card at her.

'I am from the police. There's no need to worry. We'll go and check it out, and let you get on with your day.'

The woman smiled. 'Wow, that was really quick. Good luck then.' Gradually the crowd moved on.

As soon as they were out of earshot, Taverner spoke urgently into his phone.

'Right, we have had a positive sighting of Harriet Lucas at 3, Knight Lane in Robin's Hood Bay. I request armed response back up immediately as the suspect Jake Delamare aka Gary Pedley is armed and dangerous. We have a hostage situation, so I want a hostage negotiator as well.'

Finn heard a flurry of responses before Taverner rang off looking grim faced.

'They will be here in about twenty minutes.' He gave Finn despairing look. 'God, the roads are bad, I suppose. I don't know about you, but I hate waiting around. It's highly irregular but what do you say to doing a recce round the back?'

Finn nodded. Anything could happen in the time it would take for the services to get there. It only took a few seconds to kill someone. The wait would be excruciating. He had to do something. This was as good an idea as any.

'Come on then, let's go.'

'How about you cause a distraction? I'll hide out of view and try and take him when he comes out.'

Finn nodded and advanced around the back of the property through a narrow alley. The garden was fenced and there was a gate at the rear which was open. Finn scanned the back of the property and noticed a small greenhouse to one side. He crept inside and began smashing the windows with a stick, trying to make as much noise as possible, and avoiding the shards of glass as they fell. A curtain flickered upstairs, so Finn continued to make as much commotion as he possibly could. Taverner moved into position at the side of the rear door, but behind a pillar, waiting for Delamare to come out. Finn ran out of glass panes to smash, so started throwing ceramic plant pots, again making as much noise as he could.

Harriet could hear the racket and realised that she now had an opportunity to escape whilst Jake was distracted. She tried to break free from her ties, hoping that they were loose as Jake had tied them hastily. She manoeuvred herself so she was stood up on the bed, backed onto the wall and guided her hands towards the nail she had used previously. The knots were looser and this time she was able to prise the rope apart quickly. Within a few seconds she had freed her hands, removed the tape from her mouth, then set about untying her ankles. Then she crept towards the door and opened it. Slowly and gingerly she slipped into the hallway, scanning the area as she went, her heart thundering as she moved, as stealthily as she could. Jake was nowhere to be seen, presumably downstairs wondering whether or not to break cover to investigate the noise outside.

Taverner lay in wait, his hand holding the gun ready.

The back door slowly opened, and a foot appeared.

Taverner leapt into action, coshing the gun over Jake's head, missing as he ducked. The gun fell, skittering across the floor as Jake punched Taverner full in the mouth and viciously kicked him. Taverner lunged at him as Finn advanced, holding a large plant pot ready to smash over Jake's head. At the same time, blue lights flooded into the area and the sound of sirens filled the air as a police helicopter came into view overhead. The bloody cavalry had arrived and not before time. Jake looked up, panicked and made a run for the back fence whilst Finn and Taverner gave chase. Finn rugby tackled Jake to the floor, Jake fell on top of him and whilst Finn gathered his breath, Jake picked up a large brick. Taverner was about to come at him from behind when a gun shot rang out and Jake screamed in pain, clutching his leg as he fell to the ground. There were shouts and cries as the garden was flooded with police officers with guns trained on Jake, and all hell broke loose. Finn turned to see Harriet in the doorway, still holding the gun.

Epilogue

Finn trained his binoculars on the field as the horses rounded the bend on their second circuit in the Malton Cup at Wetherby. He was tracking the bay horse with the white star marking on his head, Star Light, with Gavin Clary, conditional jockey on board. It was October and the National Hunt season was in full swing, so he was especially busy coaching and mentoring his conditionals. He was particularly anxious that Gavin had a good ride on the promising hurdler trained by Vince Hunt and owned by Guy Montague. After the poor few months the town had endured, with two murders, the strain of the police investigation and the mistrust that had generated, he really hoped both Gavin and Vince would do well. They all needed a boost, especially Gavin. Guy Montague had inherited his brother's title and had overcome an attempt by Gary Pedley to nobble his best horse, Fort William, by getting the jockey to eat Life balls injected with a sedative. Fortunately, the police had arrived in the nick of time to stop Davy Hughes eating one and Fort William went on to win the Group race by an impressive five lengths. Guy had invited Vince, Daisy, Neil, Hattie, Tony Murphy and even DI Taverner to the meeting. All eyes were trained on the big bay horse and Gavin, who was wearing Guy's distinctive red and yellow hooped colours.

Gavin was in fourth place tracking the leaders as the horses came up to the third from last fence. Gavin manoeuvred the bay to the outside of the track where the ground was better and moved up as Star Light shot over the penultimate fence, pulling into second place and gaining ground on the leader, Lavender Hill. Finn muttered under his breath. Come on, come on, Gavin. Don't give up. Just keep going. Come on!

Star Light looked to be full of running, but so too, did the big grey, Lavender Hill, but coming up to the last fence, the grey horse made a huge leap from way out and struggled to clear the fence. In contrast, Star Light jumped cleanly and landed well ahead. Lavender Hill was given a sharp slap by his jockey and started to come back, so the pair were neck and neck twenty yards from the finish line. The crowd were shouting encouragements. Vince was chewing his cheek and Harriet could hardly look, but Gavin kept his focus and then pushed Star Light harder and harder. In a riot of colour, mud, sweat and noise, Star Light won by a clear head. Marvellous!

Vince and Daisy hugged each other, and Guy gave a satisfied smile and accepted Harriet and Finn's congratulations. Taverner shook Guy's hand. Vince dashed off to sort out Star Light and have a debrief with Gavin.

'Bloody great race, well ridden,' shouted Finn as Gavin and Star Light made their way into the winner's enclosure. Gavin beamed back. There was no trace of the depressed, suicidal young man, he had been when Finn first met him. Now the future looked very bright, for all of them.

Guy Montague was delighted. 'I've made a decision to celebrate every success after the horror of the last few months, so I'd like you all to come back to my box for a drink,' he said to the whole group. 'I'm just pleased that the wretched business is over.'

It certainly was a relief to everyone. Jake Delamare aka Gary Pedley was locked up after a brief stay in hospital to remove a bullet from his calf. It was a superficial injury designed to stop rather than kill, but it had enabled Jake to be arrested.

In Guy's box, waiters circulated with trays of canapes and flutes of champagne.

'Remind me, how did you learn to shoot like that?' Taverner asked Harriet.

'Oh, just from competing. I used to do the modern pentathlon, you know where you have to show jump, run, swim, fence and cycle. I used to be in the junior British team but had an injury, so had to give it up. Obviously, we didn't shoot proper rounds, we used laser guns, but the principles are the same.'

Taverner nodded, amused by her modesty. 'Well, I think you did extraordinarily well. Are you fully recovered?'

Hattie grinned. 'Yes. I just feel a bit of a fool, that's all. I really thought Jake and I might get to write that cookery book together and he really did seem very glamorous.' She was actually mortified when she thought about how taken in she had been by Jake. She'd even unwittingly given him information about the investigation. What an idiot!

Finn laughed. 'Never mind, Hattie. We can all be wrong about people.' He was thinking about Kimberley and how she had turned out to be not exactly what she seemed. He had decided not to pursue their relationship.

Guy tapped his champagne flute with a spoon, and everyone turned to look at him.

'I want to propose a toast to Hattie, Finn and DI Taverner for catching the murderer of James Clary and my own dear brother, Tarquin Montague.' Guy looked momentarily sombre. The funerals had been held a month or so ago and both men had been laid to rest. 'And I can't thank you enough for stopping me becoming Gary's third victim.'

The police had found detailed plans on Gary's computer which outlined the mechanics of the braking system on Guy's Jaguar. Gary had plans to disable the brakes and cause a fatal car accident. Then Gary planned to stake his claim to the Montague inheritance as he was convinced that he was the old Lord's illegitimate son and heir. DNA tests, however, said otherwise.

'I still don't really get it,' said Daisy. 'I mean Gary did well as a chef, he could have been successful in his own right, so why kill Wolf and Clary?'

'Money, vengeance, maybe, for how he was treated,' explained Taverner. 'He didn't have the money to back any of his projects. He started off using Clary to give him information on how the horses performed on the gallops. Jimmy did the maintenance on them and planted small cameras disguised as birds. He then studied the horses at work at his leisure. When Jimmy gave him the wrong name for a horse, he identified the horse in the hood as St George rather than Rock of Gibraltar, Gary lost a fortune. That's why he killed Clary. The lads literally swapped St George's hood and tried it on Rocky, so he

176

thought he really had been hoodwinked, you see. When Guy's father died, he thought that all he had to do was kill Tarquin and later Guy and then stake his claim to the Montague seat. But Tarquin was already suspicious and questioned Perdita about Clary's contacts. He thought that Delamare looked like his old cook's son, Gary. Even though Gary had had plastic surgery, he still recognised him. It seems that Gary heard about Tarquin's suspicions and realised he was going to tell Finn and Hattie about him. That's why he killed Tarquin. His goal then was to humiliate the Montague family by preventing Fort William from winning the big race at York and then tamper with Guy's car, so he would have an accident. Gary had years of being bullied when he moved schools, from a prep school to a local comprehensive, and his mother struggled to provide for him when they were turfed out of Montague Hall, so I'm afraid he was obsessed about regaining the money and the status he thought he was due. He also thought he really was Lord Montague's son. He even had a pair of cufflinks commissioned with the Montague coat of arms engraved on them, he was so sure. It just burnt away at him, I guess.'

Guy looked thoughtful. 'I suppose my father was at fault. Gary's mother certainly told him that Gary was his son, probably as a way of milking him for money. It could have been true. My parents were ill matched and let's just say, Dad sought his comforts elsewhere.'

Daisy nodded. 'Still, at least Neil has been exonerated which is brilliant.' Daisy beamed at Neil who tightened his arm around her.

'And my brother-in-law, Drew. He was guilty of buying tips off Clary and also lost his shirt on St George. All he was doing was trying to amass some money to set up his restaurant. Never mind, I hope he makes a go of things now.'

Guy had agreed to give Drew a business loan for the restaurant he was desperate to open and had also increased his sponsorship of Neil's show jumpers and was planning on expanding his stud and blood stock investments. So, in the end everyone's futures were secured, even Harriet's.

'So, when do you start your new job?' Daisy asked Hattie.

'In a week or so. Can't wait. Perhaps, I'll write that cookbook after all.'

Harriet had finished her degree and had been successful in joining the Professional Jockeys' Association as a dietician. It had been her dream job, but she and Finn had also been approached by the BHA and were asked if they would formally take on a role at the Integrity Team, investigating irregularities in racing, if and when they arose. Both had agreed. Finn was employed by the BHA as a jockey coach anyway, so could easily be seconded in the future and the PJA were happy to assist their colleagues, too. It was all very hush hush, of course, so no-one knew apart from the BHA staff. Their jobs meant that they had access to the racing world quite legitimately. In the meantime, they would both continue in their present roles.

Vince took a sip of champagne. He looked at Taverner and Tony Murphy. 'I reckon these two could do their sleuthing professionally, don't you? They could teach you lot a thing or two. Next time, you'd do well to take advice from them.' He was still sore about his daughter's boyfriend being viewed as a suspect and could not resist having a dig.

Taverner inclined his head graciously. 'Well, they certainly helped in this case.'

Tony Murphy merely raised an eyebrow. After all, he had negotiated with Finn and with the PJA regarding Harriet's role to do just that.

Daisy gasped in surprise. 'Next time? There won't be a next time. Nothing like this could possibly happen in the future. Besides, both Finn and Hattie will be far too busy in their jobs to run around solving crimes for the police.'

'I'm sure we will be,' replied Harriet.

'Absolutely,' Finn added, exchanging a look of perfect understanding with Harriet. They couldn't help wondering what their next case would be.

About Charlie De Luca

Charlie De Luca was brought up on a stud farm, where his father held a permit to train National Hunt horses, hence his lifelong passion for racing was borne. He reckons he visited most of the racecourses in England by the time he was ten. He has always loved horses but grew too tall to be a jockey. Charlie lives in rural Lincolnshire with his family and a variety of animals, including some ex-racehorses.

Charlie has written several racing thrillers which include: **Rank Outsiders, The Gift Horse, Twelve in the Sixth** and **Making Allowances.**

You can connect with Charlie via twitter; @charliedeluca8 or visit his website.

Charlie is more than happy to connect with readers, so please feel free to contact him directly using the CONTACT button on the website.

www.charliedeluca.co.uk

If you enjoyed this book, then please leave a review. It only needs to be a line or two, but it makes such a difference to authors.

Praise for Charlie De Luca.

'He is fast becoming my favourite author.'

'Enjoyable books which are really well plotted and keep you guessing.'

'Satisfying reads, great plots.'

Printed in Poland
by Amazon Fulfillment
Poland Sp. z o.o., Wrocław

58497438R00103